This Bitter
TREASURE

S.W. HUBBARD

CHAPTER 1

Tuesday, September 6.

It's my favorite day of the year.

No, it's not my birthday. Or my anniversary. Sean and I don't have one...yet.

It's the day after Labor Day this year. The recognized end of summer.

The first day of school.

I haven't set foot in a classroom for over ten years, but this day still feels like the beginning of a new year. A time to start fresh, learn something new, leave last year's mistakes behind. And heaven knows there has been a raft of them.

I look down and admire my feet in my cute ankle boots. What's a new school year without a new pair of shoes? They're much trendier than my usual footwear. But September is a time to reinvent myself.

Maybe I'll sign up for a yoga class. Or learn to knit with Natalie, my dad's new wife. Nothing as demanding as what Ty is doing right now. Or Jill.

Of course, there's the whole matter of learning how to be a member of the Coughlin family: a wife, a daughter-in-law, a sister-in-law. That's reinvention on a much bigger scale for an only-child bachelor-girl like me.

I glance at my cell phone: disturbingly blank.

"Why do you keep checking the time?" Adrienne asks. "Your appointment is at two; you won't need more than fifteen minutes to get there."

"Appointment? Oh, I'd forgotten about that." I'm still not used to seeing Adrienne sitting at Jill's desk. I try not to get wistful thinking about my former assistant enrolled in graduate school at

NYU. I miss her terribly, but I'm excited for her and I know she'll do great. It's Ty I'm worried about. "I'm thinking about Ty. His first class is almost over. I'm dying to know how it went. Do you think I should call him?"

Adrienne shakes her head. "Wow, Audrey—I didn't peg you as the kind of mom who hops in her SUV and follows the school bus on the first day. Did you pack a heart-shaped note in Ty's Elmo backpack?"

The vision of Ty in an Elmo backpack, even at age five, cracks me up. "I see him as Power Rangers all the way." But even though Adrienne is right that I'm being ridiculously over-protective, I know that Ty has been very nervous about his debut as a college student. He's been out of the classroom for more than five years. Twice in recent weeks he's tried to defer his enrollment at Palmer Community College to the spring semester, claiming that Another Man's Treasure Estate Sales is too busy to spare him. But no one he knows—not me or Adrienne, or his cousin Marcus or his grandmother—would let him off the hook. So today's the day— Intro to Statistics, 20th Century Art, and Writing Skills.

"I think he said he had the art class first. That'll just be looking at slides. How hard could it be?" Adrienne squints at her computer screen, putting the finishing touches on a flyer she's designing for our next estate sale.

"It's not just the classes, it's the whole scene. You know, the other students."

Adrienne chokes on her green tea. "Audrey, the man is six-one, a hundred and ninety pounds. He survived a year in Rahway State Prison. You honestly think someone's going to bully him at Palmer Community College?"

I turn away. Adrienne means well, but she doesn't know Ty the way I do. Of course, no one he meets on campus would dare mess with him physically. But Ty is much more sensitive than his impressive physique would lead you to think. He's keenly tuned to other people's reactions. He senses disdain, has a divining rod for condescension. He's worried that he's not up to this challenge, and even more worried that the students and professors will immediately perceive his weakness.

And Ty does not like feeling weak.

I can relate.

But Adrienne's right. I can't call him after every class like some hysterical helicopter mom. Luckily, he was away for Labor Day weekend, so he'll have to stop by the office on his way home to pick up last week's paycheck. I'll debrief him then. I return to my Accounts Payable to keep myself busy until my afternoon appointment to provide an estimate at a house in Melton, one of Palmer County's priciest towns.

Soon Adrienne rises to retrieve something from the printer and I catch a whiff of her expensive perfume. Adrienne has raised the style quotient of our office by about a thousand percent. The Tory Burch flats she wears cost more than what I pay her for a week of part-time work. But I don't have to feel guilty for her paltry pay. Adrienne's Wall Street husband, my future brother-in-law, is her family's support. Adrienne begged for the job when Jill announced she was leaving, and the rest of the Coughlin clan chimed in loudly that working as my assistant was the perfect solution for both of us. Adrienne would have a job to put her talents to good use. Her husband and his parents would be satisfied that the job is flexible enough so the kids wouldn't suffer. I would get an over-qualified marketing expert who had once worked in the corporate world.

And Sean would look good for bringing a wonderful woman like me into the family.

So hiring Adrienne became my first test of Coughlin solidarity. In the face of that much pressure, could I behave rationally by interviewing a range of candidates and choosing the most qualified? I soon realized that when the Coughlins set their minds on something, resistance is futile.

"How's this for Saturday's sale?" Adrienne slides a colorful flyer in front of me. She's obviously spent a lot of time on it. Too much time. The net result is quite pretty, but too cluttered to be legible from a distance. And printing up fifty of these will use up half the expensive ink in our printer. I feel a bead of anxiety-induced sweat trickle between my breasts. Telling Adrienne's she's done a project incorrectly is not a management task I relish.

"Uh, it's lovely, but…"

Adrienne's eye's narrow. "But what?"

"Well, you've used a lot of colors, and some of these design elements make the text hard to read from a distance."

Adrienne's mouth tightens. "I think it's foolish to scrimp on printing costs," she sniffs. "You've got to spend money to make money."

Spoken like a woman who's used to spending money that other people earn. "True, but remember the flyers are just a small part of every sale's marketing plan. Spending more on them isn't the best use of our promotional budget."

Adrienne snatches back the flyer. "Well, if what I'm doing isn't important, why did you ask me to do it at all?"

I take a deep breath. Adrienne's only been on the job for two weeks, and we've already had a few of these contests of will. I cannot let her intimidate me. She may have better clothes sense and better decorating sense than I do, she may have once worked for Estee Lauder, but I know how to run my business.

I hand her the flyer. "Fewer colors. Bigger type."

Before she can respond, I grab my messenger bag and head out for my appointment.

Out on the sidewalk, I feel like kicking myself. If I head to Melton now, I'll be forty-five minutes early for my appointment. I'm such a ridiculous coward! I stand up to Adrienne, then run away because I can't bear to sit in the office with her while she sulks. I'm not cut out for dealing with high-maintenance women.

I guess I may as well stop by Caffeine Planet for a latte to kill some time. As I walk the few blocks to my favorite coffee emporium, I mull my management problem. The thing about Adrienne is she doesn't need to work. People who are desperate for a job to pay their bills *listen* to their bosses. People who want a job as a distraction from shopping and redecorating don't. But I have no one but myself to blame. In the heady first weeks of my relationship with Sean, I wasn't rationally analyzing pros and cons. Life was nothing but sunshine and roses. What could go wrong with hiring the wife of Sean's brother? Why not ingratiate myself with my new family by providing the perfect part-time job that everyone agrees Adrienne needs?

I'm still madly in love with Sean. His sister-in-law...not so much.

I turn the corner to North Main and the cheerful blue and green Planet sign beckons me. When I open the door, I'm bowled over by the wonderful aroma of rich, strong coffee. Who couldn't love this? You really have to wonder about people who say they don't drink coffee. I place my order for a medium latte, which at the Planet is just that—none of this bogus venti, grande nonsense— and make a little chit-chat with the baristas. I know them all by sight, if not by name. Instead of moving over to the coffee delivery area, I decide to pop back to the restroom while my drink is brewing.

A woman with a dancing toddler is ahead of me.

"Momeee, I have to go-o-o-o ba-a-a-d."

"Just hold it for a second, honey. We have to wait our turn."

The little girl, already low to the ground, crouches and peers under the two stall doors. She points to the stall on the right. "A lady is sitting on the ground in there. She shouldn't do that because the floor is yucky, right Mommee? Right?"

The mother and I exchange a glance, but at that moment the door of the stall on the left opens, and the mom herds her daughter in. I crouch down and look under the other door.

I see a pair of crumpled, blue-jean clad legs. One bare foot is visible.

Between two toes protrudes a hypodermic needle.

CHAPTER 2

I tug on the stall door, but of course it's locked. Bending down again, I gingerly touch the naked foot. The skin is warm, so hopefully the girl has just nodded out, not OD'd. I rush out to the counter. Luckily, the crowd has thinned and I can speak without causing too much of a commotion. I gesture to the older of the two baristas, who can't be more than twenty-three or four. "You'd better call 911. A girl has collapsed in the restroom. She's got a needle in her foot."

The barista's eyes widen. "Amber!"

"Oh my God, Amber, why wouldn't you stop?" The younger barista runs back to the ladies room.

"Call 911," I command, but the older girl hesitates.

Her colleague starts shouting from the back. "I can't reach her. I can't open the door. Call! Call an ambulance!"

The older girl takes a deep breath and reaches for the phone.

Once I hear sirens in the distance, I grab my coffee and head out to meet my client. I don't need to be in the middle of this drama; I've got enough of my own.

I settle into the driver's seat of my Honda and take a nerve-settling breath. What a morning!

I've always loved that my hometown is a mix of stylish and tacky, wealthy and gritty. But shooting up in a main street café at nine-thirty in the morning is a lot more grit than I'm comfortable with. Don't people even make an effort to hide their illegal activities anymore? I'd like to call Sean...hear the sound of his voice...hear him tell me that young women shooting up is the exception, not the new normal. But I know how he feels about personal calls during his workday. Unless I have a severed limb, I wait for him to call me. He usually checks in late in the afternoon so we can make plans for our evening. His place or mine, dine in or dine out? So I resist the urge to call him for reassurance and head south out of Palmyrton.

Melton is not so much a town as a sought-after zip code. What passes for the commercial district is a row of tiny shops in a few Victorian houses too close to the street to be desirable as residences. There's a gift shop that sells high-end tchotchkes, a café that sells high-end scones and tea, a tiny church used only for high-end Christmas, Easter and weddings, and a post office with one clerk. It's the kind of post office the Postmaster General keeps wanting to close to balance the budget, but the influential residents of Melton will never allow that to happen. They wouldn't want to merge with neighboring Palmyrton. Then their preppy kids would have to rub shoulders with the hoi poloi in the Palmyrton Little League, and their pure-bred dogs would have to play with mutts like my Ethel at the Palmyrton dog park.

And their drug addicts—and I'm sure Melton has its share— would be hauled off unceremoniously from the Vera Bradley section of the Cachet Boutique instead of being driven quietly home.

Sean says Melton insists on having its own police department so residents can call the cops every time a raccoon sets off their motion detector lights. But I need to put a lid on my attitude because running an estate sale in Melton is bound to add beaucoup bucks to the bottom line of Another Man's Treasure. And with Sean and me trying to buy a house, I need all the cash I can earn.

My client's house is lovely from the outside. A sizeable Tudor in a neighborhood of widely spaced gracious homes, it was probably built in the 1920s to house lawyers and stockbrokers and bankers and is still occupied by that ruling elite today. The curving flagstone walk and quaint mullioned windows set off a thrum of anticipation in my core. This is a house with profit potential.

Just as I raise my hand to the bird-shaped knocker, the heavy oak door swings open. An awful smell wafts out before I even step into the house. I'm used to old people's houses smelling bad, of course: cats, mothballs, mildew, must. The scent of this house is

familiar, but not one of those. I step into the house and shake hands
with the woman who's called me there.

"Hi, you must be Audrey. I'm Kara Lyman. Come on in."

The foyer is dim compared to the bright sunshine outside. I
follow the voice, feeling like I'm stepping into a void. A smelly
void. God, what is it? Sickly sweet with an undertone of decay. It's
a smell I know well, but not one I associate with estate sales. Like
not recognizing Ruby, my Zumba instructor, when she showed up
in my dad's chess clinic.

Once my eyes adjust, I can see that Kara is maybe early fifties,
a generation older than me. Her color-coordinated sweater and
slacks are stylish, in a country club mom kind of way. The foyer is
grand, with a polished parquet floor and a thick Persian rug.

"Thank you so much for meeting me here on such short notice."
Kara runs her hands through her hair, but the bob is so perfectly
cut that every strand falls right back into place. "As I mentioned on
the phone, I need you to do an inventory of the house's contents
and give me a rough estimate of the worth." She talks as she walks,
leading me into a large formal living room.

"It's a lovely home. Has it been in your family since it was
built?" I ask.

"No, my parents bought it shortly after they married, in the mid-
fifties."

My heart rate kicks up. Sixty years of very tasteful acquisitions.
My gaze rests on a Philip Guston painting over the fireplace.
"Your parents collected early twentieth century art?"

Kara glances over her shoulder at the painting, indifferent to its
beauty. "My father was the collector. He died in 1989. There
haven't been any more purchases since then."

I take a seat opposite her in a rose damask covered wing chair.
The room is immaculate, but the smell persists. Why can't I
identify it?

"I'm happy to give you an estimate, but you should know there
are no guarantees. The sale could bring in much more, or much
less. A lot depends on timing. When will you be putting the house
on the market?"

Kara shuts her eyes and takes a deep breath. "I have no idea."

Before she can elaborate, we hear a crash and a cry of pain from
the rear of the house. Kara jolts up from her seat. "Darlene?" She

rushes to an archway in the back of the room. A heavyset woman in pink and aqua nurse's scrubs appears and they talk quietly.

That's the smell! The horrible hospital smell of sickness and death. After my dad's stroke and my own brushes with serious injury, I've spent too much time in hospitals. These are memories I try to block, but the nose knows. Someone in this house is terminally ill, and Kara is already planning the estate sale. Does she expect me to run it while the poor old soul is clinging to life? Will I have to put "not for sale" signs on the oxygen tank and the IV pole? I've seen plenty of people who weren't heartbroken by their relative's death, but this is *cold*.

Kara returns. "Where was I? Oh, the timing of the sale. As you can see," she waves in the direction of the nurse, "my mother is in hospice care. She... I don't know..." Kara's cellphone starts an insistent trilling. She purses her lips and pulls the phone from her pocket. "Yes, Cassie? Well, what do you want me to do? I'm in New Jersey."

High-pitched, teenage girl keening floats through the air.

"Cassie, you'll just have to ask one of the other girls for a ride. You have to handle it yourself. There's nothing I can do." Kara ends the call in mid-screech.

She leans back in her chair, shuts her eyes, and lets the phone slip from her fingers. "I'm losing my mind," she murmurs.

"You have kids?"

"Three—the youngest is only fifteen, the middle one is in the midst of college applications. My husband is in sales and travels constantly. We live in Pittsburgh. And my mother is dying here, all alone. And I can't move her to a nursing home because, against the advice of her lawyer, she made it a condition of her will that if her children put her in a nursing home, she would leave all her money to St. Hubert's Animal Shelter." Kara's lip trembles as she opens her eyes to meet mine. "Honestly, I'm about ready to let the dogs have it, because I can't take this stress. Driving back and forth, seven hours each way. Never in the right place at the right time. Ugh."

Her well-groomed façade has cracked and I see the frazzled woman within. "Are you an only child?" I ask.

"Ha! It would be easier if I were. I'm the second of four. My older brother should have been the executor. If he had lived, none of this would be happening." Two slow tears slip down her cheeks. "My younger siblings, Rachel and Tom, are twins. Tom is...has... issues. And Rachel, Rachel is The Baby." Kara makes air quotes. "She was born an hour after Tom and nearly died. Her whole life we all treated her like a fragile little flower. Now we—I'm— paying the price."

Kara takes a deep breath and clenches her hands. "I can't believe I'm telling you all this. You must think I'm nuts."

"No, I'm used to it. People have a tendency to tell me all about their families. Something about turning over all their stuff to me is...freeing...I guess."

Yes, I'm used to being a psychotherapist to bereaved, and not so bereaved, survivors. But Kara is not a survivor. Her mom is still alive. "So, you're not thinking of having the sale before...."

"Oh, no! But I've been coming to New Jersey once every ten days or so. It's exhausting. I have to make the most of each trip, try to get as much done as possible. I have to be totally prepared, have everything ready. When, you know, it happens."

I want the job. I can tell from the two rooms I've been in that there's lots of good stuff here. But geez, the idea of inventorying this poor woman's possessions while she's clinging to her last days of life.... What will I say if she asks who I am, what I'm doing? Without sounding critical, I need to encourage Kara to wait until her mom has passed before starting the job. "We could sign a contract now, then you could just call me from Pittsburgh and I'd get started...when the time comes."

Kara's hands grip the arms of her chair. "It's vital that I get an inventory now. It's a complicated estate. As the executor, I'm responsible. I need to have everything inventoried and the sale ready to run. My Realtor already has a buyer for the house. She told me your company would empty the house and leave it clean as a whistle. Isn't that what you do?"

"Yes, of course, but usually—"

Before I can elaborate, Kara lets out an exasperated huff. "You're not interested. I'll have to find someone else."

Whoa, Nellie—not so fast! "I want the job. I can start the inventory as soon as you sign the contract."

There's another metallic clatter. Kara flinches, but doesn't rise this time. "My mother is restless. She's not really aware of what's

going on. Sometimes the aide has a hard time keeping her calm."
She gives her head a little shake to regain her train of thought.
"You wanted to me sign a contract?" She extends her hand.

I pull my standard contract out of my bag. Kara grabs a pen
from the end table and moves to sign it.

Geez, she really is in a hurry! "You should read it first," I warn.

"I'm sure it's fine. My Realtor recommended you." She hands
the signed contract back. "Can you start right now? There's quite a
bit to go through."

"Today? I hadn't planned on it, but I guess I could work until
five." New job or no new job, I'm still determined to make it back
to the office in time to intercept Ty after his classes.

"Good. How long will it take you to get me an estimate?"

"It depends on how much research I have to do. Items of
exceptional value I'll sell through specialized dealers, not the
general sale. Maybe a few days, maybe a week."

"I'm returning to Pittsburgh tonight, but the aide will be here
every day. She can let you in. Let me introduce you."

"The sick room—there's nothing for me to see there, I
imagine?" I hope.

"Actually, the room Mother is in now used to be the study.
There are some antiques, some paintings and books. You will need
to go in."

I'm not too good at keeping a poker face. Kara must notice my
distaste.

"Don't worry. The aide will know the best time, when Mother
has had her meds and is sleeping."

Kara's phone chirps. "That's the alert for my lawyer's
appointment. Come and meet Darlene and I'll leave you to your
work."

I follow her to the far side of the room, and a cluster of framed
photos catches my eye. "But are you sure you're ready? You need
to remove items of sentimental value and other things you don't
want sold."

Kara surveys the living room with an unamused laugh. "There's
nothing sentimental about this place. My mother's good jewelry is
in the safe deposit box. Everything else is up for sale."

People say this all the time, but when the house has been
emptied to the bare floorboards, they come to me demanding to

know what I did with an envelope containing a lock of baby hair, or a circa 1945 newspaper article about Aunt Bessie serving in the WACs. I point to the photos. "Snapshots, letters, souvenirs—what do you want me to do with them?"

"Sell the frames. Toss the photos. Toss anything you find." Her voice contains not a shred of doubt.

"But your siblings? Maybe they have mementoes they want preserved?"

Kara's restless eyes meet mine. "Believe me, there's nothing in this house any of us wants to preserve."

CHAPTER 3

Darlene, her frizzy hair yanked back from a broad, plain face, acknowledges our introduction without much interest and says Mrs. Eskew won't be reliably asleep for at least an hour, so I head upstairs to begin. There, the stench of illness isn't so bad. It doesn't take long for me to become totally engrossed in the inventory. There are five bedrooms on the second floor. A quick glance shows the master is at the near end of the hall, but I save that for last. The next three bedrooms are tastefully decorated with antiques and perfectly coordinated custom bedding and drapes. Guest rooms, now that the kids are grown. But one bedroom has been maintained as a shrine: tennis trophies, swimming trophies, golf trophies, crew trophies—all engraved to Parker Eskew. This has to be Kara's oldest brother, the one who was supposed to be the executor. A blue Columbia banner. An award from Rotary. Some kind of fraternity certificate. And framed photos, scores of them. Parker in his scull. Parker with a tennis racquet on his shoulder. Parker in a group of tuxedoed young men. He resembles Kara, but in the way a Doberman resembles a mini pinscher. The face is similar, but it's a whole different breed. His vitality practically leaps out of the picture frames. In none of the photos does he look any older than late twenties. I wonder what happened to him?

It will be our job to discard all this after the sale. Kara's pain when she mentioned her brother seemed genuine, yet she doesn't want to keep any of his things. Maybe she already has the treasures that are meaningful to her. You can't keep everything. But people feel heartless discarding the memories of the departed.

And it's a good thing they do. That's what keeps Another Man's Treasure in business.

This room has the most personality, but the fewest items of monetary value. The bed, dresser, and nightstand are slightly dated Ethan Allen. I can sell them, certainly, but they won't bring much. I open a dresser drawer expecting it to be empty. Instead there are some neatly folded Columbia sweatshirts and tees. I open another drawer—please don't tell me she saved his underwear and socks—but it's full of scrapbooks and photo albums.

I shut it gently and leave the room.

In the master bedroom, there's plenty to inventory. A collection of Chinese cloisonné, a series of Audubon prints, a closet with five Prada and two Chanel bags and some timeless St. John suits. There are four small worn spots in the shape of a large rectangle. Something has been removed from the top of the dresser—a jewelry box? I open the dresser drawers. The two small top drawers are empty, but the lower drawers are filled with lingerie. This must be where Mrs. Eskew kept the jewelry that Kara says is now in a bank vault.

I finish in the bedrooms and notice a raised panel door that blends with the wainscoting in the hall. I try the handle, but it's locked. I'll have to ask Kara about that. There's also a narrow staircase that leads up to the third floor. I walk partway up, but I'm driven back by the heat. No air-conditioning up there. I think I'll save that for another morning when it's cooler.

I head down the broad main stairway. There's a landing where the stairs turn, with a niche containing a lovely sculpture of a nymph gracefully perched on rocks. I pause to take a photo. This will require some research—I know nothing about sculpture. I crouch to line up the shot just as Darlene emerges from the study/sickroom. She has her cell phone pressed to her ear, and an orange prescription bottle in her other hand. "It says fifteen milligrams," she says. "Twenty. Yeah? Well, you try taking care of her with no meds. Fine."

She walks out of my line of sight. Then I hear the rattle of pills shaken out of a bottle.

CHAPTER 4

I descend the stairs and stand hesitating in the foyer. Should I go to the back of the house and see if now is a good time to inventory Mrs. Eskew's sickroom? I'd much prefer to slip out the front door, but honestly, the task won't be any more appealing tomorrow.

I start down the hallway, but a long table with a collection of stone figures soon catches my attention. They're gargoyles! How cool is that? I pick one up—whoa, really heavy—and study his face: big bulging eyes, pointy ears, and a teasing grin. The back of the figure is rough and uneven, showing where he was removed from whatever building he once guarded. I pick up another. This one has a dragon's snout and wings emerging from his shoulders. I wonder how much they're worth? 'Cause if they're not too expensive, I may have to buy one for the new house we're searching for. Sean would love it.

I'm a few steps from the study, when the door flies open. Darlene and I spring away from each other, equally startled.

Her eyes narrow. "I didn't know you were out here."

"I just came down from the bedrooms. Is this a good time to inventory the study? If not, it can wait until tomorrow."

Darlene sighs. "No, you may as well do it now. She's asleep."

"If I'm interrupting your break…"

"I don't get a break." Darlene holds the study door open and waves me in.

The room is dim and suffocatingly hot. The decaying smell catches in the back of my throat. How can Darlene stand to sit in here all day? I creep forward. A high hospital bed with the head raised sits in the center of the room. At first glance it appears empty, the old woman lying in it is so wizened and pale. I can see the blue veins of her scalp through the scant tufts of silver hair that remain. Her breaths are rasping and so far apart that they don't seem capable of sustaining life. I avert my gaze and make my way to the bookcases that cover two walls.

A decorator can impart style, but books speak the truth about a house. Matched sets of leather-bound classics: fake culture. Slightly frayed editions on eclectic topics: a true reader. Meticulously organized books with perfect dust jackets: a collector. Readers are more fun, but collectors bring in more money, of course.

I shine my flashlight across the shelves. John Steinbeck. Willa Cather. Wallace Stegner. Someone had a passion for authors writing about the American West. My heart rate kicks up. Good lord, could that be a first edition of *The Grapes of Wrath*? I climb the rolling ladder to give the volume a closer look.

"What made you go after that one?"

Darlene's voice startles me so much I nearly topple off the ladder. I got so excited by the book, I forgot she was even in the room. First editions are one of my favorite topics and I could easily wax on about them, but I bite back my words. A book would be easy to steal, but hard to sell for someone who knows nothing about rare editions. I slide the Steinbeck back into its place. I'm starting to see the scope of the job. This room alone could take me all day if these shelves are filled with valuable first editions. Clearly, I'm going to have a hard time cataloguing all these books under Darlene's inquisitive eye. I'll have to ask Kara how she wants me to handle the book collection.

"Just an author I like. I'm kind of a book geek." I come down the ladder. "Have you been taking care of Mrs. Eskew for long?"

"Three months." Darlene stands with her arms folded, watching me. Chit-chat about her patient is not on her agenda.

There's a nice little Queen Anne table next to the bed. I'd like to look at it, but a stainless steel tray filled with pill bottles rests on top. How can a dying person require so much medication?

"You want me to move that?"

"If you don't mind." I feel Darlene's eyes boring into my back as I open the drawer to look at the dovetail joints and run my fingers over the finish.

"You think someone's gonna wanna buy that?"

"Mmmm. Probably. There's a good market for smaller pieces like this."

"Like, for more than twenty bucks?"

I shrug, hoping I'm projecting indifference. In reality, I know a dealer who will pay $800 and sell it in a shop in Mendham or Summit for $1,200.

"Well, I wouldn't give more than twenty bucks for any of this dark, depressing old junk," Darlene says. "If I had money, I'd go to Ikea and buy all new fresh, modern stuff. I like modern. I wouldn't want some dead lady's old shit."

I cringe at "dead lady." But poor Mrs. Eskew doesn't stir. "Lots of people agree with you," I say. "But luckily there enough who like antiques…or a bargain… to keep me in business."

"Yeah, I know all about finding bargains at garage sales." Darlene nudges a frayed footstool with her white Crocs. "I'm sick of that. Sick of second-hand everything."

I move to a huge desk that has been pushed aside to make room for the bed. It's Chippendale revival, made of nice mahogany, but pieces like this don't fetch much these days. Now that all anyone needs to run a business is a laptop and a cellphone, the market for desks with this much square footage has shrunk to nothing.

"When you planning on having this sale?" Darlene follows me, keeping five feet between us.

I cough. "Not until…."

"She'll be gone by Friday. Saturday, tops."

My eyes widen. "But Kara just went back to Pittsburgh."

"I *told* Ms. Lyman. She don't wanna believe me. Says the doctor is giving her two, three weeks. No way."

"You've taken care of a lot of dying people?"

"Twenty-five, thirty. You hear that sound she's making when she inhales?"

We pause and listen to the intermittent scratch of sandpaper on wood emanating from the bed.

"I don't care what the doctor says," Darlene continues. "That sound means she's on the way out."

I open my mouth to speak, but what can I possibly say?

"Guess you think that's mean, huh?"

"Just realistic, I'm sure." I scurry over to the oil portrait between the two windows, sending up a silent prayer that when my time comes, I won't have Darlene watching over me. "What will you do when this job...ends?"

"If I'm lucky, the agency will send me right out on another one. I got three kids. I can't afford days off."

She flicks her stringy ponytail. "I'll probably get another job pretty quick. I'm in demand 'cause I'm...you know."

Brutally honest? I wouldn't think that'd be a selling point in a home health aide. I peer at her above the iPad I'm using to take pictures and notes. "Uh...I'm sure you're good at what you do."

"That doesn't matter. I meant, I get hired a lot 'cause I'm white. Lots of the other girls are Haitian or Jamaican. Don't get me wrong, I think they're nice. But lots of the old folks don't want a black nurse."

I stop what I'm doing. "Surely it's illegal to request someone by race?"

"Yeah, I think it is. They say stuff like, 'Must speak perfect English.' Like, my friend Georgene is way smarter than me. She was a registered nurse back in Jamaica. But sometimes she don't get the jobs, and I do."

Darlene keeps talking as I shine my flashlight on the painting of a dour old man in 18th century garb. I'm looking for the artist's signature, but all I can see is a tiny brass plate screwed into the frame, which reads "Bartholomew Eskew, 1735-1791." Cool—an ancestor painting. Won't Kara want to keep this? If old Bartholomew were my great-great-great-great grandpa, I'd keep him.

"This job hasn't been so bad," Darlene continues. "At least she's light. Changing her diapers isn't so hard. The four hundred pound diabetics with gangrene are the worst."

She sinks into a chair. "And the ones with Alzheimer's. They stay up all night and roam around the house. They try to escape. They reach in their pants and throw their shit at you. The old men beat off all the time."

With her eyes half-closed, she keeps talking. "Yeah, this job's not so bad. I hope the old gal hangs on a few more days."

I want to run screaming from the room. I'd rather work in a coal mine than have Darlene's job.

CHAPTER 5

"Tell me all about it!"

By the time I get back to the office, Adrienne has left for the day and Ty's car— a three-year-old Nissan Sentra that's his pride and joy—is parked out front. Finally, I get to hear the report on his first day of school. And after my encounters with the drug addict at Caffeine Planet and the home health aide at the Eskews' house, I'm ready for some happy news.

Ty tucks his paycheck in his back pocket and shrugs. "I dunno. It was a'right. Just school. Without all the nonsense rules."

"C'mon, Ty—you gotta give me more than that. How was 20th Century Art?"

He grins. "The teacher talks like Jill. 'Matisse's The Da-a-ance is the first m-a-a-sterpiece of the ce-e-e-ntureee.' "Cept she's hotter. Statistics, the teacher's an old dude, but he's okay. He started right in teaching and I understood everything. So far."

I'm encouraged by his enthusiasm. "What about the writing class?"

Ty's expression darkens. "'S okay. But I don't wanna be there."

"Writing was never my favorite subject either, but it's useful in business to be able to write well."

"I don't mind taking English. I'm mad I got put in the dumbass class. Even when I was doing bad in high school, they never put me in with the dumbass kids."

"Ty! It's not a class for slow learners. Remedial just means you have a little catching up to do before you're ready for the freshman writing class."

"'Cause I don't talk right."

"You talk fine. It's just…nonstandard."

"So this class is to help me talk white?"

"No!…Well, maybe. Kinda."

Ty grins and the smile spreads to his big brown eyes. "Marcus can turn it on and off. When he's out with us, he talks regular. 'Yo, whattup…let's chill with some Stoli' Then when he's with his friends from work, he's all, 'Nice to see you again. Would you care to partake of a cocktail?' I ain't goin' there."

I crack up. Ever since Ty's cousin Marcus got his first job at a Wall Street bank, he's gotten a little pretentious, and Ty busts him for it. "I promise I'll never ask you to utter the phrase 'partake of a cocktail.' But you want to learn the business, right? Meet with clients, negotiate with dealers. You don't want to be still hauling heavy furniture when you're forty."

"I guess." Ty sighs. "Will you tell me when I make a mistake? But just you. I don't want to hear it from her." He points to Adrienne's empty desk.

I rest my hand on his arm. "Just me."

Ty turns his back and busies himself straightening some boxes in the corner. "I think I did something stupid," he mutters into the cardboard.

"What? Tell me."

"In the English class, I wrote about stuff that I shouldn't have. She asked us to write about why we decided to enroll in college this semester. I should've just written something basic, like I want to go to college to do better at my job. Instead, I, I…"

"You told the truth?"

That he had gotten bored with high school and dropped out. That he had fallen in with older guys he wanted to impress. That he drove the car when they robbed a convenience store. That his misadventures had brought him a felony conviction that would shadow his whole life.

"So now she knows a lot about me. Too much."

I'm curled up on Sean's couch researching prices for Mrs. Eskew's nymph sculpture and paintings while he cooks our dinner: salmon and couscous with some kind of greenish sauce. Roasted Brussels sprouts, which I never even knew I liked. If he went to the farmer's market, maybe there will even be an apple tart. My lonely days of eating carry-out Pad Thai straight from the box are over.

I resisted being taken care of, resisted mightily. But now that I've surrendered, I've discovered being in love is nice. Really nice.

I offered to help cook, but Sean says I slow him down. So I lean on the island that separates the living room from the kitchen and tell him about my new job. "The people aren't so nice, but the house is loaded with great stuff. This job will finally get Another Man's Treasure on track to meet my profit projections for the year. We could actually be up five percent over last year if those books and paintings are as valuable as I think they might be. I'm researching prices right now."

Sean reaches across the counter and strokes my arm. "You're so sexy when you talk numbers."

"You're so sexy when you sauté."

I love watching Sean cook. His big hands move with amazing dexterity, the chef's knife flashing over a pile of herbs. His sandy eyebrows draw together as he examines something simmering in a skillet. He is as intense about our meal as he is about every crime he investigates for the Palmyrton police department.

I've turned my attention back to my laptop when Sean speaks. "Have you checked your email? Has Isabelle sent us any listings to look at?"

My throat tightens. "Uh, no—nothing today. She says this is a slow time for new listings." I feel terrible for lying, but I can't show Sean the links to the houses that our real estate agent sent me this afternoon. They're awful little split-levels and Capes with tiny boxy rooms and dismal 1970s kitchens and baths. We've been searching for weeks, so I know Sean will insist on going to look at them. And they both have four bedrooms, which he wants. And they both have big yards, which he insists upon. All this for the prospective kids that he can hardly wait to have and I am terrified of.

I'd be perfectly happy with the adorable renovated two-bedroom carriage house with a secluded patio and no lawn whatsoever that Sean firmly rejected in late July. I still fantasize about that place—a perfect little love nest for two.

"Audrey, we've got to find a place to live." He looks up from stirring and his blue eyes meet mine. "I hate never spending the entire night with you."

My heart melts and I get up to give him a hug. I can't spend the entire night at Sean's place because of his building's no-dogs policy and he can't get a decent night's sleep at my place because my bedroom is only big enough for double bed. So we pawn my mutt Ethel off on my dad when we can, and when we can't we fool around like teenagers and then I go home to my place or Sean goes home to his.

"Maybe we need a different Realtor," he murmurs as he wraps his arms around me.

"No!" I pull away. "Isabelle said she'd have some places for us to look at soon. She has first crack at new listings coming on the market." The truth is, after I passed on her latest listings, Isabelle suggested that maybe, just maybe, I ought to run the listings past my partner before rejecting them out of hand. "Darling," she'd said, "he might see potential there that you're missing. Is he handy?"

In fact, Sean is handy. And he's tapped into a network of moonlighting cops and firefighters and building inspectors who know how to do just about everything. But I know how anxious Sean is for us to get settled. I don't want him to talk me into a place that we'll regret just for the sake of having our housing problems resolved. I'll know "our" house when I see it. And it won't be some dreadful Disco era bi-level on the far edge of nowhere.

Dinner is delicious, and as Sean presents me with a slice of fruit tart and a cup of decaf, my phone rings.

I glance down, unwilling to take a call from anyone annoying who will kill our mellow mood.

It's Jill!

"Hi, honey! How's school?"

"Oh, Audrey, I'm so upset. My friend, she died. I can't belie-e-e-ve it." Choking sobs come through the line, loud enough to make Sean stop stirring his coffee and take notice.

Her friend died? She's only been at NYU a few weeks. How good a friend could have died? And of what? The crying escalates. Maybe a fellow student got hit by a car? "I'm sorry, Jill. Were you there when it happened?"

"What? No, of course not. I'm here, at school. I would have stopped her if I'd've known."

Hmmm. Sounds like a suicide. Just like Jill to feel responsible for everyone's stability. "Don't blame yourself. There must've been other people she could have turned to for help."

"Not the friends she has now. I'm the one who's known her since kindergarten. We were best friends all through middle school. But in high school...." And the rest of the sentence disappears in tears.

"Wait, who are you talking about? This isn't someone from NYU?"

"No-o-o. It's Amber. Amber Pileggi."

Amber? Why does that name sound familiar?

"Didn't you hear? It happened right in Caffeine Planet. People in Palmyrton are posting all the RIP messages on Facebook and Twitter, but no one will say exactly what happened."

"Oh. *That* girl." The words slip out involuntarily, and instantly I regret them.

"What do you mean? Do you know something."

"I don't. I just heard someone got sick there this morning." Yes, I'm lying to Jill. But if she finds out I was on the scene, she'll pester me for every little detail. And honestly, what do I know? I saw her foot. I saw the needle. This gory detail will only make Jill more emotional. "I heard it might be drug-related."

"Augh! That's what I was worried about. Amber had a problem with pills."

Let Jill believe that. She doesn't need to know the truth is even worse. "Honey, I'm sorry about your friend. But don't let this bring you down, okay? You need to stay focused on school."

"I know." Her sobbing subsides. "I just needed to talk to someone who would understand. I haven't made the kind of friends here that I can flip out on. At least, not yet."

"You can always flip out on me."

"Thanks, Audrey. You're the best." Jill gives one last sniff. "I feel better now."

"What was that all about?" Sean asks after I hang up. "Is Jill okay?"

"Do you know what happened to the girl who died in Caffeine Planet this morning? I was there when we found her in the rest room."

Sean fixes me with his penetrating stare. "You were there? Why didn't you mention it?"

"I wanted to call you when it happened because I was kinda freaked. But I hate to bother you at work. And honestly, by dinner tonight, so much else had happened that I forgot about it. Why? Is it more than an accidental overdose?"

He stabs a forkful of tart and chews methodically.

"Sean?"

"I can't discuss it, Audrey."

"I saw the needle. It was heroin, right? Are you involved in the investigation?"

Sean places his silverware carefully on the plate and keeps his eyes focused on his coffee.

"C'mon, Sean. Can't you just confirm what she died from?"

"So you can tell Jill and she can tell the immediate solar system? No, Audrey, I cannot tell you."

Like a kid who's told she can't have a cookie, I now really, really want the cookie. "Is the investigation a big deal? I mean, sad to say, but overdose deaths aren't that uncommon anymore, right? So why is Amber's death unusual?"

"Audrey!"

I see our happy dinner heading south. My curiosity over Amber's death isn't worth a fight with Sean.

I stand up and clear the plates. Clean-up is my job when Sean cooks. "Okay, Mr. Confidentiality. But I'll remember this next time you need a tip."

Sean slips his arms around my waist and nuzzles my neck. "What I need is a tip on a bedroom that can hold a king-size bed."

I twist to face him. "There's one about twenty steps from here."

"What time do you need to leave?"

"Ethel should go out by eleven."

Sean backs me out of the kitchen. "Forget the dishes. I'll do them in the morning."

CHAPTER 6

The next day, I return to the Eskews' house ready for a full day of inventorying.

I ring the front doorbell twice, but no one answers.

The home health aide is supposed to be here to let me in. I'll be really ticked if I came all this way for nothing.

I try the doorknob and it turns in my hand. Apparently Darlene simply left it unlocked.

Armed with my research, I'm eager to resume work on the book collection. I tap lightly on the sickroom door. Darlene pokes her head out. "I see you got in. Mornings are hard. I have my hands full with her, so I'm just going to leave the door open for you. Give me another half hour and you can work in here."

I busy myself in the foyer until Darlene reappears. She nods me into the room as her fingers fly over the screen of her cell phone. As she types, she clucks and sighs and moans so much that I know something must be going haywire in her personal life. Is it possible to eavesdrop on someone's texting? Finally she slams the phone down. "Oh, for God's sake!"

Surely, I'm meant to respond to that. "Is there a problem?"

"My youngest. He's telling the school nurse he's got a stomachache, and now she expects me to drop everything and come get him. What does the damn school even have a nurse for if they can't handle an upset stomach?"

She looks at Mrs. Eskew, who lies comatose, barely breathing, then glances at me. I hastily turn my attention to the books.

"I've gotta go outside to make a call," she says to my back. "I'll be right back. Don't worry. She won't wake up."

I open my mouth to protest, but Darlene is not paying attention to me. Before she's even out of the room, I see her phone pressed to her ear and hear her say, "You have to get him and stay with him. You know he can't stay home alone."

A few moments later, I can see Darlene's hot pink smock through the crack in the Venetian blinds as she paces back and forth on the patio talking into her phone and gesturing emphatically with her free hand.

She must be trying to get someone else to pick up the sick kid. I try to imagine myself in such a bind—trying to manage my kids' problems from a distance, always worrying about what's going on at home while I'm at work. My hands stop flipping through the book I'm holding. I worry so much about Jill and Ty and Sean and they're adults. How will I ever cope with being fully responsible for some tiny person's life? My father never knew how to cope with me. What if it's genetic?

I shiver.

Below me, I hear a voice. "I always knew it would come to this."

My hand freezes on a book. Darlene is still outside. Who spoke?

I look down at the bed. Mrs. Eskew's eyes are wide open. "How have you managed on your own?" she says, looking intently at someone in front of her. But the room is empty.

Slowly, I descend the ladder and creep toward the bed. "Mrs. Eskew? Are you all right?"

"Jean-Claude? I will meet him finally. How does the boy amuse himself? Have you told him...." Her voice had been surprisingly strong, but now it trails off.

I stand over her. Her eyes, intensely blue in her colorless face, lock with mine. "Put that book down," she says quite distinctly.

I look at my hand, surprised to see that *Tender is the Night* is still in my grasp. I set it on the bedside table.

Mrs. Eskew's eyes track my motion. "I despise Fitzgerald."

"Overrated," I agree. Should I be talking to her? Will she be frightened of this stranger in her room? She's suddenly remarkably alert. I was under the impression that even when she was awake she wasn't aware of her surroundings. But clearly that's not true.

"Where's that woman?"

"Darlene? She just stepped out to make a call. I'll go get her."

I turn and a claw-like hand reaches out from the covers and latches onto my arm. "Forget that fat bitch. Who are you?"

"My name is Audrey, Audrey Nealon. Your daughter hired me to…" I can't say dispose of your estate. "…organize your book collection. You have some very fine volumes."

"Huh. I'm surprised Kara didn't haul them all out to the curb. The girl hasn't read a book since Nancy Drew." She relaxes the iron grip on my arm. "Have you come across *The Grapes of Wrath* yet? My husband bought a first edition for seven dollars in 1955. Now it's worth thousands."

"Twelve thousand, five hundred actually. I've done the research."

"It's just as well to sell it. My remaining children are philistines, all of them." Her breathing becomes shallow and ragged. "Jean-Claude would have appreciated these books."

Her hand clutches the blanket, trying to wring strength from it. I look toward the door. Surely Darlene should be back by now.

"Mrs. Eskew, I'd better go get your nurse."

"No. That cow, she doesn't listen. She won't give me…"

Then, as suddenly as she awoke, her eyelids flutter and her hand falls limp onto the blanket. My God, is she? No, no—her chest is moving and the raspy breathing has returned.

I back away from the bed and nearly step on Darlene. I didn't even hear her come back.

"There you are! She woke up. She was talking to me."

"Yeah?" Darlene clearly doesn't share my amazement. She places her fingers on Mrs. Eskew's wrist to take her pulse. "She does that sometimes. Wears her out though."

"I thought she was totally out of it, but she talked to me about her books. She made perfect sense." I don't mention the old gal's focus on her most valuable volume.

"Mmmm. Sometimes she's totally clear, sometimes not."

"At first she didn't even know I was in the room. It was like she was looking straight at someone and having a conversation."

"Was she asking about Jean-Claude?"

"Yeah! Who's that?"

"Her grandson who never got born. She talks to him and his mother, Leonie. They're waiting for her on the other side. I tell her, 'Just go ahead and let go. They'll show you around'."

I look at Darlene uneasily. Is she serious?

"That's why I know she's close to passing. When they start seein' the ones who went before, it's definitely time."

I cough. "You've experienced this… phenomenon… before?"

"Sure. All the time." Darlene bustles around straightening the bedding, then plops into her bedside chair.

"So you believe that's true? That our dead relatives are waiting for us in—" I don't want to say heaven. I'm not sure I believe in heaven, certainly not one with angels and clouds. "—on the other side."

Darlene shrugs. "Guess no one really knows what happens after we die. No one's lived to tell about it. Ha! But I can tell you this— when it comes close to the end, I've seen my patients start talking to their dead husbands and parents and sisters and kids. Even their dead dogs. I've seen it time and again. So I guess someone's there."

I can't help but think of my mother, dead since I was three. Will I see her when I'm ready to cross over? What if I don't want to?

"Do they only see the people they cared about? What if…?"

"Your relatives are assholes? Yeah, I worry about that. I sure don't want to run into my old man again. I had enough of his beatings and bullshit here on earth. I don't need to have it again in eternity."

This conversation is totally creeping me out. Time to change the subject. "Did you get everything worked out for your son? Is he okay?" I ask as I climb back up the library ladder.

Darlene makes a sound that's half groan, half laugh. "My youngest, Kenny, he was born with cerebral palsy. Damn doctor didn't notice the cord was wrapped around his neck until he already had the oxygen to his brain cut off. So he's got some learning disabilities and bad fine motor skills. That means he can't tie his shoes or cut his meat or pour his juice. My other sons think I baby Kenny. They think he oughta be able to stay home by himself, take care of himself. But he can't. He really can't."

"Your sons are your only back-up? No grandparents who can cover for you?"

"My mother's a drunk. I wouldn't trust her with a gerbil. My middle son's good with Kenny. He's going to stay home with him today." Darlene sighs. "I just wish JJ didn't have to miss his classes. He goes to Palmer Community College."

I turn my head so Darlene doesn't see the disapproval that I'm sure is written across my face. I think of all the times my father came home from teaching at Rutgers railing against parents who expected their college student kids to cut classes to run family errands. But clearly Darlene is between a rock and a hard place. What should she sacrifice—her older son's education or her youngest son's safety?

"How many classes is he taking?" I keep making small talk as I catalog the books: Faulkner, O'Connor, Plath.

"Only three. We can't afford more. He works forty hours a week as a busboy at the Palmer Heights Country Club too. Pay's pretty good over there. Helps me keep the electricity on." She shifts her wide body in the chair. "I wish Rob, my oldest, would take a job there. But he's got big plans, that one. Just like his dad. All talk."

My God, I wish I were done in this room! Between the smell and the effort to find a topic of conversation that's neither creepy nor tragic, my head is about to split. I climb down and move the ladder. Only one more section of shelves to go.

Darlene observes me through narrowed eyes. "Guess you're not planning on hauling all these off to the Goodwill, huh?" She picks up a frayed paperback copy of a Janet Evanovich mystery from the bedside table. "That's where I got this. They have a pretty good selection over there, four for a dollar."

"That's a good deal," I agree.

I feel Darlene's eyes on me even though I'm facing the shelves. It's like she's trying to peer right into my brain. "These books you take somewhere special?"

"There are dealers…" I trail off noncommittally.

"Dealers. Yeah. I guess there's dealers for everything. Everything anybody wants, there's gotta be someone willing to deal."

CHAPTER 7

I'm sitting in the parking lot of the Palmyrton train station awaiting the arrival of the 6:03 from Manhattan. Jill is coming home from NYU to attend Amber Pileggi's visitation. She's begged me to go with her. I can hear her voice echoing in my head. "Pu-le-e-e-eze, Audrey. It'll be so awful. Funeral homes scare me. But I have to go."

Funeral homes don't thrill me either. But I miss Jill so much, I'm willing to accompany her on this depressing obligation. Then we can go out to dinner and she'll spend the night at my place before taking the train back to the city in the morning. It will be the first evening Sean and I have spent apart in weeks.

There's a whistle and the NJ Transit Midtown Express barrels into the station. Hordes of business-suited commuters pour out of the double-decker cars. Gray suit after gray suit, men and women both. And then I see a flash of chartreuse and magenta. There she is!

"Jill!" I wave to flag her over to my car. She picks up speed like a crazed greyhound, scarves and beads and tote bags streaming and jangling as she tears across the parking lot. She smacks into my arms and we clutch each other like reunited war refugees. It's only been six weeks, but our separation feels like a lifetime.

Jill's tears are always close to the surface, but even my eyes well up as we hug. "I miss you SO much," she sobs.

"I miss you too, honey."

She straightens up. "How's Adrienne doing?"

I've anticipated this question and I made up my mind that I would be very cautious in complaining about Adrienne to Jill. The last thing I want is for Jill to feel bad about her decision to leave

AMT and go to grad school. "She's okay. Getting the hang of things."

Jill's mascara smeared eyes narrow and she peers at me shrewdly. "You're not getting along."

The girl could get a job with the CIA interrogating terrorists. "Let's wait until dinner and I'll tell you all about it. What time does the viewing start?"

"It's already started. We'd better go straight there before I lose my nerve."

I hand her a tissue. "Fix your makeup. You should have known better than to wear mascara to a funeral."

On the drive to the O'Malley Funeral Home, Jill fills me in on Amber Pileggi's short, sad life. "We met on the first day of kindergarten. She was obsessed with horses and books and so was I. We played My Little Pony and Little House on the Prairie, two little weirdoes in our own little world. And we stayed that way, right up until freshman year. Then Amber got a boyfriend and left me behind." Jill sighs. "I don't blame her. I would have done the same thing if someone as hot as Anthony Lanza noticed me."

"She dumped you for a guy? I hate girls like that."

"She didn't, not really." Jill stares out the window and falls silent. "By sophomore year, I was hanging out with the drama club geeks. I tried to get her to work on a play, but she wouldn't. We never had a fight or anything. We would still talk sometimes. But you know how high school is. Everyone in their own clique. But we would still hang out sometimes, just us two, until…."

"What?"

"Senior year we went to the mall together. Amber was driving and texting with her boyfriend at the same time. She drifted out of her lane and we got in a pretty bad accident. Amber broke her ankle in a couple places and I got whiplash. She didn't want to tell the cops she had been texting, so she just said she and I were talking and she got distracted. After that, we really drifted apart."

Jill sighs. "Then I went off to college, and she stayed here at went to Palmer Community. Then I came back, but with all my problems I couldn't, I didn't…."

I reach for her hand and give it a squeeze while I drive. Jill's decision to drop out of the Rhode Island School of Design has always troubled her. The official story is that when her aunt, who had helped to raise her, died unexpectedly, Jill fell apart and came home and finished her degree at Ramapo State. But over the time she worked for me, I've figured out some other pieces to the story. Becoming an artist was Jill's mother's dream, not Jill's. Jill has an artistic eye, for sure, but I don't think she was ever very passionate about art, and she felt out of her element at RISD. But Jill has always been a good student, and dropping out and transferring to a less prestigious school must have felt like a failure to her. That's why I was so pleased when she chose to go to NYU to study psychiatric social work. This was totally her choice. She's found her true calling.

"When I was finishing up at Ramapo, I ran into Amber in town. She had dropped out of Palmer Community, and was working at the Burger King on Route 10. She looked like crap—really skinny and pale. But she was still the same sweet Amber, ya know? We went out just the two of us and it was like middle school all over again. We laughed and got silly. But as the evening went on, she got—like—strange, restless. She kept checking her phone and I got annoyed. Finally I said I'd better go and she just waved with one hand while she was texting with the other. And that was the last time I saw her."

Jill sniffs. "I should have known—"

"No, you shouldn't have known anything. Rudeness is not a sign that a friend is having a crisis."

Jill stops talking. We drive three blocks in silence.

The funeral home parking lot is packed and we squeeze the car into the last available space. Jill clutches my hand as we walk toward the entrance. There's a line to get in that stretches out the door. "I don't know if I can do this."

I give her a reassuring squeeze. "I got you covered." But I'm nervous myself. Every funeral I've ever been to has been for an old person. Every funeral except one: Cal's. But my ex-boyfriend's death seems like it happened in another eon. Life really does go on. That's what's so tragic.

We join the end of the long line. Ahead of us, people are murmuring. When they realize they don't know us, the woman in the group nudges her husband and they all fall silent. I have to suspect they're discussing Amber's manner of death.

We shuffle forward, the day's heat radiating up from the sidewalk. What small talk can we make waiting to pay our respects to a family who's lost a twenty-four-year-old daughter, a girl who should be just starting off on her life's adventure?

The door opens and a group of mourners streams out, one older woman weeping loudly as two men support her. Jill tightens her grip on my arm. I hope this won't be us in a half-hour.

Finally, with a frigid blast of chrysanthemum-scented air, we step into the lobby. I've never been in this particular funeral home, but it feels horribly familiar nevertheless. Why do they all smell the same? Why do they all sound preternaturally quiet? Why do they all have a dark-suited man with an expression of smarmy concern to direct the mourners?

We step in a room so filled with massive floral arrangements that at first I can't even spot the coffin. When I do see it, my worst fears are realized—it's open. There's a kneeler in front of it, and the line is pushing us forward making it awkward to avoid the coffin-side prayer.

"I can't do this," Jill stage-whispers. "I can't look at her dead bod-e-e-e."

"If you want to talk to her parents on the other side, I don't think we have a choice."

As the line inches forward, I see people repeating the same ritual: sink to their knees, bow their heads, make the sign of the cross, and rise with a sad shake of their heads. Then they hug a middle-aged couple and a teenage boy, obviously Amber's parents and brother. The room is packed with clusters of mourners who linger even after paying their respects. There are two priests and many elderly and middle-aged people. But oddly, there is no one Amber's age. Jill is the youngest person in the room.

Now there is just one couple ahead of us. Jill can see Amber's body, her dark hair spread across the white satin pillow, her slender hands artfully arranged around a rosary.

"Oh my God, Audrey, she looks so, so—"

Dead. Amber looks horribly dead. Her dry lips are caked with an awful shade of lipstick no young woman would ever wear. Her face is sunken and waxy, devoid even of the relaxed expression of sleep. "Don't look," I whisper. "You don't want to remember her like this."

Now it's our turn and I nudge Jill forward and lower myself next to her on the kneeler. "Shut your eyes and count to ten," I murmur under my breath. But when I glance sideways, Jill's eyes are wide open and two big tears slip silently down her cheeks as she gazes at her friend. She sways slightly and I haul her up, worried she might collapse on me.

But Jill finds some inner reserve of strength as we approach Mr. and Mrs. Pileggi. "I'm so sorry," Jill says as she hugs the father. He nods woodenly, numb from being embraced for perhaps the two hundredth time. He doesn't seem to know who Jill is.

As I shake the father's hand, Jill moves on to Amber's mother.

"Oh my God, Mrs. P—I can't believe this!" Jill extends her arms, waiting for the hug.

What she gets instead is a sharp slap across the cheek.

CHAPTER 8

Jill reels backward, too stunned even to cry out.

Amber's mother advances and I pull Jill into a protective embrace. What the hell is going on?

"You! How dare you come here?" Mrs. Pileggi shrieks.

Her husband looks as perplexed as I feel. Several other relatives step forward to hold Mrs. P. back. She writhes in their grasp.

"You did this! If it weren't for you, this would never have happened to my baby."

"Me? Mrs. P, It's Jill. Jill, Amber's high school friend. Don't you remember?"

That explains it—the mother must have Jill confused with one of Amber's druggie friends. That's why there are no young people here. All her fellow addicts stayed away.

But Mrs. Pileggi doesn't back down. "I know who you are. Before you caused Amber to crash her car, she was fine. After the accident, she was in so much pain she had to take the pain pills. And then, and then, the needle—" Mrs. Pileggi's wailing becomes incoherent, but in between gasping sobs, we all hear one word clearly.

Heroin.

"Heroin?" Jill begins to tremble in my arms. Her cheek still bears the bright red handprint of her friend's mother. "No...no, I loved Amber. I would have helped her."

"You started this," Mrs. Pileggi screams. "You helped kill her."

"That's enough." I make eye contact with one of the relatives holding Mrs. Pileggi's arm. "She's hysterical. Jill was Amber's childhood friend. She hasn't even seen her for over a year. We're going to leave now."

The crowd parts, and I pull a weeping Jill out of the room.

Dinner in a restaurant is clearly out of the question. I drive straight to my condo, order Thai to be delivered, and pour us each a big glass of Pinot.

Jill has stopped crying and is gazing blankly into space. "I had no idea she was using heroin. I thought it was just pills. Shooting up! Oh my Ga-a-wd, Audrey—how could she? How could she stick a needle in her arm? She was afraid to get a flu shot!"

"They start out snorting, then move up to the needle."

Jill looks at me like I've suddenly acquired a knowledge of nuclear fusion.

"Hey, I'm engaged to a cop. I've picked up a few tidbits."

Jill wraps her fingers around her wine glass. "I can't believe Amber was a junkie, like the sad people I see on the subway late at night. I know the news is full of stories about suburban heroin addicts, but it didn't seem real. It didn't seem like it could be happening in my hometown."

I put my arm around her shoulder. "I think it happens everywhere, Jill."

"And her mother blames *me*." Jill's eyes well up again and her lip trembles.

"Don't go there, Jill. Amber's mother is irrational because of her grief. She needs to blame someone so she doesn't blame herself."

"No, Audrey—she's right. I helped Amber along this path."

I put my hand under Jill's chin and force her to look at me. "If you're going to be a social worker, you can't keep taking everyone's burdens onto your shoulders. You didn't cause her to crash the car."

Jill slumps beside me and keeps talking. It's as if she didn't hear a word I said.

"No, I didn't cause the accident. But afterwards, we each saw a different doctor. My doctor gave me muscle relaxers and Percocet for my whiplash. I took the pills for two days, but I hated the way they made me feel…like a jellyfish floating in the ocean. So I went to my mom's acupuncturist and to the physical therapist and every day I felt better and better. Then I told Amber I wasn't taking my pills anymore."

Jill takes a deep shuddering breath. She burrows her head into my shoulder and her voice comes out muffled and choked. "She asked me to give her my leftover pills. She said her ankle still hurt really bad and her doctor wouldn't take her seriously, wouldn't renew her prescription. I believed her. I gave her my pills, Audrey. I knew it was wrong, but I felt sorry for her. And I didn't want to come off like Miss Upright Citizen. I gave them to her. I helped her get hooked."

Jill peeks up to see how I'm reacting. Honestly, if she'd done this recently, I'd be horrified. But it happened when she was seventeen years old, an insecure teenager who couldn't stand up to a demanding friend. "Oh, Jill! Of course, you shouldn't have done that, but you were just a kid. And a few leftover pain pills didn't instantly turn Amber into an addict."

Jill curls into a ball. "Mrs. Pileggi accused me in front of all those people at the funeral home. Now they all think I must be some kind of drug dealer. And in a way, they're right."

I pull her into a hug. Now is not the time to break the news that life sucks and then you die. "You don't even know those people. You don't owe them an explanation."

Jill struggles up off the couch and wanders into the kitchen in search of a paper towel to mop up her tears. "I still can't get my head around her shooting up heroin. The accident was nearly five years ago. I wonder how long she was using pills before she moved up?"

"What Amber did is very common. Sean says that's why we have a heroin epidemic in New Jersey. Doctors write prescriptions for pain meds at the drop of a hat. By the time the doctor refuses to renew the prescription anymore, the person is hooked and starts buying pills from dealers. Eventually, the addict turns to heroin— buying black market pills gets too expensive. Apparently, heroin is really cheap right now."

Jill looks like Ethel when she spots a squirrel. "Is Sean investigating Amber's death? Do you know for sure that's what happened to her?"

Uh-oh. I shouldn't have talked so glibly about Sean. Now Jill will expect me to get her inside information. "I know the cops are investigating her death. But Sean will never talk about specific cases he's working on. What I said before about the heroin epidemic—that's general stuff that's come up when we're talking or out with his friends."

Jill's eyes open wide. "How far into her past will they look? Maybe she told someone she got those pills from me. Am I going to get in trouble?" She grabs my phone from the coffee table and holds it out to me. "Call Sean and ask him what the cops have found out."

I don't take the phone. Sean is at a Yankee game with his buddies tonight. They've been riding him about how much time he spends with me, and I'm not eager to horn in. He deserves to have a night off from thinking about work and worrying about my problems. "He's out with his friends, Jill. There's nothing he can do tonight."

Jill turns her big sad eyes on me. "Audrey, ple-e-eze. Mrs. Pileggi blames me for what happened. Fifty people heard her say that at the funeral home. Someone's going to tell the cops. I bet they're going to come looking for me. Maybe I should just confess and get it over with." She paces back and forth across my living room. "What if they arrest me? I'll be kicked out of school. I'll never be able to be a Licensed Social Worker with a felony conviction."

"Jill, stop! You're blowing this totally out of proportion. What you did was just a case of teenage poor judgment. If the cops arrested people for that, we'd all be in jail."

"But I feel so guilt-e-e-e." She plops back on the sofa. "I want the cops to investigate so that what happened to Amber doesn't happen to other people. But I don't want to get in trouble. I'm scared."

The doorbell rings with our Thai food delivery. "Let's relax and eat dinner now. I'll talk to Sean in the morning. I'll try to persuade him to tell me a little bit about what's happening in the investigation, and then I'll call you. There's no reason for you to tell the cops what you did all those years ago. It's not going to change the outcome of the investigation one way or the other." What I don't say is that once Sean hears information, he can't unhear it, so I'm not going to tell him about Jill passing along her pills. I don't want her distracted from grad school.

There's simply no reason for Jill to get caught up in this Amber Pileggi mess.

The next morning, after dropping Jill off at the train station with more promises, I contemplate my options for the day. I have an appointment to give an estimate to the heirs of a modest house on the west side of Palmyrton, and I need to return to the Eskew place to keep cataloguing the contents. Now that I realize how much of value the house contains, I know I'll need help every day. Though I'd much prefer to work with Ty, the best strategy would be to take Adrienne with me and let Ty handle the new house on his own. He's eager to take on more responsibility, and I'm ninety-five percent certain the house will contain nothing but old furniture and housewares, no antiques or art. It will be a good project for his maiden voyage. I text him with the plan, and head to the office.

Adrienne shows up at nine-fifteen. Our deal is that she comes in after her kids get on the school bus and leaves in time to meet them when they get off. I'm pretty sure school starts at eight, but I don't say anything, not even when I see that she's stopped at Caffeine Planet on her way here.

If I expect her to apologize for being late, I'm dreaming.

"I can't believe how slow the service is at Planet," she complains. "With every cup of coffee they sell, they have to tell the entire story of that girl who died in their restroom."

"Oh? What *is* the entire story?"

"The part I heard was that she worked there briefly a few months ago until they had to let her go because she kept missing her shifts. Then someone else said that a young mom took her child in the restroom to pee and found that girl on the floor with the needle still stuck in her foot. Can you imagine? You stop for a latte and a smoothie on the way home from nursery school and you end up having to explain to your kid what a junkie is!"

I stare at her as I speak. "The junkie's name is Amber Pileggi. She and Jill knew each other since kindergarten. I went with Jill to the viewing last night."

Adrienne has the sense to look abashed. "Oh, wow—I'm sorry, Audrey. I didn't know. How awful."

Luckily, the phone rings to break up our awkwardness. Adrienne pounces on it while I get organized for round two at the Eskew home. Then Ty walks in.

"Whoa, look who just stepped out of the J.Crew Catalog," Adrienne greets him as she hangs up the phone.

Ty is wearing khaki pants and a blue polo shirt and he looks quite nice. It never dawned on me to tell him what to wear to a customer meeting, but he seems to have figured it out.

Ty gives Adrienne the look I call the prison death stare, intended to reduce annoying people to a puddle of submission. Unfortunately, it never seems to work on Adrienne.

She peers over the edge of her desk to check out his shoes. He's chosen his most muted Jordans, which provokes a quizzical cock of her eyebrow. Really, did she expect penny loafers?

"You look very professional," I tell him before she can comment further. "Let's go over the checklist." Ty and I huddle and review the questions he's to ask and the items he's to take note of. Adrienne has set aside any pretense of working and is openly eavesdropping. I know she dearly wants to be the one going on this assignment. I'm sure she thinks her Ella Moss top and Kate Spade shoes would make a better impression on my client. Maybe they would.

Or maybe the client would think I must charge too much if my staff dresses that well. Or feel that their possessions aren't worthy of an estate sale.

The bottom line is, Ty has earned this opportunity and I'm going to give him his chance, even though letting go is hard for me.

Very hard.

"Okay, I got it," Ty says after I've reviewed every conceivable permutation of customer requirements.

"And if she asks you if she can take stuff out of the sale after the estimate—"

"I know, I got it."

"But if it's really just an oversight then—"

Ty stands up. "Audge, I got this."

Time to stop nagging and send him on his way. Still, I can't stop myself. "If you're not sure about anything, just call—"

Now Ty gives *me* the prison death stare.

I cover my face with my hands. "I'm sorry. Go."

When Adrienne and I arrive at the Eskew house, the door is again unlocked for us.

"Brace yourself," I say as we step into the foyer.

"Wow." Adrienne pirouettes to get the full effect. "This place really is Old Money, huh?"

"Old and plentiful, and that's good for us. Let's head upstairs. I want your opinion of the designer handbags in Mrs. Eskew's closet."

Adrienne's eyes light up when she sees the quilted Chanel bag. "A classic—these never go out of style." She drops to her knees and roots through the floor-to-ceiling shelves looking for more bounty.

"Look—I found a box full of keys. Maybe one of them opens that locked closet in the hall."

Adrienne digs through them looking for a likely match. She tries a couple with no success, then gives a grunt of satisfaction as the door creaks open.

"Wow, smell that! It's a cedar closet."

She steps in and I follow her. The walls of the closet are made of smooth wood that exudes a fresh, forest-y smell. There are built in shelves and closet poles suspended at various heights.

"Look! Evening gowns!" Adrienne's face lights up. She reaches for an aquamarine silk dress on a padded hanger. "Oh my God— this is a vintage Balenciaga! It looks like it's from the sixties. So *Mad Men!*" She holds the gown up in front of her and the full skirt drapes around her like a queen's vestments. She strokes it the way I pet Ethel, full of adoration.

"That color would be gorgeous on you."

"I love aquamarine. My eye is always drawn to this shade." Adrienne has a dreamy expression on her face. "This is like a magic carpet to a bygone era when women really cared about elegance. When no one went out shopping in yoga pants."

I choose not to take that as a dig directed at me, since Adrienne never sees me when I'm prowling Whole Foods in my black spandex. It's not really kosher, but now I want to see the dress in action, not just as a relic on a hanger. "Try the dress on. I bet it would fit you."

"Seriously? I can try it on?" Before I have a chance to change my mind, Adrienne yanks her stylish little knit dress over her head, revealing her perfectly toned body and perfectly matched bra and panties. She steps into the gown and I try to zip it up. As slender as Adrienne is, the zipper won't go all the way up.

"Geez, Mrs. Eskew must have always been very skinny. But it still looks great on you. Turn around."

Before my eyes, Adrienne is transformed from attractive soccer mom to stunning princess.

"Wow, you look amazing."

"I gotta see myself!" Adrienne darts out of the closet, a little girl playing with the ultimate dress-up trunk.

"There's a full-length mirror in the master bedroom," I say as I prepare to follow her. On my way out of the closet, something catches my eye. The inside panel of the closet door is gouged with deep scratches. I run my hand over the scratches that radiate out from the doorknob and continue along the doorframe. They're certainly not recent. Perhaps a pet got shut in here years ago. Ethel did quite a number on my laundry room door when I accidently closed her in there and went out for the day.

"Audrey, where are you?" Adrienne calls.

I close the closet door and find my assistant preening before the big mirror in the master bedroom.

"It's fabulous." Adrienne swishes the fine silk back and forth and twists to look over her shoulder at the beading on the back of the gown. "I wonder where she wore it? No one dresses like this anymore except for the Oscars."

"And the Met Museum Fashion Institute Gala," an amused male voice says from behind us. We both spin around.

A tall, lean man with a mane of wavy brown hair and dark, straight brows leans casually against the door frame. "You wear it well." His eyes, startlingly similar to the color of the dress, rake over Adrienne. "I can remember standing right here watching my mom get ready for the opera. My job was to keep track of her martini for her. I think that particular dress might have seen Maria Callas in *Tosca*."

This must be Kara's younger brother, Tom. I feel like I should be apologizing for our inappropriate behavior, but he's clearly not angry. In fact, he's smiling in a very mellow way. "I was about four at the time, but I'd say you wear it better than dear old Mom."

Now that I look at him more closely, I see his hair is touched with just a few strands of gray. He must be in his early fifties, but he projects a much younger air than Kara. His jeans ride low on his hips and his oxford shirt is top quality, but frayed in an artful kind of way that I myself have never been able to achieve. My old clothes just look worn out.

I step forward and hold out my hand. "Hi, I'm Audrey Nealon, and this is my assistant, Adrienne Coughlin. Your sister hired me to catalog the house to prepare for a sale. We just discovered the dresses and couldn't quite resist...."

He takes my hand and gives it a squeeze. "Tom Eskew. Oh, no problem." His gaze quickly leaves my face and moves to Adrienne's. "It's nice to see someone having a little fun in this house for a change." He tilts his head. "Where did you find that dress? It wasn't in Mother's closet, was it?"

"In the cedar closet in the hall. There are quite a few ball gowns in there."

The dark brows arch above those extraordinary eyes. "And how did you get into that closet? With a battering ram?"

Adrienne and I step closer together in instinctive solidarity. "Adrienne found a bunch of keys in that little box." I point to the green cloisonné now resting on the dresser. "One of them fit the closet."

A lazy smile appears. "Well, aren't you ladies amazing? Beautiful *and* clever."

Adrienne tosses her hair. "Imagine wearing something this glorious to go to the opera. Now people go in jeans. It's sad."

"Tragic." Tom keeps his focus on Adrienne. "I'd tell you to keep that dress, but as my sister keeps reminding me, it's not mine to give."

Adrienne laughs off his attention. "Oh, where would I wear it? It's a little over the top for the PTA Tricky Tray." She slips past him to go back to the closet where her own clothes await. "Time for Cinderella to get back to work."

Tom turns his attention to me. "That Darlene person told me I'd find you up here. I'm glad to see my sister did a better job hiring an estate sale agent than she has hiring a nurse."

Seems to me the only thing he knows about us is that Adrienne looks good in his mother's gown. What does he know about

Darlene? Unaccountably, I feel the need to defend her. "Darlene's job is a lot harder than mine," I say.

"I suppose. Sitting by my mother's bedside is no picnic, I grant her that. Of course, she doesn't have to pretend to be heartbroken. That's the part I find challenging."

Geez, tell me how you really feel! Tom must notice that he's made me uncomfortable. He flashes a big smile. "Family drama. The Eskews have cornered the market. So, tell me about this sale. How big will it be?"

I strive to look noncommittal, but I'm having trouble arranging my expression. If you want to win big, play poker with me. "Your moth—uh, your family—has some lovely art and antiques. Some I'll sell in an estate sale, some will go directly through dealers."

Tom drops into an armless slipper chair under the window and crosses his legs. He's wearing Gucci loafers, slightly scuffed, with no socks. "Those ball gowns—are they worth anything?"

"Vintage couture can be quite valuable. I'd never put them in the general sale. I'd dispose of them through a dealer. "

"Ball park—how much?"

"I haven't done the research yet."

Adrienne chooses that moment to reappear. "I just Googled that dress. It's part of the 1969 collection. A similar gown sold for $15,000."

I could slap her. I really could. I glare at Adrienne then turn back to Tom. "My pricing research consists of more than a Google search. Many factors come into play."

I was hoping to squelch the avid gleam in Tom's eyes, but no luck. "How long will all that take?" he asks.

"I'm doing all the advance work now. We'll be ready to move immediately once...."

Tom heaves a sigh. "My mother started dying the day my brother Parker crashed his plane. She's been at it for thirty years now. Don't count on her to be in any great rush."

Crashed his plane? Is that how the golden boy with the shrine bedroom died? I'm curious, but I let Tom's remark pass.

"The stuff that's going to dealers—couldn't you start selling that right away?"

"I believe your sister wants to wait."

His handsome face darkens. "Why should it all be up to her to decide?"

The answer, of course, is that Kara is the executor and probably also has her mother's power of attorney. But his question was rhetorical, and I'm not interested in getting involved in the family dynamics. Kara hired me, and she's the one I answer to.

Unfortunately, I didn't make that clear to Adrienne. "We could sell those dresses through a dealer without bothering Mrs. Eskew, right, Audrey? I mean, she wouldn't even be aware—"

I jump in to shut her up. "Kara hired us to catalog the contents of the house. That's what we're doing until we hear differently from Kara."

Tom trades a knowing look with Adrienne. "Well, the boss has spoken." He stands up and glances around his mother's former bedroom and sighs. Is he looking for something or remembering the way it used to be in his childhood? "I'll leave you ladies to your work."

With more self-awareness of her transgressions than Adrienne usually displays, she scurries back to the cedar closet. "I'll finish recording everything in here, Audrey. Since I was late this morning, I thought I'd just work through lunch. I brought an apple and some almonds. You go meet Sean."

I'm not arguing. If anyone has the skills to catalog a closet full of designer clothes, it's Adrienne. Sean has agreed to meet me at Melton's only eatery, a tiny gourmet deli with a few sidewalk tables. Sean's not there yet, so I pull out my iPad to pass the time. After researching some vintage couture prices, I decide to Google something else that I'm curious about. I'm engrossed in reading when Sean arrives.

"You look horrified. Are you discovering some of the paintings at the Eskews' house are worthless?"

I attempt a smile. "No, I'm reading Parker Eskew's obituary. He's the oldest son. Today his brother mentioned that he died in a plane crash. He was piloting a small plane on his way to Hilton Head. His wife died with him. She was eight months pregnant. Her name was Leonie Savatier. Survived by her parents, Clothilde and Jean."

Sean leans over to look at the photo in the obit from 1988. Parker grins at the camera, his shoulders thrown back, his arm around his bride, a lovely, petite brunette in a frothy white veil. "Guy looks like a douche."

"Sean! He was only twenty-eight when he died."

Sean crams himself into one of the café's delicate wrought iron chairs, a grizzly at a tea party. "Let me guess. He had an MBA from Harvard. Was a bond trader. Just bought his own plane. Was on the way to North Carolina to play in some golf tournament."

"Close. Wharton...hedge fund manager...tennis tournament. Okay, he doesn't sound like my kinda guy either, but it's still a tragic death. The baby would've been the Eskews' first grandchild."

Sean's jaw clenches. He hates any mention of harm coming to children. "That's what I mean. You don't risk your wife's and your child's life because you want to strut and fly your own plane. If they'd gone to North Carolina on United, that kid could be getting married around now."

He's right, of course. Parker seems like a guy with a big ego, and maybe that ego was the death of him. No wonder Kara seems resentful of her role as executor.

"I ordered us a spinach salad and the grilled veggie wrap," I tell Sean. "We can split them."

Left to my own devices, I would have ordered a roast beef and brie, but Sean's on this vegetarian before six kick, so I humor him. We chat about the Yankee game and the Eskew job, but I avoid any mention of my issues with Adrienne.

"So how did Jill survive the funeral?" Sean eventually asks.

I tell him about the awful scene and Mrs. Pileggi's accusation. "Now Jill feels it's her responsibility to figure out who got Amber hooked on heroin. What if her doctor was running a, a, what do you call it? A Pill Mill?"

Sean's fork hovers in mid air. "You tell Jill we can handle this without her assistance."

I stab at the bacon in his half of the spinach salad. "But Sean, I need to reassure her that the police are taking this seriously. Tell me honestly—don't you guys figure good riddance when a junkie dies?"

Sean's face hardens. "When the junkie is a fifty-year-old homeless guy who ODs under the Jersey Transit train overpass we do. When the junkie is a twenty-four-year-old whose mom is a paralegal for the biggest law firm in town and whose dad is the contractor who remodeled the mayor's kitchen, we take it a little more seriously. The Palmer County Drug Task Force is handling the investigation. And, yes, we're following up on her doctor."

Good. This is what Jill needs to hear. But I know she'll want specific details. Sean said, "we", not "they." "Are you part of the Task Force?" I ask in my most innocent what's-up-at-the-office voice.

Sean massages his temples. "Yes, Audrey, I am. And it's the hardest job I've ever done."

"Really? Why?"

"Because heroin in Palmer County is way out of control. And no one knows what to do about it."

We both stand up and he pulls me into a hug. "You stay away from this, baby," he murmurs through my hair. "There's one thing every junkie has in common. They're desperate. Desperate to stay ahead of their need...their pain. Desperate for the next fix."

"That's so sad." I burrow into his chest, breathing in his warm, clean scent.

He pushes me away and holds my shoulders. "Desperation isn't sad, Audrey. It's dangerous."

No sooner does Sean drop me back at the Eskews' than Jill is calling me to find out what I learned from him. Just as I feared, she's not particularly reassured that Sean says a competent team is investigating Amber's death.

"But Audrey, what about Amber's doctor? Did Sean know if he's legit?"

"They're on it, Jill. You don't have to worry."

"And the Caffeine Planet connection? Why did she choose that place to shoot up?"

"Apparently Amber worked there for a while. Adrienne told me that. Did you ever see her there?"

"No, but I've never been a Planet fan. They have a lousy selection of green tea. I told you, the last time I saw her, she was working at Burger King. I wonder how she got a job at Planet? Are the cops looking into that?"

"Jill, c'mon! Sean can't tell me that."

A long beat of silence.

"Jill?"

"Audrey, I really appreciate that you talked to Sean. I do. But I think I'd better come out there—"

"No! Jill, you need to focus on school. There's nothing you can do here, and if you start nosing around, Sean will find out about it and I'm the one who will be in hot water."

"But I need to know who she was hanging with. There must be some connection between Caffeine Planet and the heroin."

"That's a big leap."

Jill lets out a huff of air audible through the phone. I can picture the determined expression that goes with that sound. I call it her "I'll do it myself, said the Little Red Hen" look.

"I'll just have to network. Someone's gotta know someone who knows."

After I hang up with Jill, I wander down the hall to Mrs. Eskew's sickroom. During lunch, a random thought had popped into my head: I remembered that yesterday I had placed *Tender is the Night* on the bedside table when Mrs. Eskew told me to put it down, and I never did put it back on the shelf with the rest of the Fitzgeralds. I should do that, so it doesn't get misplaced. When I poke my head in the room, Darlene is not there. Straining my ears, I hear her clattering around in the kitchen. Good. I'm not in the mood for more small talk with her. Now, with any luck, Mrs. Eskew will be sleeping.

As I approach the bed I hear her scratchy breathing, even fainter today than yesterday. Her eyes are shut and her mouth hangs open slightly. I can see her tongue.

I avert my gaze. She shouldn't have to lose every last shred of dignity.

My eyes search the end table on the left side of the bed. I'm sure that's where I placed the book when she told me to put it down, but now nothing is there but the lamp and a little china dish. Maybe on the other end table? But no—that's where Darlene keeps all Mrs. Eskew's meds and supplies. There's no room for anything else. My heart beats a little harder. That book has to be in this room somewhere.

I climb the ladder to the Fitzgerald shelf. But even as I do, I know the book won't be there. Darlene wouldn't know where to reshelve it. And sure enough, there is still a *Tender is the Night*-sized gap in the Fitzgerald section. Just then, Darlene returns.

She jumps when I speak to her from above. "Hi, Darlene. I came in here to reshelve a book I left on that end table. But now it's not there. Have you seen it?"

Her face hardens. "Why would I know where it is? I don't touch anything in here except the bed and the meds."

"I didn't…I mean, I, I just wondered if you noticed it there after I left yesterday?"

Darlene shrugs. "I wasn't paying any attention. I can barely see that table from where I always sit." She continues, her voice still combative. "Maybe her son took it. He was here this morning. He asked me to leave so he could have some private time with his mom."

Slowly I descend the ladder. Tom Eskew. That makes sense. After the way he was grilling me on the value of those ball gowns, it's easy to imagine him slipping a valuable book out of the house. Crap! How am I supposed to handle this?

"Was Mrs. Eskew awake?" Maybe she would know if Tom took the book. Maybe she even gave it to him although that seems doubtful after she called all three kids philistines.

"Oh, yeah—was she ever! I had a hell of a time calming her down after he left. That's always how it is."

"They argued? But she's so, so—"

"You'd think he could cut her a break at this point, but I hafta say, the old bird really gives as good as she gets."

"How so?"

"She's hangin' onto her money. Won't let any of them get their hands on all of it even after she's gone."

"What do you mean?"

Darlene waves her hands. "I don't understand this stuff. Somethin' about trusts and fixing it so the money is theirs but they can't spend it all the way they want. She won't be needing it where's she's going, so what does she care?" She bustles around the room, dropping a basket of clean sheets on a chair. "But a lot of rich people are like her. They want to stay in charge even after they're dead." She turns her back on me and begins folding.

I look at the figure in the bed, so tiny, so helpless. It's hard to imagine that she thinks she can control anything anymore. As I gaze at her, Mrs. Eskew's eyes open. Her mouth moves, but I can barely hear the sound she makes. I lean closer.

"I'm sorry," she whispers. Her hand fumbles to get free of the covers. I lift the sheet and she clutches my wrist. Her fingers feel like ice-cold bones. "Forgive me." Her grip tightens. "Please forgive me."

Panicked, I glance over my shoulder at Darlene, but she has earbuds in and her head bounces to music only she can hear.

"It's okay," I say to Mrs. Eskew. "Everything's all right."

When I speak, her eyes snap into focus. I sense that she realizes I'm not who she thought I was a moment ago.

"I'm afraid," she says. Her voice is clear and quite firm. "They don't understand. I had to...no choice. But they blame me...I'm afraid..." Her lips keep moving, but now I can't make out what she's saying. "Only Parker was brave." Her eyes widen in her skeletal face. Even as frail as she is, I couldn't shake her grasp if I tried. "Don't leave."

A shiver runs up my arm as if her terror is being conducted right into me. I long to get away from her but feel I'd have to peel each one of her fingers off my wrist to escape. "Darlene!"

The volume of my voice makes Mrs. Eskew flinch. Darlene pauses.

"Darlene, come here, please."

She yanks the earbuds out and approaches the bed. "What's wrong?"

"She's upset. She says she's afraid because someone won't forgive her."

"Mmm. Let's not get going on that or I'll never get her settled." Darlene takes Mrs. Eskew's other hand and strokes it gently. "What are you telling Audrey, Mrs. Eskew? She's just doing a little work in the house. Sorting out your books and paintings, remember? We talked about that yesterday, didn't we?" Darlene's voice is sweet and sing-songy, her gestures surprisingly tender. Gradually, Mrs. Eskew's grip on my arm loosens.

The old woman looks into Darlene's face. "Where were you? Why did you leave me alone?"

"I was right here in the room, Mrs. E. Just folding the laundry."

"I can't be alone," the old lady scolds. Her head strains forward, but she barely has the strength to keep it elevated. "It's not safe."

"No, you're not alone," Darlene says. "I'm here. I'm always here."

Mrs. Eskew's eyes search Darlene's face. Apparently she finds the reassurance she needs. Her head falls back on the pillow and her eyes close. In seconds, her breathing is slow and regular.

Darlene and I back away from the bed.

"Who's she afraid of?" I ask.

Darlene glances heavenward.

"Yeah...that, but I got the feeling there was someone real, right here in the house."

Darlene shrugs and turns back to folding laundry.

"What does she want forgiveness for?" I persist.

"Everything she ever screwed up." Darlene snaps a pillowcase. "Just like the rest of us."

CHAPTER 9

Adrienne and I went to the Eskew house in separate cars so she could leave in time to meet her kids' school bus. On the drive back to Palmyrton, I mull over the missing book, the encounter with Tom Eskew, and the disturbing scene with his mother. I've pretty much made up my mind that I should call Kara and let her know what's going on. If her mother is terrified of someone, if her brother is stealing, don't I have an obligation to let my client know?

When I open the office door, I discover I'll have no privacy to make this difficult call. Ty is hunched over his desk, his brow furrowed. Uh-oh—what could have gone wrong?

"Hey. How'd it go?"

Ty starts up, then grins. "All cool. The house was real clean. Furniture nothing special, but a nice collection of tools. Some Depression glass and Pyrex that the lady didn't even know were worth something. Here's the signed contract."

I feel the glow of pride and relief a mom must feel when her kid makes it through the class play without flubbing a single line. "This is fantastic! She signed without having any questions?"

"At first she asked where you were, but once I told her Bakelite costume jewelry was worth some scratch, she started to take me serious."

"Ly."

"Lee what?"

"Serious*ly*. You told me to correct your mistakes."

Ty scowls, then leans back in his chair and cracks his knuckles. "I got too much to remember."

I can see that he has his statistics book open on the desk. "Are you doing your homework?"

"Yeah. I can't afford to waste time, and it's quieter here than at home. I still have to read a chapter of my art book and do some grammar problems....questions...whatever you call 'em."

"Can I help you with anything?"

"Nah. I'm good." He pauses. "Why is it seriously? What's wrong with just serious?"

"Seriously is an adverb. Adverbs modify verbs. You were describing how our client takes you. Take is a verb. So you need the adverb, seriously."

He gazes at me like I'm explaining the reproductive cycle of gypsy moths. "How do you know that? And why does it matter?"

"Language has rules. Math has rules."

"Why? Who gets to decide what's right and what's wrong?"

He's got me there. "Think of it this way. Basketball has rules, right? Rules are what make it a game. Otherwise, it would just be a bunch of tall guys tossing a ball around. Someone established the rules, and now everyone agrees to play by them. And when a player breaks the rules, he gets penalized. That's the same as grammar."

"Teachers the only people who penalize you for breaking grammar rules."

"Not true. Employers, clients—they judge you on that. Might not seem fair, but it's true."

Ty digests this for a minute. "Hmmm. I guess. Rules of basketball make hella more sense, you ask me."

He goes back to his statistics and I work on researching dealers for the Eskew collections. But I can't focus. I'm still thinking of the way Mrs. Eskew clung to my arm. Her terror was real.

Ty glances up from his book. "Why you starin' into space like that?"

So I tell him what happened at the house today. "I think I should call Kara and let her know how troubled her mother is. But I don't know how to tell her about the book. I don't want to accuse anyone unjustly."

Ty shakes his head. "Stay out of it, Audge. When my grandma's oldest sister was dying, she kept hollerin' that there was a man with a beard in her room tryin' to steal her clock. There was no man, no beard, and no clock. She was havin' hallucinations, just like a drug addict. The doctor said it happens all the time with sick, old people."

"Really? Because Mrs. Eskew seemed genuinely terrified of someone real."

"It's real to her, just not to anyone else. And there's nothin' you can do except try to distract them and call them down."

"Hmmm. That's what Darlene did."

"See, it's under control. You do your job, let her do hers."

"How about the book?"

"You're not even sure it's gone. Maybe tomorrow you find it stuck on another shelf."

I reach out and pat his hand. "You're wise beyond your years, Ty."

"Yeah. Tell me 'bout it."

We work in companionable silence until I hear his phone beep the arrival of a text. Then Ty snorts.

"Why's Jill think I'd know anything about that?"

"What?"

"She's askin' me do I know about drug dealers workin' outta Caffeine Planet."

His thumbs fly over his phone keyboard. Ty is adamantly anti-drug and Jill knows it. He seems to be typing an awful lot to tell her no.

He snorts again.

"What's the matter?" I ask.

"She wanna find out where low-life smack-heads hang, she asks her only black friend!"

I know better than to tell Ty he's being hypersensitive, but honestly, he is. "She's trying to network—"

Ty's scowl lifts, and he tosses down his phone. "Never mind. It was a group text. She asked a buncha people."

"As I was saying, Jill's obsessed with finding out who turned Amber on to heroin. Amber's mother blames Jill."

"That's whack."

"I know, but Jill can't let it go. She's bugging me to ask Sean about it. She wants to skip classes and come out to Palmyrton to see what she can find out."

Ty flips the page of his Stat book. "Jill gotta learn she can't fix everything and everybody. She's even worse than you."

When I get home, Ethel all but bowls me over.

"I'm sorry I'm late, darling. What's first, walk or dinner?"

Ethel tears into the kitchen and sits by her dish. She's not one to waffle over her decisions.

"I wish I could take you with me to this new job. But it's not like Harold the Hoarder's place—it's very fancy schmancy. The Eskews wouldn't approve of you."

Ethel cocks her head and holds her tail high. I scratch her ears. "Way to embrace your mixed breed heritage, Ethel. Those Eskews might have a high-class pedigree, but it hasn't made them any happier."

As we walk through the neighborhood, my phone pings the arrival of an email. It's a real estate listing from Isabelle. "Three bedrooms, two baths, finished basement, large yard. Perfect for you. This won't last. Let's look tonight. Bring your partner."

The picture is tiny on my phone, but it doesn't look bad. The neighborhood is nice, the price within our budget. I forward the message to Sean and ask if he can meet me there. Seconds later he responds. *Be there in 15.*

I look down at Ethel. "What do you think, girl? You should have a say in picking it out. Let's go for a ride in the car."

You don't have to ask Ethel twice to go for a ride in the car. She nearly wrenches my arm out of its socket in her eagerness to get back to my garage. On the drive over, she rides shotgun, her ears blowing back in the soft evening breeze.

"Would you like to have a fenced back yard, Ethel? Someplace where you could chase squirrels off-leash?"

She gives me a big doggy grin.

Of course a house with a yard would be great for her, and would make life easier for me too. No more midnight walks in freezing weather. But a yard means other things. A swing set. A sand box. Picnic table space for twenty.

My hands feel sweaty on the steering wheel.

I arrive before Sean and Isabelle. Ethel and I get out of the car and gaze at the house from the curb. It's a shingled Cape Cod, cream with taupe shutters. A curving brick walk leads to a front door decorated with a dried flower wreath. Window boxes planted with cascading geraniums dress the wide front windows. There's a screened porch to the side where a wind chime tinkles in the breeze.

Undeniably charming. But I've been in Capes like this before. They all have small boxy rooms and no closet space.

"Hellooo, darling!"

Ethel and I turn to see Isabelle striding toward us in her power pumps.

"Isn't this simply delightful? I thought of you instantly."

Ethel prepares to launch herself onto Isabelle's immaculate silver gray pantsuit, but I pull her back in the nick of time. "It's cute," I admit. "Looks kinda small though."

"Very deceiving. The inside is surprisingly spacious. Open floorplan. Roomy master. Partially finished lower level."

Isabelle continues to pepper me with real estate speak until Sean pulls up and parks his unmarked police car behind the real estate agent's Mercedes.

I see Sean's face light up, and I know it's not me and the dog he's thrilled to see. He really likes this house.

I tie Ethel's leash to the front porch railing and we go inside.

The current owner's décor is a little cutesy for my taste. All those floral armchairs and ruffled window treatments make it hard for me to visualize living here. But Sean and Isabelle are talking nonstop about the furnace and the roof and the property taxes.

Sean suddenly notices my lack of participation. "What do you think, Audrey? This open living room/dining room is good, right?"

"Yeah. But it's got wall to wall. I thought we wanted hardwood."

Isabelle marches to a corner and yanks up a loose end of carpet. "All hardwood underneath, and perfectly protected by this carpet. No problem at all to pull it up."

Sean steers me into the kitchen. "Wow! Really a good size. Plenty of counter space. I could whip up some meals in here!"

"The range is electric. I thought you wanted gas."

"Easy to replace," Isabelle answers. "There's a closed gas line behind the stove. I checked."

The woman has an answer for everything. I guess that's why she's the sales leader in all of Palmyrton.

The full bath on the first floor has been redone. Isabelle points out the upgrades. I keep my mouth shut about the strange shade of green in the accent tile. We poke our heads into two reasonably sized bedrooms, then head upstairs.

"They've created a fabulous master suite up here," Isabelle says as she flings open the bedroom door.

"Look, they've got a king-sized bed in here, and there's still plenty of room." Sean spreads his arms.

I open the closet door expecting a pokey little nook, and find an expansive walk-in. The master bath has a double vanity and an extra large shower.

"Now look at this," Isabelle says, opening another door. "It's a bonus room! You could use it as a home office. Or a little nursery. Keep the baby up here with you while you're nursing, then move him to one of the downstairs bedrooms when he's old enough."

I feel faint.

"Wow, perfect," Sean agrees. "I was a little worried about the master being so far away from the other bedrooms."

Really? It never even crossed my mind. What does that say about me?

The house tour ends with the finished basement (perfect for a playroom, Sean and Isabelle agree), then I get Ethel and we head out to the backyard.

Lawn like a putting green. Flagstone patio with a gas grill. Colorful flower border. Big shady tree. All surrounded by a white picket fence. My hand loosens on the leash as I take in the splendor. Ethel spies a squirrel and springs into pursuit.

She zooms around and around the yard barking joyfully while the squirrel watches, safe on a high branch.

"Ethel has spoken. This place is perfect," Sean says. "Let's put in an offer."

"What? Right now? We haven't even talked about it."

"What's to discuss? It has everything we want."

"You're being impulsive, Sean. Making an offer on a house is a major decision."

"This place won't last," Isabelle says. "It's priced to sell. It just came on the market yesterday and there's been a lot of activity already. As you know, there's not a lot available in this price range."

"See, Isabelle agrees. We have to move fast. You snooze, you lose."

I feel cornered. I want to growl and bare my teeth the way Ethel does when the vacuum pursues her from room to room.

I grab Ethel and snap her leash on. "I want to sleep on it. We'll call you tomorrow, Isabelle."

Since we came in separate cars, we each had fifteen minutes alone to hone our arguments before reuniting at my condo.

"We can't commit to spending $350,000 until I run the numbers," I say as I let Sean in.

"You already ran numbers when we agreed on what price range we could afford." Sean shuts the door just short of a slam.

"Now we need to look at property taxes for this particular house, estimated utilities, projected repair and maintenance. Did you notice they were supplementing the AC upstairs with a window unit? That drives up the electricity."

Sean puts his hands on his head like he's trying to keep it from exploding. "Fine." He grabs my laptop. "Create a spreadsheet, miss math whiz. Isabelle said we can call he any time before ten."

While I enter figures into Excel, Sean keeps up a running commentary on the excellence of the house—the solid construction, the sunny rooms, the spacious master bedroom. I murmur agreement as I type.

"And it's only two blocks from Lake Valley School. Our kids wouldn't even have to ride the bus."

My fingers freeze above the keyboard. Having kids is a touchy subject with us. I haven't ruled it out, but the prospect terrifies me, and Sean knows it. Speaking about our prospective offspring as a done deal is not cool. I slowly lift my head.

He realizes he's made a tactical error. "I mean, that's a long way off. But the house does have a very convenient location. To shopping…and everything."

I type in a few more figures and swing the computer around so Sean can see the screen. "If we qualify for a mortgage that's 1% above prime, our monthly payments would be $1,800."

"That's good. We can swing that."

"But we might not get such a great rate." I don't want to mention it, but Sean has a few marks on his credit history after his messy divorce. "If we have to pay just half a percent more, look what happens to our payments."

Sean squints at the screen. "We can still manage. I'm due for a raise in the spring. Your business is really picking up. You've been crazy busy. And this Eskew sale..."

"My business is seasonal, Sean. You know that. We need to have enough cash flow to pay our bills in December and January, not just in July and August. We can't make an offer until I call the bank tomorrow and see what kind of rate we can get. If the rate's too high, we can't afford this house."

Sean stands up and pulls me out of my seat. "Take a chance, Audrey. For once in your life, don't be so rational. This house is perfect. It's the house we can build our life together in. The money will work out. Have a little faith. Call Isabelle now."

I stand stiff, refusing to melt into his embrace. "Money has nothing to do with faith, Sean. You either have enough or you don't. Do you want to start our marriage arguing about money every month, pinching every penny?"

"Of course not, but—"

"Then let me call the bank in the morning. If we get a good rate, we'll put in an offer right away."

He strokes my hair. "You're so stubborn."

"Yeah. Nothing like you."

CHAPTER 10

True to my word, I have the mortgage broker working on our rate by 8:30 in the morning. While I'm working and waiting for him to call back, Adrienne finally strolls in.

"Good morning." I look pointedly at the clock on the wall, which reads nine-twenty-five. "Or should I say, good afternoon?"

Adrienne stops dead. "Well! I would think you'd be a little more flexible when I just drove twenty miles out of my way to deliver your other employee to school."

"What are you talking about?"

"Ty was calling you but your phone was off. He called me to ask if I knew where you were. I could tell from his voice something was wrong. Turns out he loaned his car to his sister and she didn't bring it back when she was supposed to so he had no way to get to school and he has a test today. So I drove him."

I feel like a creep. A bum. A total cockroach of a human being. "Oh, Adrienne—I'm so sorry! That was s-o-o nice of you. Did he get to school on time?"

"Oh, yeah—I took the Beemer." Adrienne tosses her Louis Vuitton tote on the desk. "I didn't know Ty even had a sister. He never mentioned her before, and he didn't say much on the drive."

"She's his half-sister. She's much older and she's kind of...unreliable." I don't know that much about Charmaine, and what I do know, I'm unwilling to confide in Adrienne. Charmaine and Ty share the same father and she has drifted in and out of Ty's life as unpredictably as his dad has. Ty's Grandma Betty, his maternal grandmother, doesn't have much use for Charmaine, but no matter how much Betty warns Ty off his half-sister, Ty remains stubbornly loyal to her. So I'm not surprised he loaned her his prized car. And I'm even less surprised that she didn't return it. I am, however, stunned that Adrienne went out of her way to get Ty to class on time.

"I hope she turns up by the end of the school day," Adrienne says. "I can't pick him up. Jimmy has a soccer game this afternoon."

"You've done more than your part, Adrienne. I really appreciate it. I'll pick Ty up this afternoon."

"Why did you have your phone off?" she asks.

I dig my phone out. The screen is black. "Damn. It's been on the fritz lately. Time for an upgrade, but I've been procrastinating. I hate transferring everything and setting up the new phone."

"Go get a new phone today, and I'll set it up for you tomorrow." Adrienne pulls her hair back in a tortoise shell clip. "So what's on the agenda today? Are we working at the Eskew house?"

I'm not sure why she's such a bundle of helpfulness today, but I'll roll with it. "Yeah. Let's see how much we can get done before I have to get Ty."

When we get to the Eskews' house there's an old beater car in the driveway. It's been rear-ended so the trunk is bashed in and doesn't close completely. The back bumper dangles and looks like it's been wired on with a bent coat hanger. To think I worried that my Honda Civic was an eyesore in this neighborhood! Someone is visiting, but it's clearly not a friend or family member of the Eskews.

Again, Darlene has left the front door unlocked for us. Adrienne and I walk in and immediately hear raised voices.

"I can't give you more. The phone bill is due tomorrow. I can't risk losing my service."

"Mom, c'mon—it's just for a day. I'll pay you back tomorrow."

"How can you pay me back tomorrow? What's happening between now and then? Huh? You winnin' the lottery?"

"Don't worry about it. I have a plan. Just take my word for it."

As my eyes adjust from the bright sun outside to the dim foyer, I see two people at the end of the hall that leads to Mrs. Eskew's sickroom. I recognize Darlene's broad back and bright colored smock. The tall, thin young man she's talking to looms over her. Must be her son.

I was planning on working in the dining room today, which is accessible directly from the foyer. I'm not sure if Darlene and her son have even noticed our arrival. Should I announce myself or just get to work?

"Your word, your plan! You must think I'm as stupid as that skank who follows you everywhere. Well, I'm through with taking chances for you."

Adrienne and I exchange a glance. Whoa—I'm staying out of that. Before we duck into the dining room, we hear one last exchange.

"You want me to leave JJ out of it, so do what I say."

"My nerves are shot. I can't risk it again—"

"Do it."

Adrienne steps into the dining room and lets out a low whistle. "Geez, you could hold a Downton Abbey dinner party in here."

I gesture to a breakfront the size of a Manhattan studio apartment. "I'll catalog everything in there. Why don't you tackle the kitchen? You're so knowledgeable about cookware."

Adrienne accepts the compliment and the assignment. She exits through a paneled swing door and calls out, "Butler's pantry! Should I do that too?"

"Start in the kitchen and see how far you get."

I turn to my project. The shelves behind the glass doors of the breakfront are filled with Haviland, Wedgewood, and Tiffany, but I'm more interested in what the drawers might hold. I slide one open and pull back the dark purple velvet cover. Forks, knives, and spoons each in their own niche gleam at me. I pick up a knife. Heavy. Just as I suspected: sterling silver. Silver plate you can't give away these days. No one wants to be bothered polishing it. But this is the real deal—92.5% silver through and through. Each piece bears an intricate monogram: a large E flanked by a smaller H and a P.

That pretty much destroys its value as silverware. Rich people who want their own engraved silver don't shop around looking for the cast-offs of other rich people with the same initials.

But this silver is worth plenty if the Eskews are willing to melt it down. Silver is going for $15 a troy ounce these days. I'll need to weigh representative samples and do the math. I start to count. The knives each fit into their own groove: 20. But the forks and spoons are nested in stacks. Dinner forks: 16, Salad forks: 15, Teaspoons: 17, Soup spoons 14.

Hmm. It's not unusual to lose a spoon or scrape a salad fork into the trash, but why would the complete set of knives be present while every other part of the set has a different number of pieces missing? Could it be that someone knows that the blades of knives are made of stainless steel so they're strong enough to cut with, and only the handles are made of silver? The knives each have their own slot, so it's easy to notice if one is missing. But the more valuable pieces could be slipped out one or two at a time without anyone noticing that the stacks were shorter. How many would have to go missing before anyone noticed? Certainly there are no grand dinner parties in this room anymore now that Mrs. Eskew is so ill. Could Darlene or her son understand the value of this stuff? Is taking silverware what Darlene can't risk doing again? Another issue to consider pointing out to Kara?

As I work, I have an uncanny feeling of being watched. I turn around. A child stands in the shadows of the foyer peering into the dining room at me. Who could that be? Another of Darlene's kids? Or could Kara be back in town with her daughter? Whoever it is, I find it unnerving to be observed like a zoo animal.

"Hi." I smile and wave. "I'm Audrey. What's your name?"

She steps out of the shadows but still stays close to the doorway. "I'm Rachel," she says, twisting a strand of her wispy hair around her finger.

At least, I think that's what she said, her voice is so quiet and breathy.

Rachel? Isn't that Tom's twin sister? I take a few steps closer to her and squint at her face. There are crow's feet. My god, she's not a child, just the tiniest, most slender adult woman I've ever seen.

Certainly she's nothing like her chatty brother. She continues to stare at me, the way a kid will stare unabashedly at someone with a deformity. Except I think I'm pretty average looking, and she must realize why I'm here.

"I'm the estate sale organizer," I say, just in case she doesn't know. "Your sister hired me."

She says nothing, just keeps her big, unblinking blue eyes fixed on me.

"How's your mother today?" I'm not sure why I feel compelled to make small talk with her. Maybe I just want to force her to say something.

Rachel shrugs. "I don't like going in there. She's mean to me."

Then why are you here? To check on me? To steal a few more forks?

"Well, if you don't mind, I'm going to keep working. I have a lot to get catalogued." I turn my back and return to recording notes and taking photos. Still I feel her gaze boring into my back like the hot rays of the sun.

I finally finish with the breakfront and move toward a magnificent Federal server with intricate inlay and a bowed front. A huge Chinese bowl sits in the middle. I pick it up carefully to look for the red Imperial Reign mark.

"I've always hated that bowl."

I had gotten engrossed enough in my work that I'd forgotten about Rachel. Her high-pitched voice nearly makes me lose my grip on the bowl.

"Really? It's a spectacular example of Ming Dynasty porcelain."

"Look at those little men with their bulgy eyes. And those dragons with their long tongues. They're scary."

I've been admiring the delicacy of the painting and the vividness of the colors. I guess the bulgy-eyed guys are a little creepy, but the dragon is cool.

I turn to face Rachel. She has crept further into the dining room as I worked. "You're not a fan of dragons?" I keep my tone light.

Rachel places her hand on one of the heavy Chippendale dining room chairs. "This is where I always sat at holiday dinners. I hated having that bowl behind me. I kept imagining the dragon jumping off the bowl onto my neck. So I traded places with Tom." She points to a chair across the table. "But then I had to look straight at the bowl and see how ugly it is, and that made me cry too."

"What did your mother say?" I ask. I'm imagining Mrs. Eskew didn't have a lot of patience for antics that disrupted her dinner parties.

"Mother has always hated tears," Rachel says, casting her gaze down and tracing the carving on the back of the chair with her child-like index finger. "I was punished for crying. Parker let me sit beside him down there." She points to a chair near the foot of the table. "Parker said I'd be safe next to him."

"Dragons didn't mess with Parker, eh?" I say it as a joke, but Rachel lifts her eyes to look at me.

"No," she whispers. "Even dragons wouldn't dare to touch him."

CHAPTER 11

Adrienne and I quit work early, she to go to her son's game and I to pick up Ty.

"Don't forget to get a new phone," she warns before we part.

Since my phone is broken and we won't be able to text each other once I get to campus, I make a plan to meet Ty right outside his classroom. I allowed time for traffic that never materialized and arrive on campus half an hour early. Even though Palmer Community, with its 1960s utilitarian architecture, is a far cry from the stately campus of UVA, my alma mater, being here brings back fond memories. College is where I finally found my tribe, where I no longer felt like an orphan, math geek freak of nature. I suppose commuting here three days a week won't provide the same experience for Ty, but I hope he enjoys college.

Some of the classroom doors are open and I catch snippets of lectures as I walk down the hall. "...the vena cava carries blood back...." "the Jacksonian democrats believed..." "the programming sequence here..."

Being here not only reminds me of my own college days, but also of the rare happy childhood memories I have of time spent with my dad. Sometimes he would take me with him to Rutgers and I would sit in the back of his classroom and listen to him lecture, so proud that the man in the front of the room that all the students seemed in awe of was my dad.

I follow the room numbers searching for number 241. In the rooms I can see into, students sit in a variety of poses—some leaning forward, alert, engaged; others sprawled back, eyes at half-mast. Many are hunched over their phones, a couple are clearly dozing. I pick up my pace, eager to see what Ty's class will be like. Then I slow down—I can't very well stand outside his classroom door grinning and waving. I cross to the far side of the hall and stroll up to a bulletin board promoting summer internships, then casually glance back over my shoulder. Immediately I spot Ty's long legs and huge basketball shoes stretched into the aisle between desks. He's sitting in the second row—not right under the teacher's nose, but not hiding with the slackers in the back corner either.

The professor is pacing up and down talking about the importance of using vivid language. "Don't describe everything as 'awesome' or 'amazing'. My sandwich is awesome, my new shoes are awesome, the Grand Canyon is awesome, God is awesome. If everything is awesome, then nothing is awesome."

I chuckle because Ty always mocked Jill's ten times a day squeal of "awesome." To which she responded with a skewer of his overuse of "chill."

"So before you hand in your essays, I want you to look for the overused words, the non-specific generic words, the meaningless words."

A collective groan goes up. No one in the class seems to have noticed me lurking so I grow bolder and take a step closer. Now I can see Ty with his lips pursed and his shoulders hunched as he goes over his paper. Occasionally he erases vigorously and puts in a new word. The scrawny kid next to him taps his pen and gazes up at the fluorescent lights.

"Judah? Are you revising?" the professor asks.

The scrawny kid twitches. "Huh? I found the awesomes. I had two."

"Did you change them?"

"Change them?"

The kid has the kind of look on his face that I get when I'm on the line with the computer tech support rep somewhere in India.

The professor comes over and speaks quietly to the kid. When she's done, Ty shows her his paper. She reads, smiling slightly. "Very vivid. I can picture it."

My heart swells. You go, Ty.

She hands the paper back. "There's a grammar error in the second sentence. See if you can find it. Pronoun usage. We talked about that last week."

Rats!

But Ty accepts the paper with a good-natured shake of his head and squints at it, looking for the offending word. I fight a strong urge to rush in and fix it for him.

The professor works her way to the back of the room, disappearing from my field of vision. Now the scrawny confused kid's phone goes off with a loud blast of Aerosmith.

"Judah! Turn off your phone and put it away." The professor's voice, kind up to now, has a sharp edge.

"I gotta take this. It's important."

"You're disturbing the class."

Judah jumps up, clutching his phone to his ear. The slack boredom has departed from his face, replaced by a tense alertness. "Wait. I can't talk."

He knocks over his chair and nearly falls on his face clambering over Ty's legs in his haste to get out of the classroom. Now he's out in the hall, just a few feet from me, but he doesn't even notice I'm there.

The professor closes the classroom door firmly behind him, with a warning. "Don't come back in. I've had enough of your nonsense."

But the kid is oblivious to her anger.

"You said you'd cover for me," he shouts into his phone as he lopes down the hall. "You can't walk out now."

Ty's face lights up when he sees me sitting on a bench in the hall. "Yo, Audge."

I rise and we stroll out of the building together. "Thanks for coming all the way out here," Ty says without making eye contact.

I want to ask him what's going on with his sister, but this crowded hallway isn't the place. "No biggie. How was your test?"

"I think I did good...I mean well. Anyway, it was identifying slides in Art and I got most of them right." He gives his head a little shake. "I can't believe Adrienne gave me a ride. I didn't even ask. She offered."

"Yeah, she surprised me too. Maybe we should give her a little more credit for being nice."

Ty elbows me. "You and me the suspicious types."

"Yeah. Jill's the one who always sees the best in everyone."

"I miss her. Never thought I'd say that." Ty holds the door open for me and we head out to the parking lot.

"So how was English class? I overheard part of it before your professor closed the door. Sounds like she liked your paper."

Ty straightens his shoulders. "It's gettin' better. She says I have good organization and good description. Just gotta work on my grammar. I passed the first test, though. Buncha people failed."

"Like that kid who came charging out of the class on his phone? What was that all about?"

"Oh, him. He's always pissin' the teacher off. Keeps using his phone. Never knows what's going on. That's why I hate being in the dumbass class. If he don't wanna be in school, why'd he sign up?"

"Doesn't."

"Huh?"

"If he *doesn't* want to be in school."

"You know what I mean."

"You told me to correct you." We've reached the car and I pop the locks.

"Yeah, well, not now." Ty stretches out in the passenger seat and shuts his eyes. "I've had enough 'a school for one day."

We ride in silence for a while, but then Ty perks up and we talk over plans for the small sale that Ty is handling. When we reach the outskirts of Palmyrton, I move to put my turn signal on to turn toward Ty's house. "Home?"

He shakes his head. "Train station."

I think I know what that means. The last I heard, Ty's sister was living in Newark. He's going there to look for his car. I picture his prized black Nissan Sentra stripped in an alley somewhere in the West Ward. I'm worried. I want him to tell me what's going on, but he volunteers nothing. Something about the set of his jaw warns me not to ask.

I pull up in front of the station.

Ty turns to me. "Thanks, Audge. See you in the morning."

I look into his brown eyes. "Be careful."

His eyes narrow. "Yeah. A'ight."

When I get back to the office, there's a message on my voicemail from the loan officer at the bank. We've been approved for the lowest rate.

I call Sean with the news and he tells me to call Isabelle and make the offer.

My heart is pounding. This is it. I'm buying a house with my boyfriend.

My fiancé.

A house that's big enough for Coughlin extended family get-togethers.

And kids.

My hand trembles as I dial.

"Hi, Isabelle. We're ready to make an offer."

"Too late, darling. The owners just accepted an offer for five thousand over the asking price. I told you that place wouldn't last."

CHAPTER 12

I feel as if my diamond engagement ring just bounced down a storm sewer grate.

Gone.

The perfect house has slipped through our fingers. What will Sean say?

Of course he'll blame me. He should.

The loan officer said we had no problem qualifying for that rate.

I shouldn't have been so cautious. I should have followed my heart.

Followed Sean's heart. The problem is, I think I was following my heart. The heart that's scared to death. The heart that's not ready for the future that lies ahead.

The heart that's maybe just a tiny bit relieved. Like the way I felt when I didn't get into Princeton.

So I went to UVA. And it was great. Life goes on. We'll find a different house.

Sean will see it that way too.

I hope.

Back at my condo I bury my head in Ethel's furry neck. "Oh, Ethel, I've screwed up. Remember that nice backyard that you loved so much? I let someone else snatch it right out from under us."

She squirms away from me and whimpers.

"Are you that disappointed? Do you hate condo living after all these years?"

She turns tail and returns with her leash in her mouth.

"Let's walk over to the phone store. They let little fluffy designer dogs in there. They'd better let you in too."

Ethel marches down the sidewalk with her curved tail held high. When we reach the phone store, the gatekeeper asks me if Ethel is a therapy dog.

"She helps me cope with depression," I answer quite truthfully, and we're in. Ethel sits regally by my side as I make my purchase, haughtily ignoring a yapping Pomeranian peeking out of some chick's oversized purse.

"You were impressive in there, Ethel. Next stop: Westminster Kennel Club," I tell her as we exit the store. No sooner are those words out of my mouth than Ethel begins pulling at her leash and barking frantically. Is there a squirrel or a pigeon nearby? I see no signs of wildlife, but Ethel tears down the sidewalk pulling me after her, oblivious to the wellbeing of old ladies, toddlers, and the handicapped. What in the world is she after?

We reach the corner just after the light turns green. Ahead of us in the crosswalk I spot a familiar slouchy hat. Could it be? No— what would she be doing in Palmyrton in the middle of the week? Ethel pulls harder. My God—the dog is right. I'd know that pink and purple Peruvian sweater anywhere.

"Jill! Jill!"

She steps onto the opposite curb and spins around. Her face lights up when she sees Ethel, then shuts down when she sees me.

I reach her side and Ethel flings herself at Jill, licking her face and nearly knocking her down.

"What are you doing here?" I ask. "Didn't you have classes today? And more tomorrow?"

"I, uhm, came out to visit my mom."

"Then shouldn't you be at her house?"

"Yeah, she's going to…like…pick me up. Later. Soon." Jill's eyes dart back and forth. Then she drops to her knees and starts baby-talking Ethel.

I address the top of her head. "Jill, why are you out here? Is it something to do with Amber's death?"

She looks up at me, her eyes as wide as a kid in line to see Santa. "I wanted to talk to the baristas at Caffeine Planet to see what they knew about Amber. Oh, Audrey—she was in deep. She wasn't the girl I used to know."

"C'mon. Let's get a drink. With Ethel along, we'll have to sit outside. Then I'm putting you on the train back to NYU."

Hunkered down at a sidewalk table at City Lights nursing our craft beers, Jill tells me everything she's learned from the baristas at the Planet.

"You know that girl Caitlyn who works there?" Jill asks.

"She designs jewelry. Comes to our sales sometimes."

"That's the one. She's mad about Amber. She said Amber wasn't the innocent victim that her mother wants everyone to believe she was."

I raise my eyebrows. "How so?"

"Caitlyn told me she'd been covering for Amber the whole time she worked there." Jill lowers her voice. "Amber sold Addies."

Jill sees the blank look on my face and explains. "Adderall. It's what kids take for attention deficit disorder. Except Amber just didn't give a damn about school. No pill cures that. So she sold her Addies to kids who were cramming for tests or wanted to ace the SATs."

"How does Caitlyn know about that?"

"Because when Amber was working there, she gave another barista a sample pill, then sold her more, and the girl freaked out."

"Is that a medical term?"

"She started shaking and panicking and thought bugs were crawling on her. She ended up missing her final exam altogether."

"Geez, selling Adderall! I didn't even know that was a thing. When I was in college, we just drank Red Bull before tests." I take a sip of my beer. "So why didn't Caitlyn say anything?"

Jill purses her lips. "The girl who freaked out quit working at Planet, so Caitlyn decided not to get involved. But then things got worse." Jill leans across the table.

"I told you that Amber told me her doctor wouldn't give her more pills for her ankle. But according to Caitlyn, Amber bragged about how if she told the doctor her ankle still really hurt, he would keep renewing her pain pills. But her ankle was fine, as far as Caitlyn could tell. She'd work full eight-hour shifts and then go out to raves and dance all night."

"So she took the pain pills she got from her doctor purely to get stoned. You didn't need Caitlyn to tell you that."

Jill's eyelids start to flutter in the way that always heralds tears. "No. It's worse than that. Amber sold the pain pills she got from her doctor."

"How does Caitlyn know that? If Amber was addicted to pills, wouldn't she keep them for herself, not sell them?"

"Pills are worth more than heroin. Amber sold her pills and made enough money to buy heroin. Lots of heroin, so she could get a bigger rush."

"Honey, that's simple economics. Buy low. Sell high."

Jill's sweet face lights with anger. "Is that all it is? Remember, in the process of those *economics*, she got other people addicted."

Ouch. Who better than Jill to remind me the drug market affects real live human beings. "So who bought her pills?"

"Caitlyn doesn't know their names. But she said once she came up behind Amber in the back hall of the Planet and saw money changing hands. After that Amber was more careful. Caitlyn would see people pacing back and forth on the sidewalk and Amber would wait for a slow moment and slip outside."

"Why didn't Caitlyn say something? Even if she didn't care about the illegality of what was going on, surely it must've been rough to work with a dealer who was also an addict?"

"Yeah. Caitlyn complained to me that Amber was always late for her shifts, and so zoned out and slow when she was there. But she never told her boss."

"Why not?"

Jill sighs. "Didn't want anyone to think she was a bitch. Or a snitch. Or a narc." She bangs her empty beer mug down. "What's wrong with women my age? God forbid you would speak your mind and do the right thing instead of worrying about whether everyone else thinks you're nice. If Caitlyn had spoken up, Amber might be alive right now."

"Alive in jail. I guess Caitlyn wasn't brave enough to face that possibility." I squeeze Jill's hand. "But eventually Amber must've quit or got fired. She wasn't working at the Planet recently."

"Fired. The owner figured out she was using even though he never realized she was selling." Jill runs her fingers through her hair. "But Amber's pill customers kept coming around looking for her. Caitlyn told them to get lost, but she still never said a word to the owner."

Jill slumps in her chair. "Caitlyn found out Amber was in rehab, so she figured the problem was going to go away. But Amber was only out of rehab for six days before she started using again."

"I wonder why she went into Caffeine Planet to shoot up?"

"I think she was planning to meet a customer there. I asked Caitlyn about it, and she just shrugged, but she wouldn't meet my eye. I kept pressing her and finally she said she might have seen someone she recognized as one of Amber's customers while Amber was being taken out."

"But if Amber was in rehab, she couldn't possibly still be getting pain pills from her doctor. Could she?"

Jill folds and unfolds her cocktail napkin. "One doctor doesn't know what the other one's doing. And with all those confidentiality laws, her parents probably didn't know what the doctors were giving her." Jill waves for the check. "What time will Sean be home, Audrey? We need to tell him about this. I don't care if Caitlyn knows that I turned around and told the cops what she told me."

"I'll tell him, Jill. Your work here is done. You need to get back to school."

She nods. "You're right. I don't feel guilty about Amber anymore. I can see how she slipped into being an addict. But she chose to be a dealer."

I hug Jill as we walk out. I'm glad she's toughening up. She needs to if she's going to be a successful social worker. Still, it's a little sad.

My little girl has figured out reindeer don't fly.

CHAPTER 13

"What a day!"

Sean drops onto my sofa and stretches out. He reaches his arms out, expecting a hug. I feel terrible. Things are only going to get worse when I tell him about the house. But maybe the information Jill has given me about Amber will mitigate that.

A little.

I perch next to him and take his hands in mine. "I had a bad day too. You go first."

"There's been a rash of petty burglaries lately. Bags stolen from unlocked cars and wallets lifted from purses in restaurants and bars. The kind of thing where we're really not that sympathetic to the victim because people oughta know better, right? This stuff always happens, but there's been more than usual. Then today, we get a call from patrol, responding to a call in the Devon Park neighborhood."

"It's nice there—big yards."

Sean nods. "Lots of young families. So, this mom is sitting at her kitchen table with her camera and her laptop, sending some photos of the kids to her parents. She hears her baby cry, and goes upstairs to get him. She's back in less than five minutes, and her laptop, camera, and phone are gone. She thought she was losing her mind. Took her a few minutes to realize she'd been robbed.

"Guy had to be watching her. Came in through the sliders from the deck. She had them open—why shouldn't she? That's why people move to that neighborhood—so they can leave their doors open on a nice day.

"Then while the patrol officers are at her house, another call comes in from a house a few streets away. Lady just got back from

Costco and is unpacking her minivan. Got a big bundle of paper towels in her arms and her purse slung over her shoulder. Guy runs right into her garage, knocks her down, and steals the purse!"

"Did she get a good look at him?"

Sean shakes his head. "Happened so fast—all she could say was young, thin, white."

"So why is this your case? You don't work burglaries now that you're on the Drug Enforcement Task Force."

"Junkies. That's who's doing this. These days, no one wants to throw addicts in jail for using, but eventually every addict turns into a thief. And when they start robbing suburban moms in their houses, you better believe we're going to arrest them."

"Do you have any leads?"

Sean massages his temples. "Not yet. But it won't take long. Anyone desperate enough to rob occupied houses in broad daylight is going to mess up soon. Real soon."

Sean lies stock still on the sofa with his eyes closed. He's doing the deep breathing exercises he uses to relieve stress. "If you're certain he'll mess up, why are you so anxious?"

"Because I'm not sure *how* he'll mess up. Set off a burglar alarm and we catch him in the act—great. Grab a knife and lunge at the next lady who finds him in her kitchen—not so good. It could go either way. He's not a pro, and that makes him unpredictable."

"And unpredictable is dangerous."

"Exactly." He opens his eyes and grabs my hand. "Sorry I'm rambling. Tell me why you had a bad day."

"I will. But first, I have to tell you about Jill. I saw her today."

"You were in the city?"

"No, she was here. She came out to get more information on Amber Pileggi."

"Audrey…" Sean warns.

"I know, I know. But she actually found something out. And she wants you to know about it. And she says she's done."

Sean raises one sandy eyebrow. "What?"

"Amber was selling pills at Caffeine Planet. Pills she got from her doctors, and she used the money she made to buy heroin. It was her way of getting more bang for her buck."

Sean sits up. "How did Jill get this information?"

"Talking to Caitlyn, who works at the Planet. We know her, a little. She comes to our sales."

"We interviewed her. She never mentioned this to us."

"Didn't want to be a snitch. Hoped the whole problem would go away. Did you find pills on Amber's body?"

Sean squints at me. "That's privileged information."

"So, you did! Caitlyn said Amber's customers were still coming around." I stroke his cheek. "Does this info help your investigation?"

He pulls me into a hug. "Yes, Miss Marple. Clearly, I need to interview Caitlyn myself. I should've known not to rely on freakin' Brian Parkhurst. Man couldn't interrogate his way out of a paper bag." He pushes me away. "But you tell Jill to stay away from now on."

"She will. She's pretty disillusioned by Amber. Is it true that pills are so much more expensive than heroin?"

"Yep. People get hooked on pills, but then they can't afford the high. Heroin gets them there quicker and cheaper."

"So there's a link between the pills trade and the heroin trade in Palmyrton?"

Sean fixes me with his hard blue stare. "Interesting diversion. Why did you have a bad day?"

I decide to rip off the Band-Aid with one quick pull. "We didn't get the house. Someone else made an offer before us."

Sean jolts up. His mouth opens, then he does the yoga-breathing thing again to keep himself from saying something he'll regret. Oh-h-h, man—that means he's really upset.

"I'm sorry, Sean." I hang my head. "You were right—I shouldn't have been so cautious. Next time, we'll pounce, I promise."

He nods and pulls me into his embrace. "I know it was a great house," I murmur into his shoulder. "I'm disappointed too."

I'm glad my face is hidden when I say this. I'm not sure I'd pass his blue-eyed scrutiny.

"There will be other houses," Sean says after a long silence. "I just want this to be settled. I want us to have a home together. A home where we can start—"

Did I tense up? Did he feel some infinitesimal change in me? He pulls back enough to see my face. "It's not only about having kids, Audrey. It's not. I want us to merge our lives. Not have your place and my place, your stuff and my stuff. I want us to be rooted in this home. If you didn't truly like that house, then it's best we didn't get it."

"I did like that house. I, I..." I take a deep breath, but my voice still comes out shaky. "Maybe I'm not entirely sure what a home is. Maybe I've only thought of the places I've lived as roofs over my head. What if I don't know how to make a home?"

Sean smoothes the hair back from my forehead, his thumb caressing the tiny scar marking the attack that first brought us together. "If you can't research it and you can't create a spreadsheet for it then you can't do it, right?"

My eyes search his. "Kinda, yeah."

His lips brush my cheek and he whispers in my ear. "Have confidence, Audrey. I wouldn't have paired up with you if I didn't think you could deliver."

CHAPTER 14

One thing leads to another, and by the time Sean departs my condo, I'm pretty convinced that he's not holding the house debacle against me. But I haven't totally forgiven myself, so I feel the need to be an especially good girlfriend.

Lover.

Fiancée.

Yes, fiancée, Audrey. That's what you are.

That's how I end up at the all-night Mega-ShopRite at 11:00PM buying the ingredients for the dinner Sean plans to make for me, my dad, and Natalie. Of course, I told Sean I'd go in the morning, but I'm wide awake now so I thought I'd get the chore over with.

The Mega-ShopRite is the biggest supermarket known to mankind—about a hundred acres of food, booze, and housewares along with strange random outcroppings of yoga pants, lawn chairs, and cactus terrariums. It takes me what feels like hours to wend through the aisles because I don't come often enough to remember where anything is. Luckily, at 11:00PM, at least the aisles aren't crowded. I finally finish the scavenger hunt for all the items on Sean's list, and go to check out.

Usually, there are lots of lanes open, but this late at night, there's only one line accepting big orders. I get behind two other people with loaded carts and resign myself to a long wait.

A magazine catches my eye: "Prince Harry Eludes Capture Once Again." Ah, a chance to catch up on royal gossip! Soon, I'm so engrossed in the latest antics of the red-haired prince who reminds me of Sean that the snail's pace of the line seems like a good thing.

"Damn! I forgot the arugula!"

I glance up to see the guy ahead of me trying to get out of the line. I let him go and go back to Harry and his long-suffering girlfriends.

"You can't pay for that with your EBT card."

"Why not? It's food."

The voices are antagonistic. I look up and see the checker with her arms folded across her chest, refusing to ring up a blue frosted birthday cake.

"Custom made baked goods are not covered by *food stamps*." The checker raises her voice. "I'll call a manager."

Geez Louise—this sounds like a ten-minute delay. And I'm nearing the end of royal news.

"Fine. I'll pay cash for the cake."

The customer's voice sounds familiar. I peek over the top of my magazine. Oh, God—it's Darlene! The poor woman's trying to buy a birthday cake for one of her kids with food stamps and the clerk won't let her. I duck my head so she doesn't have to be embarrassed in front of me.

The checker rings up the cake separately, but now there's a new delay.

"Do you have the money, or what?" The bitch checker has her hands on her hips as Darlene frantically rifles through an obviously empty wallet.

"I, I had twenty dollars in here this morning. I...."

"Over-ride on Line Eight!" the checker screams, snatching the cake back.

This is horrible. I pull twenty bucks out of my wallet and thrust it at the checker. "Here. I'll pay."

The two women look at me in amazement. Then Darlene recognizes me and flushes a mottled red.

"No, you don't have to do that. Forget the cake."

"Please. It's for your son. I want you to have it."

The checker takes the cash before Darlene can object. She just wants the transaction completed.

Darlene looks down at the floor. "Thank you. I...thanks."

I want to reach out and reassure her, but my cart is between us. Before I can say anything else, she grabs the cake, puts it in her cart with her other bags, and hurries out the door.

As the checker rings my order she launches into a long tirade about the evils of lazy, good-for-nothing women who sit on their asses all day long and collect food stamps. When she gets to the part describing the parties and gourmet feasts they enjoy while lounging, I snap.

"Listen, that woman is a home health aide. She works sixty hours a week changing adult diapers and mopping up puke. She's supporting three kids and one is a little boy with cerebral palsy and today is his birthday. So how about if you just keep your mouth shut about people you don't know one thing about. Okay?"

The checker is too stunned to respond. I cram the last of my groceries into a bulging plastic bag and storm out.

When I get outside the store, my hands are still trembling with rage against that checker, and the system, and the general suckiness of a world that says a woman can't use taxpayer financed benefits to buy a blue supermarket birthday cake for her handicapped son. A light drizzle is falling and between that and the tears in my eyes, I have a hard time seeing where I parked my car.

I'm standing on the curb staring into the parking lot when I see her.

Darlene is sitting on a bench next to a sign marking the place where the Palmyrton/Summit bus stops. In thirty-four years of living in this town, I've never ridden the bus. Does it even come this late? Darlene's eyes are shut and her hand loosely clasps her cell phone. The cake box sits beside her on the bench, accumulating raindrops on its cardboard and cellophane lid. Her other bags are tumbled at her feet.

"Darlene? Do you need a ride?"

She startles. "No. I'm fine. The bus will be here eventually."

"But you don't even have a raincoat or an umbrella. Please, let me take you home."

"I called my son. He's probably on his way."

But I can tell by the way she was sprawled on the bench when I walked up that her son didn't answer her call. She has no idea where he is, and no idea if the bus is coming. I pick up the cake. "I'm giving this cake a ride to your house. Are you coming with us?"

Darlene gazes up at me through the drizzle. Her usual toughness has cracked; she looks sad and fragile.

"C'mon." I feel like I'm coaxing a frightened stray.

Without a word she gathers together her bags and follows me to my car. I make a right out of the parking lot because I remember she mentioned she lives near the high school. I'm about to ask her for more directions when I catch a movement from the corner of my eye. Darlene's shoulders are shaking. She's wracked by silent sobs.

It's dark and rainy and I really need to pay attention to the road. I reach my right hand out and make ineffectual patting motions in her general vicinity. "Really, it's okay. Don't let that horrible cashier get you down."

Darlene says something garbled. I'm pretty sure it's "I don't give a flyin' fuck about her." There, that's the spirit! But she's still crying.

Her phone rings and she answers it instantly. "Rob?"

A moment later she slams the phone into her lap and stares out the window. Occasionally, a strangled sob escapes her.

I'm pretty sure Rob is her oldest son. The one who always uses her car. The one who fought with her at the Eskews' house. The one who clearly isn't picking her up. Then something else occurs to me. In the line Darlene said she had a twenty in her wallet this morning. But her wallet is totally empty now. Does her son steal from her too?

What can I say? How can I help her?

"Turn right on Walnut, then left on Pierce," Darlene says as the hulk of the high school complex looms into sight.

Silently, I do as she directs. The homes on the street are all two family houses, but they seem cheerful enough.

"Left at the corner."

Now we are on a short, dead-end street I've never been on before. There are a series of small apartment buildings, dirty beige brick, three stories high. The tiny yards in front of them are beaten dirt and weeds. I gasp as a feral cat dashes in front of the car. In my headlights I see a critter dangling from its mouth.

"Last building on the right." Darlene scrambles to gather together her bags.

"Let me park. I'll help you carry the stuff in."

"This is close enough." Struggling with full hands, she opens the passenger door then turns to take the cake box from my hands. "Thanks again. I appreciate it."

In the harsh glow of the dome light, her face looks as lined as Mrs. Eskew's, aged by worry, not by time. "Darlene, is there some way I can help?"

"There's nothing you can do. Nothing anyone can do. Unless I win the Powerball, I'm screwed."

CHAPTER 15

Last night's drizzle has turned into a steady downpour. When I arrive at the Eskew house in the morning, there's no sign of Rachel. Good riddance—she was creeping me out. A fifty-ish woman/child with a dragon phobia is more than I can handle today. Darlene is also laying low. That's fine too. After our encounter last night, we'll both be embarrassed to see each other today. Adrienne has taken the day off—chaperoning her daughter's Science Center field trip—and Ty will be in as soon as his 8:00AM class ends. With the dining room done, it's time to move into the butler's pantry, a narrow room linking the dining room and kitchen that contains even more china and glassware. I enter and flick the wall switch. Nothing.

Using the flashlight on my phone I can see the bulb in the ceiling fixture is blackened. I wonder if Darlene knows where I can find another bulb? Probably easier to go out through the door that leads into the kitchen to look for her. As I step toward it, I hear voices.

Through the gap in the door I see Darlene and another woman in nurse's scrubs in the kitchen bowed over some paperwork.

Darlene sounds defensive. "I don't know what you're talking about."

"I have counted the remaining pills. The quantities don't square up with the medications log you've been keeping." It's the nurse talking. She must be the supervisor from the hospice service.

"Okay, whatever," Darlene answers. "Maybe occasionally I give her an extra pill. She's restless, in pain. What difference does it make? We both know she's not getting better."

I stand rooted in the pantry. Should I make a noise to let them know I'm there?

"It's not up to you to change her dosages. Only her doctor can do that."

"Fine. I'll never give her an extra pill, no matter how hard she moans."

"Just make sure your records are accurate. Any more problems and I'll report you."

The door from the kitchen to the driveway closes with a bang.

"Bitch," Darlene speaks to the empty room. She bangs dishes in the sink. Then I hear the sound of breaking china.

"Shit! Goddamn it."

This is clearly not the time for me to pop out of the pantry and ask where the lightbulbs are kept. Carefully, I back out into the dining room. I'll just go around into the living room and unscrew a lightbulb from a lamp. As I cross the foyer, the front door opens.

"Ty! Just in time." He's late, which is so unusual that I immediately start to worry that something might be wrong. But he seems in good spirits.

"Hey, Audge. Whattup?" Ty stands in the middle of the foyer, does a 360 survey of his surroundings, and lets out a low whistle. "Some crib they got."

"Yeah, we're looking at big bucks here."

"Then who was driving that hooptie that nearly crashed into me on the way outta the driveway?"

I motion for him to lower his voice as I peer out one of the narrow windows flanking the front door. No cars in sight. "It must've been the other nurse. Darlene's boss, I guess. They just had a big argument."

"'Bout what?" Ty asks in a softer voice.

I jerk my head toward the living room. "C'mon, I'll show you around." Ty follows me as I get a light bulb from the living room and I tell him what I overheard. "Darlene is hard up for money. Today her boss was threatening to report her for giving Mrs. Eskew too much pain medication. Yesterday, I overheard a conversation that makes me think her son has been pressuring her to steal stuff from the house, but I'm not sure." Then I tell him about the cake episode at ShopRite. "I guess I should tell Kara, but I feel sorry for Darlene. And I could be wrong."

Ty scuffs his foot across the Aubusson carpet. "Seems like this family's got money to spare."

"Yeah, but they didn't hire me to be Robin Hood."

"Didn't hire you to be a security service either. Stay out of it."

Ty adheres strictly to the "no snitching" credo. He'd get along well with Caitlyn at Caffeine Planet. "Maybe I can find a way to let Darlene know she needs to stop."

Ty makes a face. "Whassamatter—things goin' so good in your life right now you gotta look around for problems?"

"Actually, things aren't going that well." I fill him in on the real estate deal.

Ty stands quietly for a moment before he replies. "I don't think you were too careful. I know people who got foreclosed on because they didn't understand how much their mortgage payments were really going to be." He squeezes my shoulder. "You did the right thing to check it out."

"Thanks, Ty."

Then we head for the pantry.

"Any of these paintings famous?" Ty says as we make our way through the dining room. "That one looks like a Thomas Cole landscape."

I pause in front of the pantry door. "Wow, Ty—way to rock the art history. It's a different artist, but from the Hudson River School. Good eye."

He grins as he enters and reaches up to screw in the light bulb. "Ninety-five on that test. Got the bonus question too."

When the light comes on, I can see that the butler's pantry may not hold much of interest. The shelves are filled with hundreds of plain wine glasses and stacks of unadorned white dishes. "Looks like these were supplies for big parties. Adrienne started in here yesterday. We'll let her finish this tomorrow. Let's you and me check out the breakfast room and the home office."

We emerge into the kitchen. No sign of Darlene, but I see the shard of a broken plate on the floor. Ty pokes around the kitchen.

"I've seen bigger kitchens than this before," he says.

"Yeah, this house dates from the time when people did their entertaining in the formal living room instead of inviting everyone to hang out in a glamor kitchen."

Ty heads down a short hall, trying doors. "How come there's a bedroom back here?"

I come up behind him and peer into a cramped bedroom with an adjoining bath. "Huh, a maid's room. Nowadays, if people are rich enough to have servants, they don't expect them to sleep next to the kitchen. But it makes sense that the Eskews would have had a maid back in the day. Now Mrs. Eskew just has Darlene and a cleaning service."

Ty turns back the way he came. "What's a breakfast room, anyway? They need a separate place to eat Froot Loops and pancakes in?"

"It's like a casual dining room, where the family eats when there's no company."

"In my house, we call that the kitchen." Ty shakes his head. "Some people got more money than sense."

The breakfast room is a sunny space with two walls of windows framed by window seats and a round table that seats six. The paintings on the wall are whimsical watercolors of animals and flowers. When I look closely, I see they are all signed "Rachel." "Huh, these were painted by one of the Eskew kids."

Ty peers over my shoulder at a painting of two birds frolicking in a bird-bath. "She's pretty good. Looks just like that."

I follow his pointing finger and see the bird-bath outside in the garden with a finch perched on its rim. Rachel has a sort of art-primitive style that's at once innocent and evocative.

"And look at this," Ty says. "She painted one of her brother and sister."

The painting shows a young man in a bow tie and blue blazer with his hand on the shoulder of a little girl with blonde hair holding an Easter basket. "No," I say, "I think that's Parker, the oldest son, with Rachel herself. Kara, the second child, would never have been that much smaller than Parker."

Ty moves across to the other wall. "Here's a photograph of the same pose, kinda."

The photo shows the four Eskew children dressed for Easter Sunday. Same bow tie, same Easter basket. In the photo, earnest Kara and laughing Tom stand between Parker and Rachel. In the painting, they've been excised altogether.

"Guess Rachel decided to get rid of half her siblings. I met her yesterday. She and Tom are actually twins, but they look nothing alike. She's incredibly tiny. Kara said Rachel had been sickly as a child. It must've stunted her growth. From a distance she still looks like she's about twelve years old. Then you get up close and see the lines in her face. She is one weird chick."

I make a note on my iPad. "Kara told me that the family had already removed items of sentimental value. I wonder if they plan to put Rachel's paintings in the sale?"

"Someone might buy 'em," Ty says. "I've seen pictures a lot uglier sell." He looks at a Swiss clock on a shelf. "That's not the right time, is it?"

"Yes—ten o'clock."

"Damn! I didn't realize I was so late. I gave a kid from my English class a ride back to Palmyrton because I saw him miss the bus."

"No problem." I glance around the room looking for more items to catalog. "Ty, see if those window seats have storage inside."

He removes a cushion and flips up the seat. "All kinds of junk in here."

As we start emptying the contents, Ty tells me about his ride with the kid.

"This kid Judah started talkin' the second he got in my car and he didn't stop 'til we got to his house. All about his mom, his dad, his lousy step-father, his brothers and how broke they all are and how he never gets to use their car. TMI."

"Did he want your advice?"

"Nah. Nothing I could do about any of it. After Judah's dad took off, his mom hooked up with some loser and had another baby. But that kid's got something wrong with him, and the loser took off too. So Judah's older brother is mad at their mom for havin' a disabled kid, and he won't help out with him. Judah likes his little brother, but he gets tired of watching him all the time." Ty drags a box loaded with school yearbooks, papers and report cards to the doorway and sets up an empty one. "One good thing about talkin' to Judah. He makes me feel better about my family problems."

I keep dumping book reports and art projects into the box and attempt to sound only mildly interested. "Is everything okay with Charmaine?"

"I never thought trying to help someone could be so complicated."

"You can say that after all we went through trying to help Harold?"

"That's different. My sister's not a crazy hoarder. She's normal…but—" Ty shakes his head.

"What?"

Ty throws his hands up in the air. "I tell her what to do and she won't do it!"

I laugh. "I give you advice that you don't follow."

"Nuh-uh. Name once."

"I told you to apply for those scholarships and you refused."

"That's different. I knew I wouldn't get 'em."

In an astonishing show of restraint, I don't launch into the how-do-you-know-until-you-try discussion that we've already had too many times. But I can tell my words have struck a chord. As he works, his brow is furrowed in thought. Finally, he lets out a loud sigh.

"What's the matter?"

"Nuthin'. I guess I gotta be more patient with Charmaine. Let her come around to doin' stuff in her own time."

I rest my hand on his shoulder. "I'm still working on learning that, Ty. It's not easy."

Ty springs back into action. Enough with introspection. "Looks like the Eskews totally forgot all this school stuff was ever here."

"I'll let Kara know and she can decide if they want to keep it or pitch it."

Ty lifts the second cardboard box and the bottom gives way, scattering papers around the room. We both work to retrieve them.

Everything I pick up belongs to Parker. Third grade book report on *The Indian in the Cupboard*—A+. Sixth grade poster on photosynthesis—A+. Eighth grade report card—all As. High school essay on *King Lear*—"insightful" the teacher has written. A+.

The yearbooks that produced the weight in the box landed in a stack. Four yearbooks from Bumford-Stanley Academy 1974—

1978. I flip to the sports teams. Parker Eskew is featured prominently in every shot of tennis, golf, swimming and crew. In many of the photos he has his arm around the shoulders of another young man, a little shorter, a litter thinner, a little less intense. One photo caption reads: "Parker Eskew and Wesley Tavisson take first and second in the Palmer County junior golf invitational."

In 1978 Parker is listed as the Valedictorian, and Wesley Tavisson is Salutatorian. Under Parker's picture is a paragraph on future plans. "Major in Economics at Harvard. Row for the Harvard crew just like my dad."

Harvard? I thought Parker went to Columbia. All those banners in his room, all those photos and trophies showed him wearing Columbia royal blue, not Harvard maroon.

"What's the matter?" Ty asks. "You find something important?"

"No, just puzzling. Parker's high school yearbook says he was headed for Harvard, but all the stuff up in his room shows that he went to Columbia."

Ty shrugs. "Musta changed his mind."

"Mmm." I don't argue the point. But if Parker got into Harvard, and Harvard was part of the family tradition, why would he have switched to Columbia? Harvard is the more prestigious school, and God knows, the Eskews are all about prestige. Somehow I don't see Mrs. Eskew encouraging her son to pick the college that makes him happy and damn tradition.

Ty returns with his pile. All Parker's. Now I'm just curious. "What about those other boxes? Do they have the other kids' stuff?"

Ty flips a few lids. "All Parker."

I open the other window seat bench. "Whoa. This one is full of model airplanes." I lift one out. It's the *Spirit of St. Louis*. Underneath in meticulous printing it says Parker Eskew. I check another two, but I know what they will say.

Parker. All Parker.

CHAPTER 16

As Ty and I finish in the breakfast room, my phone rings. Kara.

"How's it going at the house? Are you almost done?" I hear cheering in the background. She must be at her kid's game although it's early in the day for that. "My brother mentioned something about Mother's old ball gowns. He seems to think they're worth something. Can that be true?"

I only met her on the day she hired me, but I can picture her anxious, distracted face as her words tumble into my ear. "I'm making steady progress. Yes, the dresses are vintage couture. They're worth a few thousand each. I haven't finished the research. But there's something—"

Kara cuts me off. "Really? Have you counted them? Where did you leave them?"

I feel like I'm having a conversation with an AK-47. "There are eight dresses. We put them back in the hall cedar closet where we found them. It was locked, so we locked it again."

"Wait…where did you say you got the key?"

"We found a cloisonné box full of keys in your mother's former bedroom. One of the keys fit the cedar closet in the hall."

"Amazing. I've been looking for that key for years." I hear a sharp intake of breath. "Did you tell my brother about the key? And what about Rachel? Has she been there this week?"

"Yes, I met Rachel yesterday. I didn't mention the key to Tom, but my assistant—"

Again, Kara doesn't give me a chance to finish before she resumes peppering me with questions and orders.

"Oh no! Tell her not to talk to Tom. And definitely don't tell Rachel about those dresses. You didn't do *that*, I hope."

This is the worst part of being an estate sale organizer. I'm often thrust into the middle of family bickering, when all I want to do is run the sale. Families initially present themselves as the Waltons. And then when I mention that Jim-Bob came by and took home grandma's crocheted potholders or dad's Masonic tie-clip, they suddenly turn into the Kardashians, clawing one another's eyes out with spite and jealousy. Often the items with virtually no monetary value inspire the greatest conflict. I remember two brothers who came to blows over a hideous Tyrolean cuckoo clock.

"No, Rachel and I didn't talk about anything that will be going into the sale. But, Kara—there's something I'm concerned about. Some of the books in the study are quite valuable. Your parents seem to have been collectors of first editions."

"Oh? You mean they're not just books that Daddy read?"

"No. For instance, he has a complete collection of first editions of all F. Scott Fitzgerald's novels."

"So that's a good thing, right?"

"Yes—except that *Tender Is the Night* has gone missing. It was there on Wednesday, and gone today."

"Did you tell Tom and Rachel it was valuable?"

"No. No one. And there's one more thing." And then I tell her about the missing silverware.

"The silver. How could I have forgotten that it could be melted down? Listen, can you move the silver to the cedar closet? Lock it in there for now."

Clearly, Kara suspects her siblings of stealing. If they're capable of theft, maybe they really have been threatening their mother. Maybe I'd better tell Kara about my encounter with Mrs. Eskew.

"I'm concerned because your mom spoke to me yesterday—"

"Spoke? About Jean-Claude?"

"Yes, and—"

"Oh, don't worry about that. It's been going on for months."

"But she seemed very—"

"Damn, my daughter's game is over. I can't think…just, just don't worry about that book right now. Bye."

"But wait—there are also some school papers and paintings…"

There's a commotion and then garbled voices. "Maw-aawm! Did you see it? Did you see my goal? I bet you missed it talking on the phone."

"Of course I saw it, darling. It was fabulous. Audrey, I've gotta run. But tell me this—will you be ready to run the sale by next weekend?"

"Possibly, but your mother—"

"Maaawm!"

"Call me tomorrow," Kara snaps.

And the line goes dead.

CHAPTER 17

Ty and I break for lunch at one.

"Sean is taking me to lunch at that little café in Melton. Want to join us?"

I'm not sure which he finds more alarming: the guest list or the tea shop ambiance of Melton's only eatery.

"Nah. Ima swing back to Palmyrton and check on Mrs. Morrone's house. Make sure we're all ready for the sale there tomorrow. You need more help here this afternoon?"

"No, I'll finish up in the living room. On Monday, you and Adrienne and I can tackle the attic and the basement. I'll see you back at the office around four."

After lunch, Sean returns me to the Eskew home. We sit in his car with the windows down and I let him nuzzle my neck. There's no one to see us carrying on like teenagers. The street is deserted; the whole neighborhood as quiet as an unused movie set. A cool breeze loosens a few yellow leaves from the big tree in the front yard and they drift lazily down.

"What time do you think you'll be done?" Sean asks.

"Maybe six. I really want to finish the living room today."

"Don't work too late. Your dad and Natalie are coming at seven."

I whisper in Sean's ear, "Are you hoping the meal you're serving is so good that they'll offer to take Ethel for the night?"

He sits up with a stern expression. "You know I genuinely enjoy their company." Then he grins and returns to pawing me. "But if I can put that idea in their heads...."

I kiss him in earnest. "You're the best." I drag myself out of his embrace and head toward the house. I've only taken a few steps when a shrill scream pierces the gauzy autumn air.

Then a woman's voice: "Oh, my God! Oh, Jesus, no!"

I look back over my shoulder at Sean who's just backing out of the driveway.

In a few bounds, Sean is at my side. "Someone screamed," I tell him.

"Get back in the car."

"No, it must be Darlene. She won't know who you are. I'd better come with you. It's gotta be that Mrs. Eskew has died."

But even as the words leave my lips, I feel a shiver of unease. Darlene has been expecting this. She's attended scores of deaths. That scream contained true terror. What's going on?

Sean is running toward the front door and I trot at his heels.

The front door is unlocked, as it has been all week. We charge into the foyer just as Darlene comes running down the hall from the sickroom. She freezes when she sees us, her eyes widen and her head whips back and forth like she's looking for an escape route.

"Darlene, what's wrong? What happened?"

Sean doesn't wait for an answer. He's heard enough about the house from me to understand where Mrs. Eskew lies and he pushes past us.

Darlene backs away from me slowly like a hiker who's unexpectedly encountered a bear. I don't have time to consider her odd behavior because Sean is inside the study now, and I hear a strangled shout from him.

I run into the room and he intercepts me. "Don't look."

But as Sean well knows, I don't take direction well. I squirm until I can see past him to the bed.

On the white pillow where Mrs. Eskew's head has rested every day there is now a red, pulpy mess.

"What...?"

Sean holds me by the wrist. "Don't take a step closer."

A yard from my feet lies one of the gargoyles, the one with the bulging eyes and impudent grin.

His lips are covered in blood.

CHAPTER 18

Sean pulls me back into the hall. He's on high alert, his head swiveling back and forth looking for the intruder who did this.

"Darlene?" I shout. "Darlene, where are you? Are you okay?" I take a step toward the kitchen but Sean's iron grip restrains me.

"Do. Not. Move." With the hand not restraining me, Sean pulls out his phone and calls in the crime using a lot of terms I can't fully process.

My knees quiver and my head swims. I lean against the hall wall for support. Who could have done such a terrible thing? Mrs. Eskew was utterly helpless, totally immobile. A thief would have no need to kill her even if he was stealing from right under her nose.

She told me she was afraid. She told me, and I did nothing, nothing to help her.

Sean ends his call and pulls his service revolver from the shoulder holster he always wears. I shrink back. I don't like his gun. He's not my lover with that thing in his hand.

"You think the killer is still in the house?" I whisper.

He nods, his gaze darting from the end of the hall leading to the kitchen to the staircase leading to the bedrooms. I know he wants to search the house, but he's reluctant to leave me. And honestly, I don't want to be left alone. I just want to hold Sean's hand and wait for the police to arrive.

But Sean is the police, and he wants to do his job.

I nod toward the kitchen. "I'll come with you," I mouth.

There's a little alcove right before the kitchen, and Sean positions me there. Then he raises his weapon and sweeps into the kitchen. I squeeze my eyes shut and raise my shoulders.

Please let the kitchen be empty. Please don't let him get hurt.

I hear Sean fling open the door to the butler's pantry and I brace myself for disaster again. But there's nothing.

"Okay, you can come in," he calls to me.

When I enter I see a half empty glass of soda and a sandwich with a few bites taken out sitting on the table.

The back door is wide open.

Sean and I spend the rest of the afternoon and well into the evening with the Palmer County police. This crime has occurred in Melton, and since the Melton PD is so small, they've turned the investigation over to the county police. Each of us is being treated as a witness, so we're being kept apart.

Over and over the cops ask me about why I have access to the house, why the front door was unlocked, and who else has been coming and going.

Over and over I explain my work, explain that Darlene leaves the front door unlocked for me, explain that the other people I've seen at the house are Mrs. Eskew's children, Kara, Tom and Rachel, and Darlene's son, whose name I think is Rob. The other nurse. Reluctantly, I tell them that my assistants have also worked at the house. I don't want either one to be interrogated as I am, but I know they both have iron-clad alibis with plenty of witnesses. Ty was at Mrs. Morrone's house. Adrienne was at her daughter's field trip.

Over and over they ask me to recount the story of what happened when I entered the house after lunch. They quiz me on the exact words Darlene spoke. Over and over I tell them about Darlene's shout of surprise, but how she didn't speak to me when we encountered her in the hallway.

"Have you located Darlene yet?" I ask.

The cops exchange glances and continue to grill me. They don't like it when I ask a question; I'm just supposed to answer theirs. What agency sent her to the Eskews? What other patients has she cared for?

I have already given them Kara's phone number, so I remind them that only she knows the answer to those questions. I've known Darlene for less than one week, but still I'm certain she didn't harm Mrs. Eskew. I tell the cops that, but all they do is nod and scribble in their notebooks.

But why did she run? I have to admit, her actions are very strange.

As the questioning continues, different cops enter and leave the room.

When one who seems a little more perceptive than the others is in charge, I blurt out what's eating at me.

"Mrs. Eskew was afraid of someone. She told me that on Thursday."

That catches their attention. I recount our conversation as closely as I can.

"She was afraid of Darlene?" one cop asks.

"No. She was mad that Darlene wasn't there. She said she shouldn't be alone. Darlene is the one who calmed her down."

"Why did Darlene leave her alone?"

"She had to make a phone call. Her son was sick. And Mrs. Eskew wasn't all alone. I was there. Mrs. E was asleep when Darlene left, then she woke up and got scared while she was talking to me."

"She was afraid of you?"

"No, she was hanging on to me, saying, 'They blame me.'"

"Blame her for what?"

I shrug.

The cop tilts his head. "And you didn't think to tell anyone about this?"

Augh! "I told Darlene. She didn't seem concerned. She said Mrs. E was simply afraid of dying."

"But you didn't agree?"

"I wasn't sure. I barely knew the woman. Then I told my assistant, and he said that old people hallucinate, and that's what was probably happening."

"Your assistant is a doctor?"

"No, of course not. But he told me about his elderly great-aunt, and…and, well, I tried to tell Kara, but she was in the middle of something and we had to hang up…and then this happened…and, oh, God! I feel awful. This is my fault. I should have spoken up. Especially because we were in the habit of leaving the door unlocked. Whomever she was afraid of could easily come in."

They stand out in the corridor comparing notes. Each time they return to me, their questions focus more intently on Darlene. How well do I know her? Did I know her before I started to work at the Eskews' house?

Again, I explain our very brief acquaintance. But then I feel compelled to elaborate. "Surely you can't believe Darlene would pound her patient's head in? Whenever I saw her with Mrs. Eskew, she was very calm, soothing. Nothing seemed to faze her."

The lead cop, who has a double scar bisecting his left eyebrow that irresistibly draws my eye, hitches his chair closer to me. "Did you see something that should have fazed her?"

Now I've managed to paint myself into a corner. "I just meant that taking care of an invalid is hard work that I wouldn't want to do, but Darlene seemed to take it all in stride. She even said that this was one of her easier cases."

"Easier than what?"

"Than a four-hundred pound diabetic with gangrene. Than an Alzheimer patient who wanders around and throws things."

"I see. So you talked to Darlene a lot, did you?"

Augh! This is what I get for volunteering more than what I was asked. "One day I was cataloguing items in the sick room. It would have been very awkward to work in the same room as Darlene and not speak to her. She told me about some of her other patients, that's all. She said she liked working for Mrs. Eskew because she wasn't difficult. She would have no reason to kill her."

"Did Darlene know when you would be returning from lunch?" the cop asks.

"No, I didn't check in with her when I came and went."

"Did Darlene have the run of the Eskews' house?"

"Nothing could stop her from walking around, but I only ever saw her in the kitchen, bathroom and hall."

The cop's gaze drills into me from under those flawed brows. "You never encountered her anywhere else in the house?"

I think of the silverware missing from the dining room. In the back of my mind there has been a niggling worry that Darlene took it. I let it go when Kara seemed to suspect Tom. But I am being absolutely truthful when I say, "I never saw Darlene in any other room."

"Do you smoke, Ms. Nealon?"

I'm startled by his sudden change of direction. "Me? No, I've never smoked."

"What about your assistants?"

"No, neither smokes. Why?"

"Did you ever see Darlene smoking on the back patio?"

"No, but—" The but slips out as I remember the time Darlene left me alone with Mrs. Eskew, when the old gal had her encounter with the departed Jean-Claude. Now I have no alternative but to finish my thought. "Once she went out on the patio to take a phone call, and I think she might have been smoking a cigarette. I could just catch a glimpse of her through the Venetian blinds."

The cop makes a note of this, and I figure they must've found cigarette butts out there. But that could explain why Darlene ran away. Maybe she was out there having a smoke break when the killer came in. She worried that she'd be blamed for leaving her patient alone. I want to say this to the cops, but I'm worried I'll make things worse for Darlene, not better. It's not my job to speculate. Surely, this idea must have occurred to them too.

My interrogator shifts gears again. "Tell me, Ms. Nealon, why do you think Kara Lyman was so eager for you to get started prepping for an estate sale before her mother had even passed?"

Ah, this is a dicey question. Since I discovered items going missing, I think I know why Kara was so hell-bent on starting the inventory. I have not mentioned the missing silverware or missing book. I figure Kara must be on her way to New Jersey. Let her tell the cops.

"I don't know. You'd have to ask her that."

"Are there valuable items in the house? Electronics, computers, cameras?"

"No, nothing like that."

"What about jewelry, small items that could be pocketed?"

"Kara put all her mother's jewelry in a safe deposit box. I'm not handling that. The house contains many valuable antiques, paintings, rugs."

"Did you discuss that with Darlene?"

"Of course not!"

But I can't help thinking about the missing copy of *Tender is the Night*. And the silverware.

Finally at 7:00PM they let us go. Sean has not enjoyed the role reversal of being the questioned, not the questioner.

"Incompetent assholes," he mutters as we leave the police station.

Our plans to cook for Dad and Natalie have morphed into being fed leftovers by the two of them.

"It just doesn't make sense," I say to Sean as we drive to their place. "Why brutally murder a dying woman? She only had a couple days left to live. Maybe a week, tops."

"It wasn't premeditated. Darlene snapped," Sean insists. "You've been talking all week about how awful her job is. Maybe the old lady made one mess too many, and Darlene couldn't take it anymore."

"But I heard Darlene shout on my way into the house. I'm positive she sounded surprised, terrified. She didn't do it. She discovered the body."

We stop at a red light and Sean turns to glare at me. "Then why did she run?"

I tell him about the cop's questions about cigarettes. "She probably worried about being blamed for leaving her post. Maybe she stepped outside on the back porch for a smoke. And the killer was watching and slipped in. When she saw what happened when she left her post, she panicked and ran."

"Ran off on foot from Melton, a town with no sidewalks, no public transportation?" Sean's not too impressed with my theory.

I stare out the window as snug suburban houses glide past my view. It's true that there's been no other car in the driveway in the morning or the afternoon, which meant that her son had dropped her off so he could have their car. "Maybe she was terrified that she was alone in the house with a killer, so she ran out and called her son to pick her up once she got away from the house."

"Or someone was already waiting for her," Sean says.

"Did you tell the county investigators that? Did you put that idea in their heads?"

"No. They made it very clear that it's not my case and they weren't interested in my analysis. So screw them. But I'm telling you, it was Darlene."

"But why beat Mrs. Eskew's head to a pulp?" I shudder, unable to get the vision out of my mind's eye. "She wasn't even recognizable as human."

"That's why I say Darlene snapped." Sean taps the steering wheel with the side of his hand for emphasis. "That kind of violence indicates rage, a crime of passion. She grabbed whatever weapon was closest to hand. Those gargoyles were right outside the sickroom door."

I shake my head. "Darlene didn't do it. She was used to all the awful things involved in taking care of dying people. She told me herself that caring for Mrs. Eskew wasn't that hard. The poor woman wasn't eating anymore. She was light. She could barely talk. No, someone else slipped into the house—the front door was always unlocked—and killed Mrs. Eskew while Darlene was out of the room. The poor old gal told me she was afraid. I didn't do anything to protect her."

Sean takes the corner faster than necessary. "Audrey, whoever killed her, it has nothing to do with you. You're not responsible."

We drive in silence for a while. Everything in Palmyrton looks so nice and normal: pots of chrysanthemums, silly Halloween decorations, back-to-school-night banners. How can this be a day on which an old woman was murdered? How can I brush that off like it's a fender bender I just happened to witness? I can't contain myself.

"Maybe it was a junkie, like the young man who robbed that woman in her garage and stole the computer and camera right off the other lady's kitchen table. When Darlene discovered the body, she panicked and ran."

Sean scowls. "Too complicated. And it completely contradicts your theory that she was killed by someone she feared."

"Maybe the intruder made a few forays into the house and Mrs. Eskew saw him. And no one believed her. But this time, she said something that made him kill her."

Sean parks in front of my father's condo and turns to face me. "You've been watching too many of those British detective shows on PBS."

Natalie sets bowls of homemade zucchini soup in front of Sean and me while Dad keeps peppering us with questions. I know what's bothering him. The situation isn't logical.

"That brings us back to Audrey's original question—why murder a dying woman? Who would benefit?" Dad has picked up a pen and a junk mail envelope and makes a bulleted list as he speaks. "Her heirs were due to inherit in a matter of days."

"Maybe they couldn't wait," I say. "The doctor told Kara it would be a couple of weeks. Darlene's the one who thought the end was closer. Tom apparently is eager to get his hands on the money. I think he may have stolen a valuable first edition. Maybe his mom accused him of that. She had moments when she was quite lucid."

Dad shakes his head. "But why risk killing her to gain a week? Or to stop her from talking about a stolen book. Often she wasn't lucid, so who would believe her? If one of the heirs is convicted of killing her, they'll never get a penny of her money."

"If one of her kids wanted to kill her, they wouldn't have needed a weapon," Natalie says as she reappears with a Salade Nicoise. "She was so weak, totally helpless. Anyone could have just put a pillow over her face, and no one would have even known she had been murdered. Or someone could have slipped her an extra pill. It would look like a natural death.

"When a person is terminally ill and expected to die, the attending physician usually just signs off on the death certificate," Natalie says. She's a nurse, and although pediatrics is her specialty, she knows plenty about death and dying. "There would be no autopsy unless the doctor suspected something wasn't right. And honestly, I think there are plenty of times when relatives help the dying person along and the doctor simply looks the other way if he knows his patient had been suffering."

Dad makes a check on his list. "Good point. If the heirs wanted to hurry the process, they wouldn't have killed her so violently."

"Rage." Sean speaks that one word and returns to picking the black olives out of his salad and tossing them into mine.

Dad nods. "I think Sean is right. Rage is the motivation."

"It might be the motivation," I say. "But it's someone else's rage. Not Darlene's."

CHAPTER 19

Although Dad and Natalie probably would have taken Ethel for the night, Sean's and my ardor has been cooled by the murder. We agree to go our separate ways, saving the dog-sitting chit for the future.

In the middle of the night, a raccoon knocks over a trash can, Ethel goes bonkers, and I find myself wide awake worrying about Darlene, Mrs. Eskew, and *Tender is the Night*. There's not much I can do about the first two, but as I lie staring at the ceiling, I experience a bolt of clarity. If Tom Eskew stole the book, he must be trying to sell it. There simply aren't that many pristine first editions signed by the author, and not that many places to sell them. I can easily check the online marketplaces, but I suspect Tom wouldn't go that route. He'd rather take it directly to a dealer and get the cash than wait around for an online auction. There are only two antiquarian book dealers in Palmer County, and I know them both. I'm sure I'll find that book tomorrow.

In the morning, I call Rare Find first. It's a business that's run like a business: regular hours, a phone that gets answered, and a website. No one there has seen my copy of *Tender*. That means a trip to Venable's Books. Mr. Venable runs his business out of two rooms in his drafty, firetrap Victorian. More often than not, the "be right back" sign is hanging on his door. There's no way to call ahead because he never answers his phone, and he certainly doesn't have a website. What he does have is a photographic memory for every book he's ever acquired. From whom he bought it …on what shelf he filed it …to whom he sold it. It's a bother to make a trip there, but if he has *Tender*, he'll certainly know who brought it in. I decide to nip over before the sale at the Morrone house since Ty has it so well under control.

Every time I walk into the jam-packed shop and see Mr. Venable peeping through the shelves at me, I'm always struck by the feeling that he reminds me of some character actor on TV or the movies, but I can never place him. Now it dawns on me: Mr. Venable looks like the stars of those funny goat videos so popular on the Internet. He's got a wispy white beard, a long face, knobby arms and hands, and a skipping walk.

"Ah yes, *Tender is the Night*." He nods at me from across the battered counter in the front of the store. "I sold it to the father and bought it back from the son. No worse for wear, thank goodness."

My breathing quickens. "What father and son are we talking about?"

"Gilbert Eskew and his son, Tom."

"You remember selling that book to the senior Eskew? He bought it in the sixties."

"Oh, he was a regular customer. Yes, indeed."

"You were friends?"

"Friends!" He gives a baa-ing little laugh. "Oh, heavens no. He wasn't a very friendly man. I managed to insult him, and he put me in my place." Mr. Venable's eyes are twinkling. He certainly doesn't seem full of regret.

"Insult him how?"

"One day when he was buying a book, I said, 'Eskew. That's an unusual name. What nationality is it?' because genealogy and the etymology of surnames are interests of mine." He leans across his desk and blinks his goaty eyes at me. "Did you know that Truman Capote is the seventh cousin of Tennessee Williams? Anyway, Eskew glared at me and said, 'American.' And he turned on his heel and didn't come back for several years. Years! Of course, by the time he did come back, I knew exactly why I'd offended him."

He pauses. Clearly he expects me to beg him to continue, so I oblige.

"After he left, I started researching the name Gilbert Eskew. Mind you, this was long before Google, back in the day when genealogical research was still a challenge." Another pause.

"What did you find?"

"My customer became Gilbert Eskew when he was eighteen. Before that, he was Jakub Eskein. Son of Moische and Sarai Eskein, a shoemaker and a laundress on the Lower East Side."

"No, that can't be true. There's a portrait of a Bartholomew Eskew who lived in the seventeen hundreds hanging in the Eskew home."

Mr. Venable wrinkles his nose. "How do you know the man in the painting is an ancestor of the Eskews?"

"There was a little brass plaque—" Then I start to laugh. How easy it is to create an impression! "Mr. Eskew must've bought that painting at a flea market and screwed the sign into the frame. So he was ashamed of being poor and Jewish? What a slap at his parents!"

"Oh, maybe they encouraged him." Venable tugs on his straggly beard.

Good grief, the old guy is infuriating! "Why?"

"Jakub was a superstar at Stuyvesant High School. That public school was a pipeline into the Ivy League for poor but smart kids. They probably all figured the name change would give him a better chance."

And then he graduated from Harvard. And married an Episcopalian. And bought a stately home. And got into a posh country club. And produced four WASP children. By then it was too late to reclaim his roots.

Despite being intrigued by this information, I can't resist a dig at my informant. "So, you solved a mystery but lost a customer."

"Only for a few years." He puffs out his chest. "It's hard to avoid me if you're a serious collector of first editions."

"Did you ever tell him you knew his secret?"

"Never told a soul until I told you."

"Why not?"

"No one else ever asked."

After I get back from Mr. Venable's, I pack up a few things at the office and prepare to head to the Morrone sale. Then I notice Ty's laptop sitting on his desk. I'd better bring it with me.

The laptop has gone into sleep mode, but when I pick it up, it jumps to life. On the screen is a photograph. A photo of an adorable baby, a few months old. He has coffee-colored skin, a headful of dark curls, and big button eyes. He stares at the camera with his little chin jutted out. He should have a thought bubble over his head, "Don't mess with me."

It's a photo of Ty as a baby. It must be.

But then I notice the fabric of the blanket he's sitting on: *Finding Nemo*.

Nemo wasn't a thing twenty-three years ago. This photo is recent. Very recent.

On my way to the Morrone job I feel dizzy with anxiety. Ty has seemed tense lately and worried about money. He kept wanting to postpone college. I assumed he was simply nervous about returning to the classroom. Now I see his behavior in a whole new light.

He's been coping with fatherhood.

How could he have let this happen? Just as everything in his life was going so well, how could he have been so careless as to knock up some girl?

And who is she? If the baby is three months old, then the mother is someone he was dating a year ago. I try to remember this time last year. It would have been right around the time I discovered my mother's ring. Right when I met Cal and got swept away. It's hard to remember what was going on in other people's lives in the days when that giant iceberg ripped apart my life. It seems to me Ty was juggling a couple different girls then. I thought it was cute. But lately, I haven't heard him mention any girls at all.

And what was going on when the baby was born? How could I have missed this? Was I so caught up in my love affair with Sean that I totally overlooked that Ty was struggling with impending fatherhood?

How could *Jill* have missed it?

We work the sale together all day, but I'm anxious and distracted. The flow of customers peters out early, and by dusk we're packed up and ready to roll. I send Adrienne home and prepare to confront Ty.

Just before we leave the empty Morrone split-level, I pull out his laptop. "You left this at the office. I figured you'd need it."

Ty slaps his head. "Thanks, Audge. I got too much goin' on these days."

"Want to tell me about it?"

He cocks his head. "Nuthin' to tell. Just school and shit."

I wouldn't classify a son as "and shit." "I saw the picture on your computer. How could you not have told me about this? How could you have hidden that you have a son?"

Ty is looking at me like I'm babbling about the Illuminati taking over the world.

"Are you crazy, woman? That's not my son. That's my nephew. Charmaine's boy."

The relief is like getting my first breath of air after a wave has knocked me flat.

"Your nephew! He looks just like you."

"I know. Everybody says so."

"Why didn't you tell me?'

"I only found out myself three weeks ago. Charmaine was living in Baltimore with the baby's father. I hadn't heard from her more than a text once in a while. I didn't know she was pregnant. Things started falling apart with the guy once the baby was born, and Charmaine came back to Newark."

Explaining the timing doesn't explain why he never mentioned his uncle-hood to me, but I let it pass. "What's his name?"

"Adelowo. It means 'the crown has respect' in Yoruba." Ty shakes his head. "I told her not to saddle him with a name nobody outside of Nigeria can pronounce, but you can't tell Charmaine nothin'. *Any*thing. I call him Lo."

"I like his name. Little Lo! He's really cute, and I don't even like babies. Much."

Ty has a gentle look in his eye that I've only seen before when Ethel has her head on his knee. He's crazy about this kid. Is that what a blood bond does? Is it automatic?

"Why didn't you tell me?" I ask again, my voice soft.

Ty paces around the tiny Morrone living room. "I didn't want you to think bad of Charmaine. I don't want my grandma to know. I don't want her sayin' I told you so."

Ty stops before me and stretches his long arms up to the top of the doorframe. "So now I gotta help Charmaine find a decent place to live. And a job, 'cause she can't count on her baby daddy. And if she finds a job, she's gonna need someone to watch the baby." He pauses and stares me down. "She's a good mother. She really is."

"I'm sure she is. You should tell Grandma Betty. She would help, wouldn't she?"

Ty shakes his head. "Grams is done raisin' babies. Besides, this baby's not her grandchild. She'll tell me to walk away. But I can't. I keep seein' his childhood goin' down like mine, know what I'm sayin'? I can't let that happen. The boy needs a man in his life. A real man."

I give him a hug. "You're the realest man I know, Ty. Lo is lucky to have you as an uncle."

He looks down at his giant feet and shrugs. My heart swells with such affection for him that I speak without thinking. "I'll babysit in a pinch. Just call if you ever need help."

When I get home from the sale, Sean has an outing planned for me.

"Put on sneakers and a sweatshirt. We're taking Deirdre's kids to the St. Bart's Carnival."

"I haven't been to the Carnival for years," I protest. "Probably since I was in middle school."

"Good news. You're coming this year. I promised the kids I'd take them."

"They won't want me tagging along on an outing with their favorite uncle." I won't admit it to Sean, but I'm uneasy around the kids. Sean is indisputably the fun uncle. But I feel they regard me as falling way short of being the fun aunt.

"Oh, yes they will. The boys don't want to ride with their sister. And I can't ride with her."

"Why not?"

Sean turns to me and grins. "I throw up."

So Sean and I and the kids set off on our Saturday evening adventure.

Even after twenty-five years, the carnival still stirs in me a mixture of excitement and anxiety. As kids, we used to hang out the school bus window, squealing with delight when the first carnival trucks pulled into the St. Bart's field. We'd watch the progress from morning to afternoon as more of the rides and stalls were set up. As opening day grew closer, everyone began to make their plans. Who was going when and with whom. That's the point at which excitement morphed to anxiety for me. I had to start scheming—begging my father for permission to go, wheedling cash from my grandparents for tickets, and worst of all, hinting and hoping that my neighbors or a friend would offer me a ride. Once I was there, I had to pretend disinterest in the games. I knew there would be nothing but trouble if I came home clutching a goldfish in a plastic bag or an oversized, neon-furred stuffed animal. Tonight, for the first time in my life, I can experience the carnival without my father's disapproval.

Chrissy's eyes are as big and round as Cracker Barrel pancakes as the bright lights of the carnival come into view.

"This is the first year she's getting to come at night," her brother explains. "Instead of on Sunday afternoon with the babies."

Chrissy lets go of Sean's hand, reminded that she's too old for that. "What was the carnival like when you were little?"

"Same rides," I say. "The Viking Boat, the Ferris Wheel, the Spinning Tea Cups."

"Same dirt-bag carny workers with no teeth," Sean mutters.

"Did you come with your brothers and sisters?" Chrissy asks me.

"I don't have any. I'm an only child. I used to come with our neighbors, the Andersons."

Sean glances over at me. "Your dad didn't bring you?"

I snort. "Dad wanted no part of it. I had to beg to be allowed to come. He claimed carnival rides are inherently dangerous because they must be designed by engineers at the bottom of their class. According to him, engineers on the Dean's List would be designing something more worthwhile."

Sean chuckles. "I can definitely hear Roger saying that. So why did he let you go at all?"

His question stops me cold. Why *did* my father let me go if he thought the carnival rides were dangerous? "Maybe that was just an excuse," I whisper. "Maybe he couldn't face being a sad, single dad among all the happy families."

Sean pulls me into a hug while the kids skip ahead. "My dad brought us, but he acted like he was patrolling the South Bronx the entire time. I guess what you fear is all a matter of perspective."

The tinny music gets louder and the scent of popcorn and funnel cakes drifts out to us as we reach the admission gate. Sean winces as he forks over a handful of twenties, and we're in. Immediately, the boys spot other kids they know and the whole pack clamors to ride the Viking Boat. Chrissy looks up at the giant canoe that threatens to loop the loop at each turn. She bites her lip.

"Let's work our way up to that one, Chrissy," I say, as her brothers run off with their friends' father. "We can start small with the parachute swings."

Sean waits outside the barrier, and we wave to him each time we fly by. The cool breeze ruffles my hair, and I feel like I might take off and soar right up to the stars. Finally, I've got the carefree part of childhood nailed.

When the ride stops, Chrissy and I stagger off, giddy and laughing. Sean scrutinizes us. "You gonna puke?"

"No way!" we chant in unison and high five each other.

The boys rejoin us, and now their pack is even bigger.

"Ty! What are you doing here?"

"Keepin' an eye on Kyle and Jamal. Grams wouldn't let 'em come alone."

I ride the Tea Cups and the Tilt-a-Whirl and begin to worry that my inner ears will never be the same. Then, Ty's cousin Kyle declares the Haunted House their next stop, and the kids roll in that direction as one.

As it gets later, the composition of the crowd surrounding us changes. Families with kids leave and are replaced by packs of guys and girls in their late teens and early twenties. Beer isn't sold at the carnival, but given the screaming and staggering of the young people surrounding us, I'd say some pre-gaming has taken place. Sean shoots a threatening glare at some guys in wife-beaters who jostle him.

When we arrive at the Haunted House, I elbow Sean. "This doesn't spin. You take a turn. I'm exhausted."

"Okay, time off for good behavior. Boys, you go first. Chrissy, you stay right in front of me. Ty, you coming?"

"Ima stay out here," Ty says. "After what we found at Harold the Hoarder's house, I don't need to pay money for nasty surprises."

As awful as that job was, it did bring Sean and me together. I had to call on him for help, then I had to push him away when he got too controlling. It took us a while, but we've finally figured out our boundaries.

Within seconds of Sean and the kids disappearing into the house, we hear their high-pitched screams from within the attraction. I chat with Ty about our profits from the sale at the Morrone house, but he doesn't answer. His eyes are riveted on the haunted house.

"What are you worried about? Kyle and Jamal can't get lost in there."

Ty nods toward the head of the line. "Whattup with those two? They're too old for this."

Two young men in their early twenties stand a few steps before the entrance and talk with their heads close together. The taller one wears a backwards red New Jersey Devils cap. He looks at some cash in his hand, sticks it in his pocket, and they enter the attraction.

"Eeew," Ty says. "Get a room!"

"No! You think?"

Ty strides closer to the exit to wait for the kids. Soon Kyle and Jamal emerge, followed by the others. Finally, Sean exits. He shoos Chrissy and the boys towards Ty and me, and steps into the shadows behind the attraction. I see him making a call. Seconds later, Backwards Devil's Cap and his friend leave the house. They separate without a word and join the crowd.

Sean lopes over to us and tosses me a twenty. His eyes are tracking the guy in the Devil's cap. "Let the kids play a few rounds of games. I'll be right back."

"Where are you going?"

"There's a team from the Drug Task Force here. I gotta check in with them."

"Sean, no—this isn't a work night!"

"Ty will help you," Sean calls back over his shoulder.

A wave of anger overtakes me as I watch Sean's back disappear into the crowd. What if I hadn't come tonight? He wouldn't have gone off with the Drug Task Force and left the kids alone. So why do it now? He doesn't want to miss out on some big arrest, so he dumps his family responsibility on me.

"Guess your boyfriend's never off-duty," Ty says.

There's an edge of disapproval in Ty's voice, disapproval that I happen to agree with. But I don't let that show. Ty and Sean have progressed from mistrust to tolerance, but they're still a long way from cordial. I don't need to give Ty fuel for his fire.

"Sean and the Task Force are working hard to shut down the heroin trade in Palmyrton," I say. The kids are running ahead of us to the games.

"Looks like I was right. Those two guys were up to something, but I guessed the wrong thing," Ty says.

I watch Sean's nephews tussling with each other, and I can't restrain my annoyance. "Sean better not leave me here for long. I can't ride herd on all three kids."

"Don't worry," Ty says. "We'll win 'em some toys."

Ty easily sinks three shots in a row at the basketball game and lets Chrissy pick the prize. This inspires the boys to face off against one another, while Chrissy cheers them on. Ty comes to stand beside me. He has a restless look on his face, the kind he gets when he's trying to work out a problem and is unwilling to ask for help.

I wait, but patience is not one of my virtues.

"What's wrong?"

"That guy that Sean's after—the tall one? I feel like I've seen him before."

"Really? I couldn't see his face clearly, but there was something sort of familiar about the way he carries himself. That kind of loping walk."

Ty rubs his temples. "I feel like there's something right on the edge of my memory. Like when I'm tryin' to remember the rules about commas."

The kids have managed to lose twenty dollars' worth of games in record time, and still Sean has not returned nor responded to my text. I'm not sure whether to be angry or worried. Is Sean merely preoccupied or is he caught up in something dangerous? Sean has managed to convince me that detectives like him face less risk than patrol cops, but he's obviously not investigating from his desk tonight.

The kids look at me imploringly wanting more money for the games, but I don't have any cash to offer. I intentionally left my purse at home so I'd be unencumbered. Now I'm angry at myself. When I was a single girl on the dating scene, I never left the house without enough cash to get a taxi back home. Now, because I'm engaged, I thought I could let down my guard. Dumb, Audrey. Really dumb.

Ty jerks his head at Kyle and Jamal. "We all outta scratch, bros. Time to head out."

"We'd better walk out with Ty, guys. We'll meet Uncle Sean at the car."

"No! Not yet! We still have some tickets left." They wave a handful of strips. "Let's ride the Viking Boat one more time, then we'll go."

Chrissy hasn't ridden the boat at all yet, and she begins to whimper that I promised to ride it with her. True, true. We don't have enough tickets for Kyle and Jamal to join us, so I urge Ty to go.

"Don't worry, we'll be fine. See you on Monday."

Watching Ty go, I know how the passengers on the Mayflower must have felt when the last glimpse of England faded from view. Now I'm on my own, fully responsible for three children I barely know. How could Sean have done this to me? If he's intentionally ignoring my texts, I'll kill him.

But what if he's physically not able to answer? What if something's gone horribly wrong?

I try to stuff my anger and anxiety deep down in my gut where they tumble and scratch at each other like two cats in a bag. The line for the Viking Boat inches along. Up close and personal, the boat is really big. Chrissy gulps as she watches how high it swings, how close it gets to vertical. And every time it reaches the apex, the riders let out a unison scream. "Aiyeeeeee!"

I've counted how many people are ahead of us. "We'll definitely get on in this batch," I tell the kids. The boys cheer. Chrissy looks green.

"I can't do it." She grabs my arm and tugs. "Please don't make me, Audrey. I'm scared. Let's go on the Ferris wheel instead."

"I can't leave the boys, honey. We all have to stick together."

"Chrissy, you're ruining everything!" Her brothers turn on her, screeching hyenas of rage.

She curls into a ball on the ground. "I can't do it. I'm sca-a-ared."

"C'mon lady," a guy behind me nudges me forward. "The line's moving."

Frantically, I scan the crowd for Sean. I've texted him our current location, but still no response. I start texting him again as the line pushes us forward.

"Just let us go," the boys plead. "Nothing can happen on the ride. It's no different from the haunted house. We'll wait for you at the exit. We promise."

The line shoves us further. I drag Chrissy to keep her from being trampled. Sean hasn't responded to my text. What should I do? This is a nightmare.

The boys reach the head of the line and hand over their tickets. They scoot through the gate.

The decision has been made for me. I guess they're right. Now that they're on the ride, what can happen?

Chrissy and I duck under the barrier and leave the line. "Okay, let's go wait by the exit for the boys."

"No-o-o-o!" She tugs on my arm. "I want to ride the Ferris wheel. The boys got one last ride. I get one too."

"But you gave up your ride on the Viking Boat."

My logic escapes her. Chrissy begins to wail at the top of her voice. "You pro-o-o-mised."

A mother passing by turns to give us a "should I call Social Services?" stare. Managing children is insane. I'm not cut out for this.

"That's enough." I try to use Sean's firm tone, but it backfires. I'm not her mother or even her aunt. I'm nobody. She sizes me up with shrewd fourth-grader eyes. Then she pivots and races toward the Ferris wheel.

I chase after her, but the crowds slow me down. Where Chrissy can slip between people, I have to dodge around them. I scream her name, but she doesn't listen. People can see the child I'm chasing, but no one moves to stop Chrissy. They watch us like we're part of the evening's entertainment.

In an instant she melts into the throng. I lose sight of her pink sweatshirt and break into a sweat. I glance back at the Viking Boat.

The boys are older and at least they have each other. What choice do I have but to follow Chrissy?

My heart races as I dodge through the crowd, and it's not because I'm running. What if I can't find her? She's ten—a little girl alone in a crowd of possible drug dealers and drunken teenagers and skeevy carny workers who are probably all parolees and pedophiles.

I will kill Sean for abandoning me like this.

He'll kill me for losing his niece.

I arrive panting at the Ferris wheel. Surely Chrissy will be there, tapping her foot waiting for me to arrive. I blink, willing her to appear when my eyes open.

Nothing.

The line contains mostly teenage couples planning to make out high above St. Bart's field. I run up to a couple in the middle of the queue. "Have you seen a little girl with strawberry blonde hair in a pink sweatshirt?"

They shrug and edge away, treating me like a panhandler on the subway.

Dear God, where can she be? The Ferris wheel is visible from everywhere on the carnival grounds. She couldn't have lost her way. Either she went somewhere else, or someone…

The possibility is too horrible to imagine.

"Chrissy!" I shout at the top of my voice, but my cry is swallowed up by the roar of the music and the crowd. Strangers surge around me. Tall, short, fat, skinny, but no little girl in pink.

I resist the impulse to plunge headlong back into the fray. Be rational, Audrey. Think. Think like a child.

Not easy for me. Even when I was a child, I didn't think like a child. What could have distracted Chrissy between the Viking Boat and the Ferris wheel? She had to pass the fishing game. I charged right by it, but maybe she paused to look at the prizes. I backtrack in that direction, pleading that a little pink flamingo will emerge from this infernal flock of starlings.

As I elbow my way through the crowd, something familiar does catch my eye: a man in a backwards red Devil's cap.

In my frantic state, I turn toward him, not consciously aware of why he is familiar, but knowing I saw him earlier tonight. Can he help?

"Hey! Have you—" I reach out my hand and catch a corner of his black hoodie.

He grabs my wrist and wrenches my arm, flinging me out of his way.

Losing my balance, I crash to the ground with a spine-jolting thump. As he races away, I realize my mistake. That was no friend; it's the guy Sean was after. The guy cutting a deal in the haunted house.

People step around me, probably thinking I'm just another drunk girl fighting with her boyfriend. I struggle to make sense of what just happened. That kid recognized me...

I pull myself upright. My God, where *is* Sean?

This has gone on long enough. I've gotta call 911. Someone has to help me.

As I fumble for my phone, something warm slips into my hand.

I look down. An angelic freckled face gazes back up.

"C'mon, Audrey. Uncle Sean is waiting for us."

A wave of orgasmic relief passes through me. She's alive!

The first wave is quickly followed by a second wave.

Of fury. The little brat is perfectly fine, while I nearly had a nervous breakdown.

Chrissy tugs me along toward the Ferris wheel. "Why were you way over there? Don't you know when you're lost, you're supposed to stand still?"

I could cheerfully stuff a wad of cotton candy down her throat, cardboard cone and all.

I grab her shoulders and spin her around to face me. "Why did you run off like that? You could have been hurt, kidnapped! Never run into a crowd again. Never!"

A heavy hand falls on my shoulder. "Ease up, Audrey. You're scaring her."

I spin around.

CHAPTER 20

"You!" I pound Sean's chest. "Where the hell have you been?"

"I was gone twenty minutes. You couldn't handle that? Why did you leave those kids alone?"

"Twenty minutes my ass! It was forty-five. And I didn't leave them; they left me."

Sean and I face off, and by the look on the kids' faces they must think they're about to see some video game martial arts battle played out right before their eyes.

Sean backs down first, unwilling to put on a show that will be reported back to his sister. We drive to Deirdre's house in cold silence, but as soon as the kids are inside, the fireworks begin.

"Is this what it's going to be like when we have a family?" I demand. "Whenever your job calls, you're going to run off and dump our kids on me, whether I can manage or not?"

"Who can't manage a ten-year-old? She weighs fifty pounds, tops."

"So I was supposed to use brute force to restrain her? That's your approach to all problems, isn't it?"

Sean grips the steering wheel as if the car might fling itself off the overpass onto Route 287 below. "A case that I've been working on for weeks was about to break wide open. I thought I could count on you to help me out for a few minutes. Apparently, I was wrong."

"You haven't told me one thing about this case. I think you saw your buddies were going to make a bust and you wanted to be in on the action. You claim to love those kids so much, but you didn't hesitate one second to ditch them and run off to bask in some glory."

Sean slams on the brakes as a traffic light turns from yellow to red. He turns to face me, eyes on fire. "That's why you think I do my job? For glory?"

I feel this argument spiraling out of control. We're both saying things that can't be unsaid. But I can't stop myself. "We're not ready to have kids, Sean. I can't shoulder the entire responsibility for their welfare while you pop in to be Fun Dad whenever it's convenient. That's was fine for your mom, but it's not going to fly with me."

When Sean pulls up in front of my condo, I spring out of the car and run to the door.

He doesn't follow.

I let myself in and collapse on the couch. Ethel jumps into my lap. With shaking fingers, I dial my father's home number. As I knew would happen, Natalie answers; Dad hates talking on the phone. Tearfully, I choke out the story of my evening. "How can I possibly have children?" I ask her. "I don't know how to control them."

"You don't control kids, you raise them. You guide them." Natalie's voice is gentle and kind, but I'm not soothed.

"Well, I clearly don't know how to do that either. Deirdre's kids ran right over me. They wouldn't listen to reason. And when I lost Chrissy, I was terrified. It was like the time Ethel got lost chasing the man who attacked me, only a million times worse. I was devastated, choked with fear, thinking of her hurt and helpless." I'm blubbering now, not sure if I'm talking about Ethel or Chrissy or both of them.

I bury my tear-stained face in Ethel's neck. "How can I possibly live like that on a daily basis, knowing something terrible might happen to our child every time he's out of our sight?"

"I won't lie to you, Audrey. Parenting involves moments of terror, no doubt about it. So does being married...owning a pet...having a friend. But what's our alternative? To live in total isolation from everyone who might bring us joy...or pain?"

"That's what Dad did for thirty years," I whisper.

"Yes, it is. And he still struggles with that regret."

"Tell him I'm coming over to have breakfast with him tomorrow. I'll bring the bagels."

CHAPTER 21

Too wound up to sleep, I roll through the TV channels looking for some fluff to numb my brain. *Law and Order*—too grim...*Big Bang Theory*—too insulting to math geeks...*Seinfeld*—I've seen that episode twenty times...*Keeping Up with the Kardashians*— I'm not that desperate. Five hundred channels and nothing to watch. I roll through again and this time a familiar face fills the screen. It's the ten o'clock New Jersey news. A peppy, hairsprayed anchorwoman speaks earnestly into the camera as a threatening mug shot looms behind her.

"Police this evening announced the arrest of Darlene Hayes, who had been sought as a person of interest in the investigation of the murder of elderly Marjorie Eskew. Ms. Hayes had disappeared from the home where Eskew was killed on Friday. She turned herself in to state police this afternoon, and after extensive questioning, they announced the arrest at 7:00 PM. Hayes is being held without bail at the Palmer County Jail."

I lean toward the TV and clutch Ethel so tightly that she whimpers and squirms away. Darlene has been arrested! What did she tell the police? Could it be that Sean was right all along? I'm loath to admit that. I hope for more information, but the newscasters are shaking their heads over the tragedy and murmuring that the police have not released any further details.

Immediately I grab my phone and look at my Twitter feed. No one can expect breaking news from TV or the creaky *Palmyrton Daily Record*. The only source with truly current news is the guy who runs the *PalmyrtonNow* website and blog. Sure enough, he's been live-tweeting from the courthouse since six. I read the stream of tweets and learn what's happened 140 characters at a time.

Darlene turned herself in for questioning. After a long interview, the police announced the arrest. Sources close to the investigation unwilling to be quoted for attribution claim that a plea bargain is in the works. Darlene will plead guilty to manslaughter.

I stare at my phone until the words on the screen blur. Manslaughter? How can someone pound an old woman's head in and be charged with manslaughter? Is "plea bargain" a red flag for another poor person gets railroaded into confessing to something she didn't do so the police can close a high-profile case?

I think this case stinks to high heaven. Justice is not being done here. Either not to Mrs. Eskew. Or not to Darlene.

Or maybe not to both.

And the one person who might be able to provide some insight into what's going on is the one person I can't call.

Ethel and I arrive at my father's place at seven-thirty in the morning bearing a bag of everything bagels and a container of scallion cream cheese. Dad answers the door wearing his moccasin slippers and pilly cardigan.

"Natalie has gone off to Sunrise Yoga," he says. "I've got the coffee made."

We sit at the table. Stir, slice, chew. When half a warm bagel fills my gut, I speak. "I don't think I can do this, Dad. I don't think I can be the wife Sean wants. I don't know how to be part of a big, traditional family. I don't know how to be a mom." I twist the diamond engagement ring on my left hand. "This fight we had doesn't feel fixable."

My father ponders this quietly. He's not one to rush in with reassuring platitudes.

"Sometimes the very qualities that attract us to another person are the qualities that drive us crazy. We seek to fill a hole in ourselves, but..."

"But what?"

Dad shrugs. "The hole is what makes us who we are. The hole doesn't want to be filled...not completely, anyway."

"So, do I want a big, traditional family or not?"

Dad gives me the sweet, sideways-sloping smile that has appeared in every photo of him from baptism to his latest driver's license shot. "You want a family. It won't be traditional. Sean knows that. It's why he's drawn to you. But old habits die hard. You need to retrain him."

"Ha! Like I've trained Ethel? The world's oldest dog who doesn't know what 'come' means?"

Ethel wags her tail, oblivious to insult, ever hopeful that some bagel scraps will soon be falling to the floor.

"Perhaps 'train' was a poor word choice. I suspect that Sean knows he was wrong to saddle you with the kids. He's probably full of remorse this morning. He'll call you eventually to apologize, and when he does, accept the apology. Don't prolong the spat."

My father and Sean, the introvert math professor and the extravert cop, are improbably fond of each other. But I won't be marrying just Sean. I gaze into my father's eyes. "How do *you* feel about marrying into the Coughlin family? You realize that if Sean and I have kids, you'll be sharing grandchildren with Frank and Mary."

He tosses Ethel the scrap she's been waiting for. "I anticipate a division of labor. Those two can handle Yankee games and the St. Patrick's Day parade. Natalie and I will manage the Museum of Natural History and Lego construction marathons."

His tone is light, but his words make my eyes prick with tears. "You've been thinking about this grandfather role, haven't you?"

He drops his gaze and gives a little shrug like a kid caught searching for hidden Christmas presents.

"Dad, I don't want to disappoint you, but I'm not certain this will really be happening. If Sean can't accept being the kind of father I need him to be, I can't...I can't..."

Two fat tears slip down my face. Dad reaches across the table and takes my hand. "Whatever decision you make, Audrey, I'll support you."

When I leave my father, I feel simultaneously peaceful and anxious. Even though Sean and I are not reconciled and I have no rational reason to believe things will work out as Dad predicts, I feel like I've off-loaded a burden. My father has offered his unconditional support, and he's shown me a path. I've decided I'll wait for Sean to call me, however long it takes. If he can't realize himself that what he did at the carnival was wrong, then nothing I can say will persuade him.

Ethel and I take a long walk in the park. When I get home, I find myself with unanticipated free time. My work on the Eskew house has certainly been put on hold by the murder. Yet I can't get the house, or the family, out of my mind.

What was Mrs. Eskew afraid of? Despite the latest news, I simply can't believe it was Darlene. I check the Internet for more news, but there are no further developments. Then part of my conversation with my dad resurfaces, the part where I said he'd one day share a grandchild with Sean's parents. I think about Mrs. Eskew's grandchild, Jean-Claude, who'd been named even before he was born. Why the French name? Who were that baby's other grandparents? I Google Parker and Leonie Eskew's obituary to read it again.

"Survived by Jean and Clothilde Savatier of Summit, NJ."

So I Google those names and learn that Jean Savatier died of a heart attack shortly after his daughter's death. He'd been in international banking. Leonie had been their only child. And with a little more digging, I discover that Clothilde now lives in a very upscale retirement community halfway between Summit and Palmyrton—Bretton Pines.

I sit and stare out my window. Sunday afternoon, the loneliest time of the week. Since my engagement, I thought this empty, unrooted sensation was a thing of the past.

Guess not.

If I'm lonely, wouldn't an eighty-five-year-old woman in a retirement home be even more eager for company? I'll ask for a tour of Bretton Pines—tell them I'm searching for an assisted living facility for my dad. Then when I'm there, I'll mention that an acquaintance is a resident, and I'd like to ask her opinion of the place. Clothilde Savatier will see me see me. I'm sure of it.

An impeccably groomed middle-aged woman greets me with a glossy brochure to begin my guided tour of Bretton Pines. The developers remodeled a Gilded Age mansion and added three wings to form a big square around a glass-roofed interior courtyard complete with a splashing fountain and towering potted palms. The great room has a Steinway grand piano and the library looks like a scaled down version of a reading room at Oxford. Each resident has his or her own private apartment, and meals are served in a grand dining room with linen tablecloths and waiters in black jackets. Geez, getting old might not be so bad if you could do it in this kind of style. I don't even enquire about the price. I'm pretty sure I wouldn't be able to keep from gasping even though my tour is purely hypothetical.

I patiently let the saleswoman run through her pitch, even asking a few thoughtful questions. Then I make my move.

"Bretton Pines is lovely and you've done an excellent job of showing me around. You know, a friend of mine is acquainted with one of the residents here. She suggested I introduce myself while I'm here. I'd like to get a sense of Bretton Pines from a resident's perspective."

"All our residents are very happy here. If the person would like to have a visitor, I'll certainly introduce you. Who is it?"

"Clothilde Savatier"

My guide stiffens. "Mrs. Savatier is quite...er...reserved. She may not want to chat."

"I wouldn't want to bother her, but my friend did specifically suggest that I look her up."

The guide looks doubtful, which makes me wonder if "reserved" is a code word for "dementia." But then she musters a smile and says Mrs. Savatier is just finishing lunch. "We can catch up with her as she's leaving the dining room."

We stand by the door as the dining room empties. There are more women than men, and they rise unsteadily from tables of four and totter toward us. Most of the ladies are wearing lacy pastel cardigans, polyester slacks, and sensible orthopedic shoes. They exit in pairs, chatting about their meal or their afternoon plans. In the middle of the room, I spot a spot a woman sitting alone. When she gets up from her table, I note her trim navy blazer, nipped in at the waist and edged in cream piping, and mid-height navy pumps with a gold buckle. Her silver hair is twisted into a chignon, her post-lunch lipstick already reapplied. How French! I'm sure that's Clothilde.

Sure enough, my guide approaches her and the old lady stops and gives me the once-over. No sign of dementia in that sharp look! She seems suspicious but her curiosity clearly has got the better of her, and she follows the guide over to me.

"Hello Mrs. Savatier," I extend my hand. "My name is Audrey Nealon. I'm acquainted with Kara Eskew."

She had been in the act of extending her hand when the name "Eskew" stops her cold. Her bright blue eyes narrow. "I read in the paper the old woman was murdered."

The guide's eyes widen. Crap—now she's going to ask what's going on.

But Mrs. Savatier pivots sharply toward her. "Thank you, Laura. You may go."

Wow! Way to dismiss a servant! She's got that nailed.

Mrs. Savatier turns back to face me. "Let us go into the parlor. You can explain the purpose of your visit there." She marches down the hall with her eyes focused straight ahead while I trail at her side. Clearly, my ruse about getting a resident's perspective on Bretton Pines is out the window. I might as well tell her the whole truth and see what happens.

The parlor, a room filled with clusters of chintz love seats and wing chairs, is unoccupied except for an old gent dozing with a book in his lap. Clothilde heads to a group of chairs in the far corner. She sits facing me and gives a sharp nod.

Start talking, and it had better be good.

So I tell her how I came to know the Eskew family, and how Darlene was there tending to Mrs. Eskew as she was dying, and everything that led up to my discovery of the body.

"So I got to see how Darlene took care of Mrs. Eskew and I simply can't imagine any reason why she would ever hurt her patient. Especially not in such an awful way. In fact, I can't understand why anyone would want to kill her when she was about to die any day. But Mrs. Eskew did seem afraid of something, I mean afraid of more than dying. But the police have arrested Darlene, and I feel like I should help because—"

I pause. Clothilde is scrutinizing me with those piercing eyes. Stop rambling, Audrey—get a grip. "I feel that I let Mrs. Eskew down. She was afraid, but I let myself be convinced that what she was saying was a normal part of dying. Now I'm not so sure. And I'm worried the police might be pressuring Darlene to take a plea bargain just so they can close the case."

Clothilde raises her perfectly plucked eyebrows. "All very interesting. But you have not explained your presence here."

No, I haven't. Maybe that's because I'm not sure myself. Except for my nagging feeling that the house contains secrets, secrets in plain sight that I'm just too dumb to perceive. I take a deep breath and keep talking. "The nature of my work gives me extraordinary access to people's lives, their artifacts. The thing about the Eskews' house is the entire place seems to be permeated by memories of Parker—his life and his death. Mrs. Eskew even spoke to me about him, and about your grandchild, one day when I was working in her room.

"I can't help thinking that maybe, somehow, her murder has something to do with Parker. With his life. Or his death."

Clothilde had been listening to me with the neutral expression of a TV shrink. Until I mentioned her grandson. Then she snaps into high alert.

"Marjorie spoke of him, our grandson?"

"Yes, it was a little weird. She seemed to be speaking directly to him. Darlene, the aide, said it's common for dying people to speak to loved ones who are already, you know, on the other side."

Is it possible to snort with a French accent? If so, Clothilde has done it.

"Foolish superstitions!"

I guess what they say about the French all being atheists is true. "She did seem genuinely anguished," I say.

"Ha! What of me?" Clothilde taps her chest. "I lost my only child, my only grandchild. She had three others, and many opportunities for more grandchildren."

Her English is impeccable, but she retains a trace of a French accent on certain words. As she grows agitated, the accent becomes more noticeable.

"That's what strikes me as so odd about the house. You'd never even know there were three other kids in the family. Everything I find is about Parker. Only Parker. So I thought if I could talk to someone who actually knew him…"

"Why should what happened to Parker and my daughter have anything to do with Marjorie's murder?"

"Whoever killed her—it was an act of rage. She was so weak, so drugged—a pillow over her face would have been enough. Instead, the killer…" I shudder. "It was very violent."

"Whatever misery befalls that family, they deserve it."

Now I'm the one with the "keep talking" look on my face.

"I despise them all. I would cheerfully pound each one with a rock if it would bring my daughter back. But revenge? What is the point?"

I'm losing her here. Does she blame Parker for piloting his own plane instead of flying commercial? "Revenge for what?" I ask.

Clothilde sits up straight and stares me in the eye. "He crashed that plane intentionally. The plane fell out of a clear blue sky. They could find no problem with the engine. There was no radio call for help. It crashed on an empty stretch of beach. No one would believe me. They said I was *une folle.*" She makes the universal sign for crazy at her temple. "They said I would not accept it was an accident because I was still grieving the loss of my husband." She leans forward and grips my arm. Her hand feels like she's been tossing snowballs.

"He killed himself and took my daughter and grandchild with him."

CHAPTER 22

This is not what I had been expecting. But Clothilde seems the very antithesis of a crazy old lady. She's smart, perceptive, and not the least bit hysterical. What she has suggested does happen—look at that German pilot who took a whole plane-load of tourists down with him. But that guy had a history of mental illness. Was that true of Parker Eskew?

"But why? Had he been depressed? He had plenty of money and a great job, right?"

"Parker never had a depressed moment in his life, I'm sure. He was a supreme egotist. His parents, especially his mother, raised him to believe he was a god descended from Mt. Olympus to grace the rest of us with his presence."

"You never liked him?"

Clothilde hesitates. "I cannot say that. When my husband and I first met Parker, we were very impressed by him. There is no denying he was quite charming…highly intelligent. But—"

"What?" I barely breathe the word.

Clothilde raises her hand to her throat and twists her pearls. "Every time I spent time with him, I came away feeling there was an emptiness at his core. My husband dismissed this as nonsense. He said I merely felt that no one on Earth was good enough for our Leonie. Jean insisted that Leonie had made a brilliant match."

"And what about the Eskews? They also approved of the marriage?"

"Ah, yes! They were delighted to be getting French in-laws. We are so chic, no? And Jean had so many business contacts that Gilbert found useful."

Her sarcasm could be cut with a knife. But this reminds me of what I learned from Mr. Venable. "I've heard that Gilbert Eskew was something of a social climber. Did you know that he'd changed his name from Jakub Eskein? He grew up poor on the Lower East Side."

"I did not know, but it doesn't surprise me. There is no shame in coming from humble roots, but Gilbert would have seen it differently." Clothilde bites her lip. "I wish my daughter had married a ditch-digger, a trash-collector. Anyone but Parker Eskew."

"But why would he have crashed his plane?"

"For years after the crash I was certain that his firm would discover some signs of embezzlement or financial impropriety. When nothing materialized in a few months, I hired a discreet private investigator to inquire in case the hedge fund he worked for was hushing it up. But there was nothing. Apparently the firm very much regretted his loss. He was one who made the storms come."

"A rainmaker?"

"*Precisement.*"

"But you still think he killed himself to avoid some scandal?"

"A humiliation that he could not endure. I'm sure of it."

"But to take your daughter as well?"

"She too saw him as a god, foolish girl. Even in his grave, he would not have wanted her to know whatever it was. And certainly he would not have wanted her to carry on after he was gone. He would have found her survival unimaginable."

"So he chose death for her."

Clothilde has been stoic up to now, but I detect a slight tremor in her upper lip. "This is what I cannot forgive. How dare he, how *dare* he, decide that my daughter and my grandson would not want to live without him?"

"The Eskews knew that you felt this way?"

"I always speak my mind. They knew, but they denied all. But I always suspected that Marjorie Eskew knew the truth, or at least suspected it."

"So maybe someone killed her to keep the secret quiet. They knew she was delirious and rambling on her deathbed. But again, why kill her so violently?"

Clothilde straightens her jacket. "Apparently someone hates her even more than I do."

CHAPTER 23

Sunday night and Monday morning have passed with no word from Sean. It's hard to keep my mind off my sadness and anxiety when I'm not even busy with work. On Monday, I putter around the office alone, balancing accounts and sorting through the stacks of paper that sprout on my desk with the relentlessness of dandelions. But this busywork doesn't fully occupy my mind. Always at the periphery are thoughts of Sean. Does he intend to never speak to me again? To walk away from our future without another word? I check my phone compulsively: a text, a missed call, an email.

Nothing.

Just past noon, Ty arrives after his morning classes. I'm ridiculously happy to see him.

"No Adrienne?" he asks, looking at her empty, neat desk.

"Sick kid. But we're not busy, so it's just as well."

We don't say it aloud, but we're both relieved to be alone together.

"Did you hear the news?" I ask. "They arrested Darlene."

Ty stretches like a very tall cat. "I heard. You talked to Sean since the carnival?"

I shake my head. "We're not speaking. I had a terrible time with the kids after you left. Chrissy ran away from me and got lost." I shudder. "I don't even want to talk about it."

Ty studies me for a moment, but he doesn't speak. Unlike just about every other person in my life, he never offers unsolicited advice. He continues the series of yoga stretches that Jill taught him. When his head is practically touching the floor, he says, "I got some details Sean might like to know. What am I supposed to do 'bout that?"

"Information? Like what?"

Ty stands up. "'Member how I told you at the carnival that I thought that dude Sean was chasing looked familiar? Well, I finally figured it out. I'm almost positive it was Darlene's son. The day I saw him at the house he was wearing a Devil's jersey."

I'm puzzled. "When did you ever see him at the house? Adrienne was with me the day I saw him."

"That day we worked on the morning room. I walked in and asked you who was driving that hooptie and you said the nurse. At the time, I let it pass because you started telling me about the fight Darlene and the nurse had. But the person driving the old car was a young, white guy in a red Devil's shirt. He looked right at me when he pulled outta the driveway. Then he sped off."

"The nurse was a middle-aged black woman. So Rob must've been there at the same time." My hand goes up to my mouth. "Uh-oh—now I get it. The nurse was accusing Darlene of overmedicating Mrs. Eskew because there weren't as many pain pills left in the bottle as there should have been. Darlene covered by saying she was just trying to keep Mrs. Eskew comfortable. But she must've given the pills to Rob. That day when I heard them arguing, I thought he was pressuring her about money. But it must've been about the pills."

Ty nods. "Rob must be sellin' what his mom gives him. So you gonna tell Sean?"

I shake my head. "I can't call him right now. Not about anything. He needs to call me to apologize first. So you call and tell him about Darlene's son."

Ty throws up his hands and shakes his head hard enough to create a breeze. "No way! I don't snitch to the cops 'bout nuthin'. I told you, and if you wanna tell him, that's up to you."

I cradle my head in my hands. "All right. I'll figure out how to handle it, but not right now." I point to a stack of boxes in the corner. "Is that stuff going to Sister Alice or the soup kitchen?"

"Alice. But I figured I'd wait until after the Eskew sale to see what else we end up with for her before I drive to Newark."

"Let's work on consolidating all that into fewer boxes," I say, eager for mindless physical labor. But while we sort and repack, troubling thoughts keep resurfacing. If Darlene was stealing pills for Rob to sell, it seems to me she'd have even less reason to kill Mrs. Eskew. Why eliminate the source? But what if Rob's an addict? Could he have killed Mrs. Eskew in a drug-fueled rage? Is that why Darlene has confessed—to protect her son? Clothilde said someone must hate Mrs. Eskew more than she does. Is it someone with a true motive? Or is it just an angry young man with lousy impulse control? That's who Sean says commits most crimes.

Ty and I work steadily, not saying much. Then late in the afternoon, there's a knock at the office door. Ty answers it, and when he steps aside, I see Kara Lyman. Her face, always anxious, looks truly haggard. She's wearing a navy blue blouse with black slacks. Maybe she got dressed in the dark. Or maybe she just doesn't give a damn.

I stand and extend my hand. "Kara, I'm so sorry for your loss. This is such a terrible experience for your family."

She ignores my gesture and my words. Without making eye contact she says, "You can return to working in the house tomorrow."

"What? But the police...it's a—" I'm about to say "crime scene," but I choke on the words.

Her gaze darts back and forth, taking in the clutter of my desk and the neatness of Adrienne's and Ty standing beside a tower of half-packed boxes. You'd think she was watching a tennis match, but no one is moving. "The police are done. They say you can return to working there. How soon do you think we can have the sale?"

I back away, rocked by a hot wave of alarm. I have no desire to return to the Eskew house right now. The truth is, I'm afraid to be there. The more certain I become that Darlene didn't kill Mrs. Eskew, the more obvious it is that the real killer—whether it's Rob or someone else— is still on the loose. And that person is not rational. He—or she—killed a helpless old lady. Why would the killer hesitate to dispatch me if I stumbled across something incriminating? But what can I tell Kara? I want to wait until the police realize their mistake and release Darlene and figure out who really killed Mrs. Eskew? I want to talk to my cop boyfriend before I return to work except I'm not speaking to him right now? Kara thinks her mom's killer is safely behind bars. Still, I think it's bizarre that she's so focused on the sale when the family hasn't even held a funeral yet for their murdered mother.

"The sale?" I stammer. "What about your mom's funeral?"

"It's a private affair. Just the family. She'll be cremated on Wednesday. So we can have the sale this weekend, right?"

I struggle mightily to keep the dismay at her brutal coldness off my face.

Kara pats her pockets. "You'll need the house key, now that Darlene isn't there to let you in."

"Must be a shock that the cops arrested Darlene," Ty interjects from across the room.

Kara shoots him a sharp look. "These people...I don't know where the home health care agency finds them. Clearly unstable."

There are a few adjectives I could use to describe Darlene, but unstable isn't one of them. However, I'm not about to debate it with Kara. "Don't you think it would be best to postpone the sale a bit until the news dies down? People have such morbid curiosity. They might come just to..."

"Gawk? Let them. I won't be there to see it." Kara plops down on a wobbly leather chair we salvaged from a sale. The top button of her blouse has come undone, and I notice a thick white scar on her clavicle. "I have buyers lined up for the house. They want to close and take possession as soon as the lawyers organize the paperwork. Then I'm going to leave New Jersey and never come back."

"I'm just not sure I can work under those circumstances. I—" I cast an uneasy glance at Ty.

"We got another small sale comin' up this week," he lies to back me up.

"I'll find someone else to run the sale at Mother's house. Just give me the cataloguing you've done so far." Kara holds her hand out.

"Give it to you?" my voice raises in outrage. "That's proprietary research. I spent over a week of work on that!"

"I'll pay you for your time." She begins clawing through her purse looking for a checkbook. "What's your hourly rate?"

Hourly rate? I'm not a clerk! Kara could never pay me a flat fee that would equal the commission this huge sale will bring. I feel September slipping from the black into the red.

Ty has moved to his desk and silently watches this debate unfold. He emits a force field of tension. He needs this job as much as I do. More, now that Charmaine and Lo are in the picture.

I put a calming hand on Kara's arm. "Let's both take a deep breath. I was just surprised that you'd expect me to get back to work so soon. Of course, I want to keep this job. Of course I want Another Man's Treasure to run the sale."

Kara lets out an exasperated huff the way people do when they get called out for standing in the express line with twenty items. "Fine. But don't drag your feet. I want this wrapped up ASAP."

"Ty and I will be at the house tomorrow," I say.

Once Kara is out the door, Ty comes to stand beside me. "Don't worry, Audge. I got your back on this."

CHAPTER 24

I've never been to the county jail, so I nearly overshoot the small sign pointing the way between a lumberyard and the Palmer County recycling center. The road takes a sudden twist and the building looms up before me—a newish concrete block structure more like my idea of a postal service processing center than a hellish Shawshank Redemption prison. No razor wire or guard towers, just a parking lot with a sign pointing the way to the visitors' entrance.

Visiting Darlene is a crazy idea, but once it popped into my head I couldn't get it to leave. So I sent Ty home early, went to the jail website, clicked on "Inmate Visitation"—God, how awful!— and learned that I could stay no longer than an hour and bring nothing with me but my driver's license. I'm not even sure what I'll say to Darlene, except I'm certain I'll be able to tell if she murdered Mrs. Eskew once I see her face-to-face.

I join a line of people—ninety percent women, one hundred percent sad and exhausted—waiting to get in to see a loved one. Inside the barren lobby, a guard checks each ID closely. Apart from a small commotion when a very large woman sets off the metal detector, no one talks although I see a few of the ladies nod to each other in recognition. I get in an elevator and ride to the third floor with the small group here to see a female inmate. We queue up, and I soon realize why the other more experienced visitors elbowed ahead of me. There are only two visitation rooms, and five of us. If everyone takes her full hour, I could be here for quite a while. I immediately pat my pocket for my cellphone so I can pass the time with email or Facebook, but then I remember I had to leave it in the car. I'm stuck with nothing but the bare beige wall to stare at.

Ty said the boredom of prison drove him crazy, and I can see why. Through the metal-screened window that separates us from the cell block, I can see about ten women sitting at cafeteria-style tables talking or staring at a small TV mounted on a column. They're all wearing beige jumpsuits and orange slip-on sneakers. A couple have gray sweatshirts. I search for Darlene but she is not among the women in my field of vision. Then the guard opens a visiting room door and lets a weeping older woman out. Through the window, I see the inmate leave on her side. She's hugely pregnant, and lumbers away from the group, going to stand beside what must be her cell. A guard lets her in. That visit lasted hardly ten minutes. I don't even want to imagine what was said.

Now that I've moved up, I can see a different angle of the cellblock, but still no Darlene. Finally, I'm next in line. Through the window, I can see but not hear a guard knock on a cell door. Darlene emerges, and when the guard speaks to her, her face lights up. Clearly she's thrilled to hear she has a visitor. I feel a pang of anxiety—she must be expecting her sons. I step into my side of the visitor's room. There are three hard plastic chairs on my side of the Plexiglas, and a telephone receiver on the wall.

I watch the guard escorting Darlene toward the visitor's room. She seems to have shrunk in the days since the murder. Her broad shoulders are slumped and her hair hangs limply. The guard lets her in and shuts the door behind her. Darlene's eyes widen when she sees me, then her whole face collapses in disappointment.

I pick up my receiver and gesture for her to do the same. She slowly places it against her ear as if she expects it to blow up.

"Hi, Darlene. How are you holding up?"

She stares at me for a moment letting the hard mask of indifference reform. Then she speaks. "I'm fine. This place ain't half bad. Watch TV and play cards all day. Food sucks but at least I don't have to cook it."

Her bravado doesn't fool me. She looks scared and lonely. Does she look innocent?

I lean toward the glass. "I came to ask you something."

"What? If I stole something else? Are you worried you left something off the list?"

That hurts, but I guess I deserve it. "Look, Darlene—I had to tell Kara that things were disappearing from the house. I never said I suspected you. In fact, when the cops jumped to that conclusion, I said I didn't think you knew the value of the books and the silverware."

"Because I'm too dumb."

Now she's trying to be ornery, but I'm not playing. "I think it was Tom or Rachel, or maybe both of them who took the stuff. But it was easier for Kara to blame you. Then the cops took her accusations one step further. I feel terrible about that. I want to help you."

"Ha! Please, don't do me any favors!" She studies her bitten fingernails with great interest.

If only I could touch her hand, get her to meet my eye. I long to ask her why she confessed, but there's a big sign saying all inmate conversations are recorded. Obviously, this is no place to frankly discuss her guilt or innocence. I have to infer the truth from our circuitous conversation. "I don't believe you had any reason to kill Mrs. Eskew. But someone did have a reason."

Darlene gazes up at the ceiling. "Doesn't really matter what you believe. What the cops believe is what counts."

Hmmm. That implies she's trying to convince the cops. "Someone was afraid. That's why they killed her."

"Afraid of that old woman? She weighed about eighty pounds."

"Afraid of what she knew, of what she was saying on her deathbed."

Darlene returns to picking at her cuticles.

Obviously, I can't ask her if Rob was in the house on the day of the murder. I decide to explore the Clothilde track. "You know how she was always talking to Leonie and Jean-Claude? Well, Leonie's mother—Jean-Claude's other grandmother—is still alive, and she has a theory."

Darlene had been steadfastly maintaining her sullen boredom, but now she can't resist showing interest.

"Leonie's mother thinks that Parker intentionally killed himself and Leonie because of some scandal that was about to break," I say. "She could never prove anything. Now she says the reason Mrs. Eskew was murdered was because she said something about

Parker that her killer didn't want heard. Does that make sense to you? Did she ever talk about Parker?"

"Are you kidding? That's *all* she talked about."

"But did she say anything about the plane crash? About why he died?"

Darlene squirms. "I don't know. I wasn't listening to her. She'd talk and talk and I'd just say, 'uh-huh'."

I feel like a teacher calling out a student for not knowing the capital of Idaho. "Darlene, please—this is important. Try to remember!"

She takes the kind of deep breath kids take when they're humoring their parents. "Sometimes she'd think she was at some kind of game or race that he was in, and she'd be cheering him on. She'd be telling him to go faster, and then she'd ask me if he won."

"And then what?"

"I'd tell her 'sure, he came in first place', and she'd relax and go back to sleep."

This is not what I'm looking for. But I don't want to plant ideas in her head about the financial misdeeds that Clothilde suspects. That will just come back to kick us in the butt. "Anything else? Anything that she said that seemed to upset her?"

"Nothing." Darlene sits back in her chair and crosses her arms across her chest.

I put my palm against the glass separating us. "I know you didn't kill Marjorie Eskew."

Her face hardens. "I agreed to take the plea bargain for manslaughter. They told me if it went to trial, I'd get life with no parole. This way, I'll be out in eight years."

"You can't let them intimidate you into saying you did something you didn't do. Did you talk to a lawyer?"

"Oh, sure. They called in some kid who looks like he's running for student council president and I'm one of his two hundred cases. Like he was going to get me off."

"Darlene, once you accept the plea bargain in court, they'll move you to Rahway. This place is like a resort compared to that prison."

"I know what I'm doing."

She stands up and gestures to the guard that she's ready to leave.

I rise too and try one last time to get her to respond to me. "Why aren't you defending yourself? Don't you want to get back home to your kids?"

I expect her eyes to well with tears, but they're flat and hard. "You just leave it alone. My kids are better off without me."

CHAPTER 25

My visit to Darlene was hardly conclusive, but I'm pretty sure Mrs. Eskew's killer is *not* safely behind bars. Nevertheless, I promised Kara I'd be at work today. I console myself with the thought that Darlene's final words, that her kids are better off without her, must mean that she's protecting Rob. And if there are no drugs left in the house, there should be no reason that I would encounter Rob there.

I hope.

I text Adrienne and tell her to not bother going to the office, but instead to meet me at the house even though I know Ty won't be able to work there this morning to be our bodyguard. I warn her to dress for dirt, but I'm sure my advice will fall on deaf ears. Adrienne's idea of work clothes is wearing last year's three-hundred-dollar designer jeans.

On my way out of my condo, I grab a heavy hammer. If Adrienne and I are together and I'm armed, we should be okay.

Kara has given me the key to the back door, and I told Adrienne to meet me here, but there's no sign of her. Just then a text arrives.

Running late. Be there in 20.

Twenty minutes means thirty in Adrienne time. Even though I don't want to be in the house alone, I'm not standing around outside waiting for half an hour. My heart pounds as I unlock the door and enter the hall that leads to the kitchen. The house no longer smells of sickness. I inhale reluctantly. Does it smell of death?

I tell myself I'm being fanciful. The scene of the crime has been cleaned, I'm sure. As I enter the foyer, I make as much noise as possible. If anyone is here, I don't want to be surprised. "Hell-o-o-o," I call.

My voice echoes in the vast, empty space.

Screwing up my courage, I climb the wide curved staircase to the second floor, then make my way up the narrow attic steps, hammer in hand. A new smell greets me as I climb: mildew, moth balls, dry rot. Not a bad smell to me—attics are exciting. They're the purgatory of a house, the last stop before the hell of the Dumpster. And just as the souls in Purgatory can be redeemed with some high-octane prayer, the junk in attics sometimes proves to be surprisingly valuable. The vase banished from the living room by a decorator too young to appreciate English Prattware. The long-forgotten baseball cards and Barbie dolls. The Oriental rug rejected in favor of Berber wall-to-wall. The finds are all the more thrilling for being totally unexpected.

But to find the gold nuggets, I have to dig through memories. The clothes people wore to the biggest events in their lives: graduation gowns, wedding dresses, Army uniforms, Eagle Scout sashes. The souvenirs of vacations dimly remembered, parties long-forgotten. Gifts and heirlooms given with love, but received with reluctance. In short, all the stuff no one has the heart to discard or the closet space to keep.

When I get to the top of the stairs, I see the Eskew attic is just what I expected—a tangle of boxes, furniture and sheet-shrouded objects that might be treasure or might be trash. A large, undivided space, the attic has a solid floor but the walls are unfinished and insulation drips down from the ceiling. No signs of squirrels or raccoons, so I begin my exploration.

As is often the case, the area around the entrance is the most crowded. People shove boxes up into the attic intending to deal with them later, then the next box gets shoved up, pushing the earlier arrivals back. The far corners stay empty.

I'm in the midst of this clutter assessing the contents—so far only mildew-y children's books, Christmas ornaments, and some lamps—when I hear a noise behind a box ahead of me.

I scream.

The box tips over. I raise my hammer.

The elfin face of Rachel appears. She stares at me wordlessly as she did the other day in the dining room.

I lower the hammer, feeling foolish. Why would she be here now, after all that's happened? On the other hand, I suppose she doesn't have a job—who would hire her?—so what else does she have to do with her time?

"Hi, there. You're here early." I can't ask her what she's doing here. After all, it is still her house. But I feel the need to break the silence with some words, however inane.

"Where's the other lady, the pretty one?"

Ouch. Way to tell it like it is, Rachel. "I'm expecting her any minute. We're going to see if there's anything up here that can go into the sale."

"The sale. Right." Rachel studies her tiny, sneaker-clad feet.

"Are you sad about selling the house?"

She slips through the pile of boxes and emerges behind me. "Happy, happy. Happy all the time, that's me. Except when I'm not."

I turn again to face her. "Do you live nearby?" I'd like to get a sense of whether to expect her visits every day this week.

Rachel gives a wide, vague wave, which might mean she lives two houses away or two towns away. "I have a condo. Mother bought it."

Before I can respond, a leaf blower kicks on outside and its high-pitched whine fills the air.

"A-a-i-i-eeee!" Rachel tucks her chin into her chest and wraps her arms around her head. She drops to the ground and rocks.

Flabbergasted, I stand before her not knowing what to do. Should I comfort her? Run outside and ask the landscapers to stop?

Gradually, the blower moves further from the house and the noise lessens. Rachel peeks out between her arms. "That's too loud. It hurts my head." Then she stands up and wanders around the attic prattling away, saying absolutely nothing that makes sense to me. Indeed, I'm not sure if she's addressing me at all or just having a chat with herself.

Suddenly, she stops murmuring and in a very distinct voice announces, "This is my throne."

I've lost track of her amid the boxes and support beams.

"Queen of all I survey," she says, and tracking her voice I see her sitting in a large easy chair by the dormer window. The chair is so deep that her tiny legs don't reach the floor and stick straight out. The light coming through the dusty window is dim, but she has donned an oversized pair of dark sunglasses.

Against my better judgment, I walk over to her. "Did you like to play up here when you were a kid?"

"Not to play. To hide. To get away from them, all of them, always telling me what to do." She smiles, but I can't tell if she's looking at me from behind the shades, or if she's traveling back in time. "Up here I could do what I wanted. Anything I wanted."

Rachel slides off the chair and continues to prowl around the attic. I return to the stacks by the door, wishing ever more fervently that Adrienne would get herself over here. I haven't turned up anything exciting yet, but there are many more boxes and piles to check.

"Look at this!" Rachel's voice pipes from across the attic.

I have no desire to quit what I'm doing, so I ignore her.

"Audrey Nealon, come here!"

Rachel sounds like a mother calling her disobedient child in the supermarket. I didn't realize she even knew my full name. So I humor her and cross to the corner where's she's standing. When I get close enough, I can see that she's pointing to a stack of boxes against the wall. Not big storage boxes, but different-sized gift boxes all wrapped in blue and white and yellow baby gift paper.

I feel a little queasy.

"These were for Jean-Claude. Mother bought them. But she couldn't give them to him." Her voice is matter-of-fact. "Jean-Claude was going to be my nephew. He was dead before he was alive."

"I'm sorry," I whisper.

"Yoo-hoo! I'm here!"

Adrienne. Thank God!

Adrienne's presence banishes all that's creepy from the attic. Her expensive perfume overwhelms the mustiness. Her pink peep-toe espadrilles and paisley boho blouse brighten the gloom. And her amusing chatter about overbearing PTA moms and jihadist New Jersey drivers brings a healthy dose of normality into the room. Rachel doesn't leave, but Adrienne's vitality mesmerizes her into silence. She perches on a stool and quietly watches us work. Half an hour passes, and when I lift my head out of a deep box full of lace tablecloths, I realize Rachel is gone.

I elbow Adrienne, nod toward the empty stool, and mouth, "Did she leave?"

"Yeah, thank God!" Adrienne answers in a normal voice. "She stood at the top of the stairs and stared at me for, like, a full minute. Then she went down. Weird. But Tom says she's always been that way."

"Oh? When were you talking to Tom?"

"Last week when I was working in the kitchen, Tom helped me move some boxes. He's very friendly."

"The two of them seem to have an awful lot of free time during the day, popping in here like they do. Doesn't either one work?"

"Who would hire Rachel? Anyway, Tom implied they all have trust funds. Except there are a lot of restrictions. He's is in PR—a consultant, so I guess he makes his own hours."

"Right. Consultant is the way rich people say they're unemployed."

"Oh, Audrey! You sounded just like Sean when you said that. And the other day, I heard him tell his mother to analyze the costs and benefits before she bought a new vacuum, and I swear I thought it was you talking. The two of you are gradually becoming one person."

Not anymore we're not. I turn away so she can't see the tears that have sprung into my eyes. I remember what my dad said about being drawn to what you lack. Sean and I have absorbed some of each other. What will happen to it if we split up?

Before I have to reply, I hear Ty's cheerful shout below. "Yo, Audge! Where are you?"

We work steadily until 1:00. Ty carries anything saleable from the attic to the second floor, and Adrienne sorts the rest for charity or trash. We get about half the attic cleared when we decide to break for lunch.

"I have an errand to run back in Palmyrton," I tell them, "so I'll eat there."

"Ima take a load to the dump," Ty says. "I'll be back by two."

"I brought my lunch," Adrienne says. "I'll just stay here."

"No!" Ty and I chorus.

She cocks her head. "What's the big deal?"

"It's not safe. Rachel is prowling around here. We don't know who else has a house key. Let's stick together. Meet us back here at two."

Adrienne shrugs. "Fine. I'll eat my lunch in the park."

I make it halfway to Palmyrton when I realize the folder I need for my meeting with my accountant is in my tote bag. And my tote bag is in the Eskew's attic.

Shit!

Now I have to double back. And I have to go into the house alone. After the Rachel encounter, I'm even less willing to be there alone. But that's what has to be done.

Back at the Eskew's house, I unlock the back door and make my way into the kitchen.

Low voices greet me.

I freeze. Is someone in this room? The door to the butler's pantry is partially open. Through the crack, I see a man's back, shirttails flapping. He's got a woman pinned up against the built-in mahogany china cabinet. Her long, naked legs are wrapped around him and her hands grip his shoulders.

It's Tom Eskew. Why did he bring his girlfriend here?

Embarrassed, I back out. Then I spy a flash of fuchsia.

I'd know that pedicure anywhere.

It's Adrienne.

CHAPTER 26

In my shock I stumble backward. My foot catches on a kitchen chair and knocks it over.

The murmuring voices in the pantry fall silent.

I want to turn tail and run, but I'm frozen. My mind can't process, my feet can't move.

After a brief period of shuffling, Tom's head pokes through the partly opened door. "Oh, hey Audrey. Didn't realize you were working here today. I was just looking for some champagne flutes. Pretty sure my mom had a few in here."

I feel my mouth hanging open stupidly. A cold sweat has broken out on my chest. My future sister-in-law is in that pantry pulling her clothes back on. In a moment I'm going to have to think of something to say to her. My brain is not up to this challenge.

Tom steps back inside and re-emerges a moment later with two tall, thin glasses in his right hand. "A friend is leaving for a job in Milan. Champagne in tumblers is no way to say bon voyage."

I stop gaping and grind my teeth to keep from screaming.

He ducks his head and gazes at me through that flopping forelock of his, holding the glasses out for my inspection. "They're mismatched, see? Surely the estate doesn't begrudge me these."

I feel like smacking the glasses right out of his perfectly groomed hands. Does he honestly think he can manipulate me the way he manipulates every other woman he meets?

"I'll be working in the attic until five," I say in a slightly louder voice than necessary. "I can use your help, Adrienne. When you're...free."

Ten minutes later, Adrienne appears in the attic. The color has drained from her face, leaving her tan looking blotchy and dirty.

"Audrey, it's not what you think."

I toss down the old golf club I've been staring at, my accountant meeting now cancelled. "How could screwing Tom Eskew in the pantry be anything other than what I think?"

"I didn't...we didn't go all the way."

"Only because I stumbled into your, your..."

She creeps toward me. "You can't tell anyone, Audrey. I don't care about Tom. It's just...I've been so..." Adrienne begins to cry. "You and Sean are still head over heels in love. Wait 'til you've been married fifteen years. Brendan doesn't even see me anymore. I'm just this woman who manages his house and his kids. He's no more aware of me than he is of the guy who pumps his gas."

It's a good thing I've dropped the golf club because if it were still in my hand, I swear I'd clobber her with it. "Brendan works seventy hours a week. You don't mind decorating that fabulous house and driving that BMW and wearing those—" I point to today's designer shoes. "And then you have the nerve to complain that he doesn't dote on you like a princess?"

"I never asked for any of this. He's the one who wants the country club life, to show off to everyone how far he's come up in the world. I wish things were still like they were when we first got married...when we were both working, when we'd come home and talk about our days. We'd make plans for the future and save up our money for the things we wanted to buy. It was—" She slumps into a heap at my feet. "Fun. We *wanted* each other. Now he just needs me because a good executive needs a lovely wife and two smart and accomplished kids."

I look down on Adrienne's shiny, dark hair. I feel a little tug of sympathy—Brendan *does* enjoy showing off his status, but I'd always assumed she was a willing accomplice. "And you think Tom Eskew wants you? He wants every woman he sees. You're nothing to him."

Adrienne cringes. I've kicked her with my words. "I know," she whispers. "I've never done anything like this before. It was a moment of madness." Her eyes are wild with fear, like the chipmunk that Ethel cornered once in my neighbor's driveway.

"You can't tell Sean." Adrienne grabs my hands in hers. "I can't lose my kids. They're everything to me."

"You want me to lie?" Adrienne doesn't know that I'm not speaking to Sean, but still I'm outraged that she has the nerve to ask me to cover for her.

Adrienne shakes my arm. "Just promise me you won't tell Sean tonight. Give me a chance to work things out with Brendan myself."

I turn away from her pleading face. There's no danger of my telling Sean anything tonight. And even if I were speaking to Sean, I don't want to be sucked into the vortex of Coughlin family drama. "Go home. I don't want to talk to you anymore. I don't even want to look at you."

Having banished my assistant, I'm left to keep working in the attic alone until Ty gets back. I cross the attic and stand looking at the gift boxes. Each one has an elaborate bow and little tags that read "welcome Jean-Claude" in elaborate script. How sad. How terribly sad. Can I really sell the twenty-year-old gifts of a dead baby? Is it less sad to toss them in the Dumpster? I pick up one of the boxes and the ancient scotch tape releases. The faded and brittle gift paper slips to the floor. Feeling like I'm reading old love letters, I open the box.

And drop it like a hot rock.

Inside, the delicate little blue sailor suit has been slashed to ribbons.

CHAPTER 27

That evening, in a throwback to our bachelorette days, Ethel and I are sharing an order of Kung Pao chicken when there's a knock at the door. Ethel's ears perk up, but she doesn't run into the foyer barking like a lunatic. Instead, her tail swishes twice across the floor and she goes back to licking the inside of the carryout container. This can only mean one thing.

I open the front door. Sean fills my tiny porch. Relief floods through me but I keep a stern face.

"Hi." His hands are jammed in his pockets and his shoulders are hunched.

"Hi yourself." I stand back and let him enter. We face each other in my cramped entrance hall.

Words tumble out of him in a gush. "I'm sorry, Audrey. What I did was wrong. I shouldn't have left you with the kids."

I nod. "True. I accept your apology."

Sean looks like he just won the Powerball. "Really? We're made up that easy?"

I turn and march into the living room, talking as I walk. "I didn't say I wasn't still mad. I just said I accept your apology. We need to talk."

When we're sitting across from each other with Ethel sprawled between us, I begin. "Look Sean, we've both been living our lives letting our jobs take precedence over everything else. But if we have kids, that's got to change."

He lifts his hands in protest. "I only—"

I cut him off. "Hear me out. I want us to have children, but I'm worried about the enormous responsibility... about the never-endingness of parenthood. I have to know that you're in it with me fifty-fifty. I can't be the default parent, the one who always picks up the slack."

Sean nods. "I understand. It was just…this case, it's so important…I got carried away."

"It's not just this case. There will always be another important case. Work isn't going to change. *You* have to change."

Sean shifts uneasily.

"If you want a woman like your mother, you'd better not marry me."

Sean snorts. "I'm well aware of that, baby!"

"Or a woman like your sister Deirdre, either," I continue. "Deirdre has a full-time job, but her husband never stays home when the kids are sick, never changes his plans when the babysitter bails."

Sean's brow creases. "I thought you liked Deirdre."

"I do, but I'm not her, Sean. I can't be her. If that's what you want," I twist my engagement ring around and around, "you need to keep looking."

Sean stands up, steps over Ethel, and pulls me out of my chair. "I've found what I'm looking for, Audrey." He wraps his arms around me and murmurs into my ear. "I can be a good cop and a good father. Pete Holzer does it. I'm going to ask him for advice."

Sean's officemate has four kids and a wife who used to be a power forward for the UConn women's basketball team. Despite my inability to dribble, I suspect I may have a lot in common with her. "That sounds like a good first step."

Sean kisses me long and hard. "How about this for second step? Let's see if your dad will watch Ethel tonight."

Now *that* is a plan.

The sun streams through Sean's bedroom window illuminating the reddish stubble on his chin. He sleeps with his mouth slightly open, his lashes brushing his freckled cheeks. How dear that face is to me!

I stretch, luxuriating in the slight ache in my thighs resulting from our vigorous reconciliation. The conversation we had in my condo was the beginning and end of talking last night. Now, in the light of day, I realize how much has happened in our days apart that I must tell Sean.

Ty's identification of Rob at the carnival...my visit to Clothilde...my trip to the jail...the slashed baby clothes.

Adrienne.

Yes, yes, yes, yes, no.

I turn on my side and touch Sean's hand lightly. He doesn't stir. I long to blurt out the whole awful story about Adrienne and Tom, but I can't. It's not that I feel any loyalty to Adrienne. It's more that I'm terrified of the consequences of ratting her out. Brendan's pain. Sean's anger. The Coughlin family circling of the wagons. I need to think this through before I make a decision. Adrienne asked me to give her a day. I can do at least that much. But how can I lie to Sean, even by omission? We've just made up. He's just promised me that he'll change.

This is too hard!

I slither toward the edge of the king-size bed. A strong arm pulls me back. "What's the big rush?" Sean murmurs.

"I have a busy day. I need to get to the Eskews' house to meet Ty at nine. Kara wants us to hold the sale this weekend."

Sean raises himself on one elbow. "Doesn't matter if her mother died of natural causes or was murdered, the sale must go on?"

"This is one weird family, Sean. A lot has happened since we were together at the carnival." So I tell him about Kara's threat to take the job away from me if I don't hold the sale this weekend. And I tell him about my visit with Clothilde.

"So I'm kinda nervous because...honestly...I'm still not convinced Darlene killed Mrs. Eskew. I think she may have confessed to protect her son."

"Say what?"

"That kid you were chasing at the carnival, one in the Devils hat? Ty recognized him. He's pretty sure it's Darlene's oldest son, Rob."

Sean jolts up. "And you never thought to mention that?"

I jump out of bed and head to the bathroom. "I'm mentioning it now. As you will recall, we weren't speaking to each other for a few days."

Sean follows me into the bathroom, hammering me for details about how Ty knows the kid at the carnival was Rob. I fill him in, then face him with my arms crossed. "Now *you* tell *me* why it matters so much. What exactly was going down at the carnival?"

Sean shakes his head. "Audrey, if every person on the Drug Enforcement Task Force told his or her spouse all the details of our investigations, and each of those spouses told one other person, the whole freakin' town would know who we're watching, who we're ready to arrest. Our work has to stay confidential."

"I'm not asking out of idle curiosity. I'm involved in this. Is Rob a dealer? An addict? Could he have killed Mrs. Eskew? Did you ever catch up with him at the carnival?"

Sean shakes his head. "We caught the other kid, his customer. Found some pills on him—Oxy. He claimed they were prescribed for his wisdom teeth. I shined a flashlight in his mouth. Stupid kid still had all four wisdom teeth. But he wouldn't give up his supplier."

"So Rob is just a small-time pill dealer, selling pills he pressures his mom to steal. Don't you have bigger fish to fry?" I ask as I squeeze toothpaste on my brush.

"He's in deeper than that. You might say Rob is in charge of demand creation for a much larger organization."

I take the toothbrush out of my mouth. "What are you talking about?"

"From what we can tell, there's a group of young people who sample pills. They give a few away, then they sell a few more, then when the customer craves more and can't afford the pills, they refer him to a heroin dealer. And get a kickback."

My eyes widen. "Was Amber part of that?"

"Yep. Until she started sampling her own merchandise. Imagine if the ladies who pass out samples at Costco ate one themselves every time they handed one to a customer."

"So we don't know if Rob is headed in the same direction. Could he have killed Mrs. Eskew when he was using?"

"PCP and crack make users crazy when they're high. Heroin addicts are more likely to be dangerous when they're coming down and there's no more candy in sight."

"So could Rob have killed Mrs. Eskew in a fury because his supply was drying up? I heard the supervising nurse giving Darlene a hard time about the pill count."

Sean puts his hands on my shoulders. "Look, there's something you need to know. There's a lot of scuttlebutt circulating about Darlene's confession and plea bargain. The county police were searching for her with no leads. Then suddenly on Sunday she comes in of her own free will for questioning. Next thing you know, the DA is talking about a plea bargain."

"Are the cops railroading her into a confession?"

"It feels like someone's exerting pressure." He rolls his powerful shoulders. "It's moving so quickly. Everyone's kinda shaking their heads. See, in a high-profile case, the DA usually talks with the victim or the victim's family to make sure they're okay with a plea. The DA doesn't want a lot of bad press."

"If your loved one was murdered, why would you ever be willing to go along with a plea? I'd want the killer to get the book thrown at him. Or her."

"Sometimes the family goes along to be spared the agony of a trial. Like if a kid or a rape victim would have to give painful testimony. But that's not the case here. I don't see why they're moving so quickly. And I don't see why the Eskews would go along."

I turn on the water in the shower to let it warm up. "Kara is incredibly anxious to wrap up her mother's estate and leave New Jersey. She says she never wants to come back. It's like she doesn't even care who really killed her mom."

Sean grabs my arm as I pull back the shower curtain. "I don't want you working in that house until we're sure what's going on."

"I have to finish the job, Sean. We need this money if we're ever going to buy a house."

His hand tightens on my arm. "What good is a house if you're dead?"

"Don't be melodramatic," I say, summoning courage I don't feel. "I promise I'll only work there if I'm with Ty." I shake myself free. "Go make me some breakfast."

As I eat my buckwheat pancakes, a text pings in from Adrienne.

Jimmy woke up with a fever. I can't come in today.

We have a lot of work to do, but I can't deny I'm relieved. Postponing the Adrienne problem doesn't solve it, but it gives me some wiggle room.

I guess her text must've prompted a sour expression on my face because Sean asks me what's wrong. I can't tell him the worst thing that happened yesterday. But I can tell him the second worst. "I found something awful in the Eskews' attic yesterday."

I sense his body tense from across the table.

"Don't worry—nothing dead. Just sad…and creepy. There was a stack of gift boxes wrapped for a baby shower. They were for Jean-Claude, Parker's unborn baby that died in the plane crash. Rachel pointed them out to me. But later, after she left, I opened one of the boxes, and the clothes inside had been cut up. I opened all the boxes, and they were all the same. Even a little stuffed duck slashed open so his stuffing fell out. I'm sure Rachel must have done it."

"Why? And when?"

"She led me over there to show me the gifts. Like she was worried I might miss them."

"What did Rachel say when you opened them?"

"We didn't open them right then because Adrienne showed up and I went back to working, showing Adrienne what she needed to do. But later, after Rachel left, I opened the boxes." I shudder. "That whole family is just so weird."

"So you don't know for sure that Rachel did it?"

I get up to pour us both more coffee. "No, but who else could it be? She told me she liked to hang out in the attic when she was a kid, to get away from her family who were always telling her what to do."

"But she wouldn't have been a child when Parker's baby died, right?"

"True. I think there's about eight years between them. So she would've been sixteen or seventeen. But she seems like a child even now. It's easy to imagine her doing something spiteful and immature."

"Spiteful against whom? Parker? His wife? Their mother?"

I shrug. "Maybe all three."

"Ah, Audrey—you don't understand sibling rivalry. Every evil deed is planned to cause maximum pain to a specific target. Did Rachel and Parker not get along?"

I consider this question. "Actually, when Rachel talked to me in the dining room before her mother was killed, she gave me the impression that Parker was her protector. That she thought he could do anything."

Sean stabs at his pancakes. "That's how I felt about Brendan. Of course, that didn't always stop me from doing spiteful things to him."

"Like what?"

"Once I put his brand new leather baseball mitt out in the backyard right before a rainstorm."

"You must've had a reason."

"I told myself I wanted him to get in trouble with Dad because I got detention in school for talking back to one of the teachers, and everyone kept saying 'why can't you be more like Brendan.'" Sean sets his fork down. His eyes are looking at something a million miles away. "I wanted to bring Brendan down a notch. I was sick of him always being held up to the rest of us as a model. The best student…the best athlete…the best altar boy. The best son."

I take his hand. I can see better now why buying a house and starting a family is so important to Sean. And maybe I can see why he pushed me to hire Adrienne. My wife is the boss of your wife. The playground battles never end. Why do I have to be part of that?

"Did your scheme work?" I ask.

"Of course not. My dad was a cop. He questioned everyone in the family about when and where they had last seen the mitt, then put together a timeline that proved Brendan wasn't at home during the window of time when the mitt moved to the backyard. Brendan was off the hook, but Dad was never able to prove whether it was me, Terry, or Deirdre who was the real culprit. We all denied doing it."

"So you never got punished?"

Sean howls with laughter. "You don't know my dad very well. He punished all three of us for a month. No TV and we had to take Brendan's turn doing dishes. But I never confessed. Still haven't to this day, so don't breathe a word of it next time you see my family. Deirdre thinks Terry did it. She still holds a grudge against him for making her miss the season finale of *The X Files* that year."

"Sean! Don't you feel guilty for not owning up to what you did? Why not admit it and clean the slate?"

He looks at me as if I'm suggesting returning Manhattan to the tribe from which it was stolen. "Ha! That was one of my most brilliant coups. And don't feel sorry for my brothers and sisters. They each made me suffer plenty back in the day."

"Okay, Mr. Family Dynamics—why do you think Rachel chopped up the baby gifts?"

"Timing is key. If she did it before the plane crash, then obviously she was pissed about all the attention being paid to Leonie and the baby. Rachel would've enjoyed the drama when Leonie opened the gifts in front of everyone. Obviously, they all would've known it was she who'd done it, but she would've succeeded in shifting the spotlight back onto herself."

"Even if it was for bad behavior. That makes sense." I clear our plates thinking about what Sean has said. When I come back to the table I ask, "What's the other timing scenario you imagine?"

"She did it after the baby's death. To express her hurt. Or her anger."

"That Parker crashed the plane and brought so much sadness onto the family?"

"Exactly."

Sean's right. I really don't understand sibling rivalry.

CHAPTER 28

"Audge, is this somethin'?"

Ty and I have resumed working in the Eskew attic, now Adrienne-free. He walks toward me holding a medium-sized watercolor, handsomely framed.

"It's got some water damage," I point to a ripple in the painting where it has pulled away from the matting. I take it away from him and study the shapes. It's an abstract expressionist rendering of a sailboat on choppy seas. "Geez, could it be..." I study the signature in the corner. "Yeah, I think it's an Arthur Dove!"

"A real one? And they just stashed it up here in the attic?"

"Mr. Eskew doesn't seem to have ever bought reproductions."

"Maybe with this one he got taken for a fool, so he tossed it up here."

"Possibly. Take it downstairs. We'll have to get it appraised."

To save time, Ty and I stopped to buy sandwiches on the way over. Now we're taking our lunch break at the kitchen table when Tom walks in. He greets us both with a great show of cheerfulness, but then proceeds to pace around the kitchen. When he's directly behind Ty, Tom makes eye contact with me and jerks his head toward the dining room. "Audrey, I wanted to ask you what you think of those Staffordshire figurines. Do you have a moment?"

I nod and rise. Ty never looks up from his turkey and cheese.

Once we're in the dining room, Tom gives me a soulful smile and starts talking. "Audrey," he extends his hands imploringly, "what you walked in on yesterday was just an impulsive encounter. Adrienne's a very attractive woman, and I..." he shakes his head, "I'm just a man who can't resist a woman's charms."

Un-freakin'-believable! He's like some bad community theater actor reciting a hackneyed script.

Tom lowers his chin and stares at me through long, dark lashes. "Please don't hold this against Adrienne. I promise I'll leave your staff alone and let you finish this job in peace."

My arms are crossed and my face is as suspicious as when someone at a sale offers me twenty bucks for an unblemished Stickley bookcase. What kind of fool does Tom Eskew take me for?

"You and Adrienne are both adults. I wouldn't care what she does if it weren't for the fact that her husband is soon to become my brother-in-law, and her kids will be my niece and nephew. So yes, if you could try not to destroy my family, that would be most helpful."

For a split second the cheesy charm vacates his face and I see a tired, sad older man. Then he snaps back into character. "Right-o," he gives me a jaunty salute.

As I turn to go back to my lunch, Tom speaks again.

"Good Lord, where did you find that?" He picks up the Arthur Dove painting, which Ty has propped in a corner of the dining room next to some other items that need my attention. Tom holds it at arm's length. I notice his hands are trembling.

"Ty found it in the attic. We wanted to check to see if it was a real Arthur Dove."

"Oh, it's real, all right. This is the painting that killed my father."

Tom sets the painting down and regards it as if it were a poisonous snake. "It used to hang in his study. Shortly after Parker's accident, when Kara and I had gone back to college, Rachel was taking a bath in the bathroom right above the study. She let the water overflow the tub. It seeped through the floor and damaged the painting."

Tom glances up as Ty enters the room, but he doesn't stop talking. "People use the term 'apoplectic with rage' figuratively, but in my father's case it was quite literal. He died of a stroke later that night."

He taps the frame with the edge of his expensive loafer. "Honestly, the damage doesn't seem that bad. It must still be worth something, don't you think?"

Ty and I exchange a glance. Damn, these people are cold!

Tom's face brightens. "Hey, you know who could tell you?" He points to the stack of school yearbooks in the corner. "I've been looking through those. There's a bunch of pictures of Parker with his friend Wes Tavisson. Wes used to hang out here all the time when he and Parker were at Bumford-Stanley. I hadn't seen him since those days, and then last year I bumped into him on the street. Turns out he's an art restorer. He has a studio in Jersey City. You should look him up. Helluva nice guy."

After Tom leaves, I do look up Wesley Tavisson. His website, RestorationArtistry.com, pops right up. His photo there shows a man with a jowly face and thinning hair, but he's still recognizable as the boy in the yearbook. I figure he can not only help with the painting, but maybe I can also pump him about Parker Eskew. When I call and tell him about the painting and explain the connection to the Eskews, he sounds as excited to meet me as I am to meet him.

Leaving Ty to finish up at the house, I set off for Jersey City.

Within fifteen minutes of meeting Wes Tavisson, I feel like I've known him all my life.

His business is housed in a gritty industrial building with a camera I must look into before a buzzer unlocks the door admits me to his workspace. I walk into an art wonderland. Paintings are everywhere—hanging from the ceiling, propped against the walls, set up on easels.

I wander through the jungle of art amazed by the changes appearing on the canvases. I get so absorbed at looking at a Chagall that I forget I'm there to meet a person. When a man materializes from behind a ten-foot high mural, I let out a little cry.

A guy with longish, dirty blond hair and a paint-stained shirt and jeans holds his hand out. "You must be Audrey Nealon. I'm Wes Tavisson. Didn't mean to scare you."

I laugh. "Not at all. I was just caught up in looking at this Chagall. And is that a Tintorello? You're stripping off the old varnish?"

"Yes, one coat at a time. The process can't be rushed. Come look at this one."

And we're off. Wes tells me about the restoring process, but more important, he asks me questions about my business and my life and listens to the answers. Really listens. That's a very uncommon quality these days when everyone is so caught up in telling you about their own fame, past, present or future. I like him.

Before long we discover we have a lot in common over and above the restoring and selling of art.

"So, you're a math major who became an estate sale organizer and I'm an economics major who became an art restorer. Does advanced mathematics come in handy in your line of work?"

"I haven't found a use for differential equations yet, but it's useful to be able to add long columns of numbers in my head when I've got a line at check-out and an old lady with seventeen items priced between twenty-five cents and a buck fifty. How about you—did your parents freak when you gave up Econ for Art?"

"Oh, honey—did they ever! But it was all their fault. I'd just graduated from Georgetown and aced my LSATs. To celebrate my admission to Harvard Law, they sent me on a trip to Italy. Well, in two weeks I called and said, 'I'm not coming back.' I talked my way into a job fetching rags and turpentine for the restorer at the Uffizi and the rest is history."

"Did they get over it?"

"Eventually they realized I knew what I was doing, but it got worse before it got better." Wes grins. "Next, I had to tell them about Antonio. But when we got married two years ago, they danced until three in the morning. What was shocking in 1982 is totally fine today."

"So true." That remark hits home. Parker and Wes were such good friends. Could Parker's sexual orientation be the scandalous secret that caused him to crash his plane? It seems ludicrous today, but thirty years ago?

"Let's have a cup of tea," Wes says, and fills an electric kettle on his workbench. "So you found a painting at the Eskew house you need my help with?" he asks, bringing our conversation back to business.

I pull the painting out of the bag I've brought to protect it. "It appears to be an Arthur Dove watercolor. It's got some water damage."

Wes bends over to study it like a doctor examining a sick patient. He clucks and shakes his head.

"Is it bad? Can it be restored?"

"Watercolors are trickier than oils. This damage is old. Why didn't they get it repaired as soon as it happened?"

I relate the story Tom told me. "Apparently, the damage upset Mr. Eskew so much he had a stroke later that night. Then someone stuck the painting in the attic, and it's been forgotten until now."

Wes arches his eyebrows. "Hardly worth dying over. The painting is still beautiful although the restoration will affect the resale value. It should still fetch thirty grand easily."

"Did Mr. Eskew have an explosive temper?" I ask, trying to sound innocent.

"Not that I ever saw. He was quite gracious to me, always encouraging me to use their tennis court even if they weren't home. But I got the sense that everyone in the family walked on eggshells around him." Wes sloshes hot water out of a Picasso mug as he hands me my tea. "House is gorgeous though, isn't it?"

"Yes, but not a very happy home."

Wes shakes his head. "Mrs. Eskew...murdered. Well—" He stops and it's obvious to me he's thought better of whatever he was going to say.

"You went to high school with Parker, right? I saw your pictures together in the Bumford-Stanley Academy yearbook. Then Tom told me you were an art restorer. Mrs. Eskew maintains Parker's bedroom like a shrine."

Wes has a sad but tender expression on his face. "Hmm. In the pictures you saw, was I gazing at Parker with slavish devotion?"

"I take it he was the superstar of your grade?"

"Yes, and I was the faithful sidekick. Parker and I did everything together." He laughs. "Well, *almost* everything. When it came time to say goodbye at the end of our senior summer, I burst into tears. I was in love with him, but I couldn't admit it, not to him, not even to myself."

"He wasn't..."

Wes throws his hands in the air. "Oh, no, no, no—the straightest of straight arrows. Parker was horrified by my display of emotion although I don't think he quite knew what to make of it. I was quite athletic, you see, so I didn't fit the fairy stereotype."

He says this with wry good humor, but I can tell those days of having to hide who he was were painful. "I hated high school," I confide. "At Palmyrton High, you couldn't be a cool girl if you were smart. I couldn't wait to get away."

Wes squeezes my arm. "You would've hated me in high school, Audrey. Being friends with Parker put me at the top of the social heap." He winks. "It's been downhill ever since."

"Was Parker really that special? There's something about hero-worship that brings out the contrarian in me."

"I know what you mean—he seems like the kind of guy you'd love to hate. But the truth is, he was smart and funny and tremendously charming. People loved being around him. He was the one who got the party started."

But was he the kind of kid who rescued birds with broken wings...or the kind who kicked them out of his path?

"Parker and his siblings were close?" I ask.

"Yeah, they were tight. They had to be—their parents weren't very warm and fuzzy."

If I thought I was going to have a hard time pumping Wes, I'm totally wrong. He seems to be loving this trip down memory lane.

"So you went to Georgetown and Parker went to Harvard? Or was it Columbia?"

"Both. He did his freshman year at Harvard, then transferred. Of course, he was instantly popular at Harvard, so I hardly heard from him. We saw each other briefly over Christmas break. Then, all of a sudden in the spring, he started calling me."

"He suddenly missed you?"

"It was strange. There was some trouble." Wes swirls the dregs of the tea in his mug.

"Girl trouble?"

"Parker didn't fully appreciate the effect he had on people. He could make them do things they'd later regret."

"Do you mean date rape?" This sounds like the kind of scandal I'm after.

Wes makes a gesture like he's searching for words that don't exist. "It was a misunderstanding."

"That's what guys all say. I'm sure Parker wasn't used to taking no for an answer."

Wes looks a little queasy. "He wasn't some drunken jock forcing himself on women. But when you were with Parker, you'd do anything to please him. You'd ski double black-diamond slopes and surf rough water. And then, when you'd broken a leg or had to be fished out of the ocean by a lifeguard, you'd ask yourself, 'What the hell was I thinking?'"

"So he coerced this girl into having sex and she regretted it? And then he called you for advice? Wouldn't he have wanted to keep it quiet?"

Wes gets a funny expression on his face, like he's suddenly seeing the second image in one of those optical illusion pictures. "I, I'm not sure why he called to tell me about it. I always assumed he simply wanted to vent. Parker simply couldn't believe the matter wasn't going his way. But this girl was more than his match. The Eskews were rich, but she was from really old, really big money. There was a building at Harvard named after her grandfather. They kept the problem hushed up, but the girl's family forced Parker to transfer. Sent a letter to Gilbert Eskew saying they'd file charges if Parker didn't leave Harvard."

"What did his parents do?"

"Oh, they backed Parker all the way. But Mr. Eskew knew he was outgunned, so instead of fighting the transfer they made it look like Parker had been wooed away by superior opportunities at Columbia. Maybe that's why Parker called to tell me what really happened. He suspected I wouldn't believe the cover story."

"So telling you was a pre-emptive strike. He asked for your sympathy?"

"And he got it. It all seems trivial now. Parker distinguished himself at Columbia. He graduated summa cum laude. Got into Wharton for grad school. Got the Wall Street job."

"And what happened to the girl?"

Wes stares at the floor the way you do when you're trying to work out a problem. Eventually he speaks. "She got her own form of justice, so I guess she was satisfied. Parker never spoke the name Sloane Trevelyan again. But I've seen her at gallery openings and museum fundraisers."

"You know her?"

Wes shakes his head. "I know who she is; she doesn't know who I am, or that I was a friend of Parker's."

"Did the experience change him?" I ask.

"Was he humbled?" Wes laughs. "All I know is he always had a beautiful woman on his arm."

"And what about Leonie, his wife? Did you know her? Were they happy? Did she know about this other girl, Sloane?"

Wes shakes his head. "I doubt it. I met Leonie once in New York when they were first engaged. She was lovely. She seemed besotted by him."

Besotted. What a word! I love Sean, but I'm certainly not besotted—not the way the two of us butt heads. But that's what he likes about me. He wouldn't want me to be besotted.

"You didn't go Parker and Leonie's wedding?"

For a fleeting moment, Wes looks like I've jabbed him with a pointy stick. "I got an invitation: Wesley Tavisson and guest. When I responded that I'd be bringing Antonio, my invitation was rescinded."

"That's awful! Parker said you couldn't bring him?"

"Not Parker. Mrs. Eskew. The RSVP cards went to her. She called me and said Antonio's presence would be 'inappropriate.'"

"What a witch! You didn't complain to Parker?"

Wes sighs. "Antonio said he wouldn't go anywhere he wasn't wanted. I didn't want to rain on Parker's happiness before the wedding. I figured I might tell him afterwards. But..." Wes's hand trembles. "I never saw Parker again."

CHAPTER 29

"Something awful happened yesterday and I don't know what to do about it. I need your advice." I speak into my Bluetooth as I drive back to Palmyrton after dropping off the painting with Wes. I've been obsessing again about the Adrienne problem. Sean has a late meeting, so I don't have to face lying to him over dinner. But I'll see him later and I need a strategy. I can't ask my dad for advice. As the clueless victim of my mother's infidelity, he'll feel that Brendan has a right to be informed. If I tell my father what I saw, he'll feel compelled to tell Sean about it himself. And that would be the worst of all worlds.

So I'm calling Natalie, begging her to meet me for coffee while my father is running his chess club meeting. I don't need a shrink to tell me I see her as the mother I never had. And listening to problems and offering advice is what moms are all about, right?

Natalie raises her eyebrows as I take a seat across from her at the Whole Foods café. That's about as alarmed as she allows herself to get.

I plunge into my story. "Adrienne and I were working at the Eskew house yesterday. I told her I was leaving early to take care of some business with my accountant, but then I got halfway back to Palmyrton when I realized I'd left something important at the house. When I came back into the kitchen, I heard noises in the pantry. It was Adrienne and Tom Eskew." I make a "use your imagination" gesture. "She begged me not to tell Sean. She claims it was just one moment of madness. But I feel terrible lying by omission to Sean. And what if Brendan finds out some other way and realizes I helped her cover up?" I shudder. "I can't stand to think about it."

I wait, an uneasy tension building. Natalie always chooses her words carefully, and if she's being this careful, she must have something very tricky to impart.

"You're right to be concerned, Audrey. Keeping secrets is not a good way to move forward in your relationship with Sean. But this." She shakes her head. "Sean and Brendan won't thank you for being the bearer of bad news. If Adrienne is unhappy in her marriage, you should urge her to see a counselor, even if her husband won't go. She's doing this for attention. I doubt that it will stop until she gets the attention she needs from her husband."

"Do you think I was too hard on Adrienne?"

Natalie reaches across the table and lightly strokes the back of my hand. "I think you have a strong aversion to infidelity. And that's understandable. But you can't know all that's going on between Adrienne and Brendan. Marriages are complex mechanisms." She pauses.

"And they can't be fixed by hacks with sledgehammers, right?"

She squeezes my hand. "You're not a hack, dear. You're just perplexed by this big, new family you're about to join."

"You can say that again. In fact, I think I'm perplexed by all families."

And I launch into my discovery of the sliced up baby gifts and my suspicion that Rachel wanted me to find them.

"I wish you could meet this woman, Natalie. You'd know how to respond to her. I feel bad, but she really creeps me out."

"Is she delusional like Harold?"

"No, nothing like that. Everything she says is based in reality. But she rattles along, chatting and chatting and it doesn't seem to matter if anyone is listening. And she's hyper-sensitive to noises. There was a leaf-blower running a few yards down from the Eskews' house one day when I was working there and she covered her ears and actually started crying. I didn't know what to do."

Natalie's brow furrows. "Describe what she looks like again. You said she's really tiny, but what does her face look like?"

"She doesn't resemble her siblings much. Her upper lip is very thin and her eyes are small."

Natalie grabs my iPad and types something, then flips the screen around. "Does she look like this?"

A variety of strange, elfin faces stare out from the screen. Even though they're all different ages, genders, and races, they bear a resemblance to one another. And to Rachel. I look above the photos: Google Images results for Fetal Alcohol Syndrome.

"Wow, you think that's what she has? That her mom drank during her pregnancy and caused Rachel's problems? But no—she's a twin, and Tom's okay. He's nothing like her."

Natalie raises her eyebrows. "FAS affects different fetuses differently. It has to do with how the alcohol is absorbed through the placenta, and the way each fetus breaks down ethanol. That's why doctors say there's no safe amount of alcohol you can drink when you're pregnant."

"So even if Mrs. Eskew wasn't a full-scale alcoholic, she still could've harmed Rachel in utero. Do you think she knew what she was doing was dangerous?"

Natalie shrugs. "Fifty years ago doctors didn't have the understanding we have today. They even used to tell their patients to have a drink to relax them during pregnancy. Still, you'd think simple common sense would tell you getting drunk couldn't possibly be good for your baby."

I lean back from the computer. "But I thought FAS caused mental retardation. Rachel doesn't seem retarded although apparently she never finished high school."

"It causes a whole range of problems: hypersensitivity, inability to understand cause and effect, inability to manage money. Mental retardation is the most severe. That's why social workers need to know about FAS. Kids get blamed for having bad behavior or being irresponsible, but if they have FAS, those behaviors can be beyond their ability to control."

"So everyone in the family blames Rachel for being a screw-up but—"

"Her mother made her that way."

My chat with Natalie makes me feel like I'm not lying to Sean about Adrienne, only stepping back and allowing her and Brendan to work out their own problems. So when Sean arrives at my condo at seven-thirty, I'm feeling guilt-free and affectionate. We've just settled in for a glass of wine when the doorbell rings. I answer it, and there stands Ty holding a yowling bundle. His eyes are wide with anxiety.

"What's wrong? Is Lo sick?"

Ty glances at the baby as if surprised to see him in his arms. "Nah, he's just mad 'cause I woke him up. It's Charmaine I'm worried about. She left Lo with me while she went to look at an apartment. She was supposed to be back a while ago. I've been calling and texting her, and her phone is off. I gotta go find her."

Sean comes up behind me. He reaches out and lifts the baby from Ty's arms. "You go. We'll watch the little fella."

He slings Lo over his shoulder like a dishtowel and rubs his back. Within seconds, the baby stops crying.

"Where's the apartment?" Sean asks.

"Fowler Street."

Sean scowls. "That's a crap neighborhood."

"Yeah, well, it's better'n Newark. And it's all she can afford in Palmyrton."

"I better come with you," Sean says.

"No!" Ty and I chorus in unison. He doesn't want to be alone with Sean. I don't want to be alone with the baby.

"Thanks, man, but I'll be a'ight." Ty reaches behind himself and pulls Lo's stroller and diaper bag into my condo. "Everything he needs is in here. I'll be back in an hour."

"Call me if you run into trouble, " Sean shouts after Ty as he lopes down the sidewalk.

Sean holds Lo at arm's length. "Hey, little man—you're kinda stinky. Let's get you changed. Bring me that bag, Audrey."

I'm mesmerized as Sean flips through the bag pulling out a pad, wipes, and a diaper. Then he lays Lo on his back and deftly removes a garment that would have stumped Houdini.

I'm shocked by the mess in the baby's diaper. "Why is it yellow? Is he sick?"

"Nah, baby poop comes in all kinds of colors." Sean looks over his shoulder at me. "You've never changed a diaper?"

"No." I feel defensive. "When would I? I've got no siblings, no cousins."

Sean laughs. "Didn't you ever babysit as a teenager?"

"Not for infants. My specialty was helping middle-schoolers with their math homework."

Sean cleans the baby up, fastens him into a clean diaper, and gets him redressed, all the while making faces and babbling away in a high-pitched voice. Lo stares at him solemnly, then suddenly breaks into a big, gummy smile.

"He likes you!"

"What's not to like?"

Sean sits the baby on his knee and begins bouncing him, all the while singing some ridiculous song about a cat who catches a mouse and blames it on the dog. The baby's chubby cheeks jiggle with every dip of Sean's knee.

"Sean, isn't that too rough? Don't hurt him!"

"Babies are tough. You can't break them. Here, hold him."

Sean hands Lo to me. Gingerly, I take him. He's like a sack of sugar with arms and legs. He squirms and burrows. I hang onto him for dear life. He tilts his head back and studies my face. I can't help but laugh.

"Oh my God—that look! I keep expecting Ty's voice to come out of him."

Sean puts his arms around us both and nuzzles my neck. "You look pretty cute with that little guy in your arms. Of course, you'd be even cuter with a redhead."

I have no response.

Sean's phone rings. As he listens, I watch him closely. His lips purse and his eyes narrow. Not good.

"I'll be right there," he says as he ends the call.

"Be right where?"

"Some Neighborhood Watch bozo stumbled onto a surveillance the Drug Task Force is conducting. I gotta get over there, Audrey. I don't want this to blow up." He grabs his shoulder holster.

"Sean, wait. You can't do this to me again! What about the baby? You can't leave me here alone with him."

"This one is too little to run away." He places both hands on my shoulders. "You have to learn to do this, Audrey. And the best way to learn is by doing, right?"

I look at the baby in my arms. For someone who can't walk or talk, he projects a decided air of self-confidence. "Do you trust yourself with me, Lo?"

His smile turns up and a dimple appears in his right cheek.

Sean kisses me on the head and ruffles Lo's dark curls. "You'll be fine. I won't be long."

Twenty minutes pass. Twenty l-o-o-ng minutes. I walk with the baby. I sit with the baby. I look out the window with the baby. He's cute, but he's really not much in the way of company. I text Ty to ask when he and Charmaine will be back. No response.

My arm gets stiff from holding Lo. Twelve pounds is surprisingly heavy after half an hour of walking. I put him back in his stroller, but he doesn't like that, so I pick him back up. Obsessively, I check my phone. Nothing from either Sean or Ty. What could possibly be happening?

At seven forty-five, Lo begins to whimper. I put him over my shoulder, as Sean did. He switches to a full-throttle cry. I bounce, cuddle, rock. The screams escalate.

Then it dawns on me. Of course, the little guy must be hungry. I go to the bag and start digging. I find a bottle—totally empty. I dig deeper looking for something to refill it with.

Nothing.

Can I give him straight-up milk? Who would know?

Natalie. I call and she gives me bad news—no cow's milk for infants. He needs formula.

"What am I going to do?"

"I'd go and get it for you, but your father and I are in Chatham at a concert. The curtain's about to go up."

"Don't hang up! Help me!"

"You'll have to go to the store and get him formula."

"Take him to the store? He's screaming! Can't you hear that?"

"He won't die of starvation en route. Just put him in his stroller and walk over to ShopRite."

At the supermarket I feel the glare of disapproving eyes. A screaming black baby with a clearly incompetent white woman. I keep my eyes downcast. I finally find the right aisle. "Okay, Lo. Dinner's almost ready, buddy."

I look at the shelves. Holy crap—why are there so many different kinds? Regular, soy, low-iron, organic, powered, liquid. How can this be so complicated? I feel my heart start to hammer.

What if I give him the wrong kind? Could I poison him? I can't call Natalie again—the concert must have started.

Another woman marches right up, grabs a container without hesitation, and tosses it in her cart. She prepares to roll off, but not before giving me a condescending glance.

She looks like a be-atch, but I'm desperate. "Excuse me, is that the best kind of formula? I'm baby-sitting and they didn't leave me enough…"

She looks into the stroller and her face softens. Confidently, she selects a six-pack of Enfamil cans from the shelf, pops one open, fills the empty bottle he's been chewing on, and sticks the nipple in his mouth.

Lo sucks the formula down with the greedy abandon of a rescued POW. The poor kid's probably afraid he may never eat again.

"Good as new," the competent mother says before handing the bottle over to me and sashaying away.

Lo polishes off the bottle as we stand in the supermarket aisle. His long eyelashes flutter and he collapses into an Enfamil stupor. I pay for this liquid gold and start the walk home. The world seems eerily silent now. I have space to think.

What is it about children that causes me to lose my grip on competence? I'm a skilled person—I run my own business. I understand math, and chess, and art, and antiques. Why do I panic when I'm confronted by the insistent needs of a child?

I peek into the stroller at Lo, sleeping so peacefully. How could this little angel be the same creature who was shrieking like a crazed wolverine fifteen minutes ago? How could timid, clingy Chrissy turn into such a demon of determination? It's the irrationality that flummoxes me. When a child desires something, all reason and logic evaporate.

No wonder my father couldn't cope with being a single parent.

How will I be any better?

When I'm a block from my condo, my phone rings.

"Where are you?" Sean demands.

"Where are *you*? I had to walk the baby to the supermarket to get him formula."

"Damn! There wasn't any in the bag?"

"It's okay. He's filled up and sleeping now. We're almost home."

"I'm sending an officer to your place in Ty's car. You need the car seat to get the baby here."

"Where?"

"Palmyrton PD. I'll explain when you get here. And, Audrey— bring a checkbook."

CHAPTER 30

The officer who arrives to drive Lo and me to the station is utterly stone-faced and without information he's willing to share. My heart thumps as we pull up. What could possibly have happened? What kind of trouble are Ty and Charmaine in?

If she's been arrested, what's going to happen to the baby?

To his credit, the cop does help me detach Lo's car seat from the base so I can carry him into the building without waking him.

As soon as I enter the main lobby, I see Ty pacing.

Good sign. If he's out here, he hasn't been arrested.

He catches sight of me and in three long strides is at my side. He looks in the infant carrier and his face relaxes, but only for a moment. Then the tension returns.

"What happened?" I ask. "Where's Charmaine?"

He jerks his head in the direction of the booking area. "She had a warrant out for her arrest."

"What! What for?"

"Two tickets she never paid. She claims she never got the notices about court dates 'cause of moving so much." Ty shakes his head. "But I know Charmaine. When somethin' bad happens, she just don't wanna deal. She probably got 'em and threw 'em away."

"But what about the apartment? What happened there that caused the police to discover the warrant?"

"The apartment was a pit. I didn't even want to go in, but Charmaine said as long as we were there, we should check it out. The building is small—just six units. The super was showing us the empty one when we heard all this noise in the apartment next door. Shouting and stuff getting knocked over and people running.

And the super's acting like he don't even hear it. So I had enough and I told Charmaine let's get outta here. The super stayed inside to fix something and we walk into the hall just when three cops are charging in and two guys from the apartment with all the noise are tryin' to run out the back."

"So the cops thought you had something to do with what was going on next door?"

"Of course. And they wouldn't listen to me. And Charmaine was givin' 'em lip. Thank God Sean showed up when he did. But by that time, the other cops had already discovered the warrant on Charmaine. So they let me go, but not her."

"Where's Sean now?"

"Busy with something. He said call him when you get here."

My call makes Sean materialize. He holds a door open to the nether reaches of the police station and gestures us to follow. The taut strain on his face and the absolute lack of pleasure at seeing me reboots my anxiety. How much trouble could Charmaine possibly be in for unpaid traffic tickets?

Charmaine looks nothing like her brother. Where Ty is tall and lean, Charmaine is short and curvy. Her skin tone is darker, her face rounder. Only in the intensity of their eyes do I see a resemblance. When she sees Ty holding the baby seat, she jumps up. The cop behind the desk glares at her.

"Is Lo okay?" she asks.

"You can see he's sleeping. But you didn't leave him with a full bottle. Audrey had to go to the store to buy him formula. What's wrong with you, girl?"

"I thought we'd be back in an hour." Charmaine's voice gets louder. "I didn't know—"

Ty waves her off. "You didn't know, you didn't know. I'm tired 'a hearing all the stuff you don't know."

Maybe Ty is mad that the cops arrested his sister, but I can tell he's even madder at Charmaine.

Sean watches the scene unfold and rubs his eyes. He pulls me away and lowers his voice. "She needs five hundred bucks in bail money or they're going to lock her up."

"Lock her up! For speeding tickets?"

"Reckless driving. She wanted to fight the tickets, but she never showed up for the court dates. So they issued a warrant. Now she has to pay the fines plus the penalties. I tried to get them to release her on her own recog, but she's missed too many court dates. I didn't want to tell Ty. He's so mad, I thought he might let her spend some time in the county jail to teach her a lesson. But then he'd be stuck with the baby, and I knew you wouldn't want him to miss school."

"If I write the check, they'll let her go?"

Sean nods. I dig into my purse for the checkbook and Sean leads me to the desk. "What were you doing there, Sean?"

"We had that building staked out. We knew there was dealing in 2B. We were waiting for the supplier to make a big delivery before we moved in. Now that's all blown."

"How did they know to run? I thought you said it was a Neighborhood Watch captain who stumbled into your surveillance."

Sean leans against the wall and tries to stretch his back. "Guy is too damn smart for his own good. He noticed our unmarked car in the neighborhood one too many times. Flagged down a patrol car and pointed it out. The patrol guys go over to check it out. When they realized what was going down, they must've looked too cheerful. Someone in 2B was watching. They started turning away customers, hiding their stash. By the time our guys caught on, it was too late. We moved in, but they took off ahead of us."

"But you know who they are, so can't you arrest them?"

"These guys are just middlemen. We're after their suppliers. We have to stop the flow. It's like a river of smack flowing into Palmyrton. The best we can hope to do is build a dam further upriver and divert the flow. It goes somewhere else, but that's not my problem."

"So now what?"

Sean takes a yoga breath. "We start all over again."

CHAPTER 31

In the morning, Ty and I are alone in the office getting organized for another day at the Eskew house. Adrienne will meet us there later. He is silent, his face rigid. I know he's angry and embarrassed about the incident with Charmaine, and I also know the best way to help him when he's in a mood like this is to leave him alone. As I continue the research I need to price all the items for the sale, Ty picks up the ringing office phone. His brow furrows, and he puts the call on hold. "Some French lady. I can't understand her name."

When I get on the line, Clothilde begins without any small talk. "I want to make a business appointment with you. This afternoon would be best. You will need to come here to Bretton Pines."

A business appointment? What does she mean by that? "You want me to organize a sale for you?"

"I have nothing left to sell, but I have plenty of resources. Come and I will explain."

"I'd love to talk to you again, Clothilde, but the next couple days are really busy. I have to run the Eskew sale this weekend. I could come Monday afternoon."

"No! That is too late. I will make it worth your while." Then her tone becomes a shade less imperious. "And I have some interesting information about Gilbert Eskew's ancestors. His real ancestors."

"What?"

"I will be waiting for you in the lounge. Any time after three will be fine."

Before I can ask another question, she's gone.

Ty freezes as we walk up the driveway of the Eskews' house. "Whose car is that?"

"It's one of Tom Eskew's—he's also got a BMW. Why? Are you interested in vintage English sports cars?"

Ty approaches the car as if he expects it to spring to life and tear off driverless. He circles it, shaking his head. He extends his hand and caresses the hood ornament. He crouches down and studies the long, narrow British license plate. He peers inside and sees the steering wheel on the wrong side. The whole time the furrow in his brow grows deeper and deeper.

"Ty, what is it?"

"This is the car from JJ's paper."

"Paper? What paper? JJ who?"

"The kid in my English class. The one I give a ride to sometimes 'cause he can never get his mother's car."

"I thought his name was Judah."

"It is, but his friends and family call him JJ."

I drop my tote bag in the driveway. "Wait, back up a minute. Darlene's middle son is named JJ. That's what she called him when she was telling me about her kids. She said he went to Palmer Community. And JJ is the name Rob used when I overheard him arguing with his mother. He said something about Darlene wanting to leave JJ out of this."

Ty's eyes widen. "You mean all this time I've been giving him rides, I never realized Darlene was his mom?"

"Didn't you ever talk about the Eskew job?" I ask.

Ty shakes his head. "JJ's one of those people who" Ty makes a yak-yak motion with his hand "nonstop. I'm drivin', I just tune him out. He never asks about my life, and I don't tell."

Typical Ty—he plays his cards close to the vest even when there's no need to. "Well, that's quite a coincidence."

Ty goes back to scrutinizing Tom's sports car. "The last class JJ came to, our assignment was to write a descriptive essay about our dream car, our dream vacation, or our dream house. Then we had to trade papers with the person next to us and give each other feedback. I read JJ's paper. He described this car. This exact car. Right down to the license plate and the hood ornament and the steering wheel on the wrong side."

I don't understand why Ty seems so stunned by this. "He must've seen the car one day when he came to pick up his mom."

Ty stands stock still with a faraway look in his eye. He's acting awfully weird.

"What's the matter, Ty?"

He snaps to attention. "JJ's never been to the Eskews' house. I remember once he told me his mom was workin' at a rich person's house and he wished he could see for himself if it was really as fancy as she said. He complains about how he never gets to use their family car—his brother or his mother always has it. That's why he has to take the bus to school. That's why he's always bummin' a ride home from me."

I still don't get what Ty is on to. "So his mom must've told him about the car, described it to him because she knows he likes cars."

Ty shakes his head. "I don't think so. The teacher's always criticizing JJ because his writing isn't specific enough. His other stuff that I read was all like, 'the shore is awesome, the ocean is nice, the sun is hot.' This paper was actually pretty good. He described every single detail of that car."

"So he must've seen it in person."

Ty nods. "And if JJ was never at the Eskews' house, then that means…"

"…Tom's car was at Darlene and JJ's house."

Why was Tom talking to Darlene? What were they planning?

I need to talk to Darlene again. But when? The sale is only two days away, and we have so much left to do.

Despite my packed schedule, I find myself sipping tea with Clothilde while Ty and Adrienne work at the house. I'm just too intrigued by the carrots she dangled to say no.

"I have been doing some reading about you, Miss Nealon. It seems to me you are a very determined person. One who is not easily deterred. I admire that."

"Research? What do you mean?"

"I may be old, but I can use Google like anyone else. I have read about these other crimes you have been involved with."

I dip my head in acknowledgement of the compliment, but an uneasy feeling stirs within me. What is she getting at?

"Your previous visit has started me thinking."

I wince. "I'm sorry, Mrs. Savatier. I didn't mean to stir up painful memories."

She lifts one hand for silence. "All my memories are painful. How can they not be? I have lost everything—my husband, my daughter, my grandson. No, what you have rekindled in me is desire. Desire to know the truth before I die. Nothing can bring my family back to me, but the truth can release me. I have wished to die for a very long time, but stubbornly I cling to life. Or perhaps I should say life clings to me. I don't believe in God. I don't believe this foolish fairy tale that I will see my family again after I pass from this world. But I do believe in *la justice*."

She stares at me so long I feel compelled to speak. "Justice."

"You can deliver it."

"Me?"

"I want you to find out what caused Parker Eskew to kill my daughter and grandson. The truth is somewhere in that house. I will pay you handsomely."

I knock my spoon off the saucer and it clatters to the floor. "Mrs. Savatier, I'm not a private detective. I'm an estate sale organizer."

"Yet you paid me a visit previously not in that role at all, no?"

I can't deny it. "That's different. I was trying to help Darlene, the caregiver. She's about to accept a plea bargain to say that she killed Mrs. Eskew. I was certain that wasn't true. But maybe I'm wrong. There's some evidence that she might have been involved."

"You are not wrong. When you find out why Parker killed my daughter, you will find out who killed Marjorie Eskew. I am sure of it. You will help both me and her."

She folds her hands in her lap and sits up ramrod straight. "And you will help yourself. I will pay you one-hundred thousand dollars."

I aspirate some tea. "What! I can't accept that kind of money from you."

"Why not? I have no one to leave it to but some charities. The Metropolitan Museum and the Red Cross will not miss it. But the money could make a difference to you, no?"

How can she possibly know about Ty's sister, about the house that got away? She can't. But accepting her money could be disastrous for my business. "The Eskews are my clients. I can't take money from you to spy on them."

"Ah, but you have already done some spying of your own, no? That is how you found out about Gilbert Eskew's name change. Well, I have done a little more research on Jakub Eskein. The librarian at the Palmer County Library was most helpful."

The old gal is full of surprises. She looks positively smug.

"Jakub was the younger brother of Myron Eskein," Clothilde announces.

"Myron Eskein? Why does that name sound familiar?"

"He was a gangster, a member of what was known as the Kosher Mafia. Apparently a movie was made." Clothilde shudders. "Gambling…loansharking…extortion—those were his specialties."

"No wonder Gilbert changed his name. Harvard wasn't likely to take the brother of a notorious criminal. Whatever happened to Myron?"

"He went to prison in 1956. Attica, the librarian said. But she wasn't able to find anything about him after that." Clothilde leans towards me. "I believe the newspaper said that when you discovered Marjorie Eskew's body, you were with your friend who is a police officer. Perhaps he can determine what happened to Myron."

I have to smile. "Perhaps he can."

"I have been looking for a scandal to explain the death of my daughter," Clothilde says. "This may be part of it. There is only so much I can accomplish from here." She waves her hand at her deluxe prison. Her gnarled hand disappears from the table and rests on her lap. When she lifts it again, she's holding a check. "If you find evidence of a crime, you will of course report it to the police. Perhaps they won't be particularly interested all these years later. But know that I will."

She places the check by my cup. "A first installment."

Pay to the order of Audrey Nealon.

$25,000.

I stand up and walk away.

CHAPTER 32

"The strangest call came in while you were gone," Adrienne says when I arrive back at the Eskew house.

"On the office phone?" Adrienne has forwarded the office phone to her cell so she can monitor it while we're all out of the office.

"Yeah. A collect call from an inmate at the county jail. Can you imagine? Do they want us to auction off the contents of their cell?"

"Adrienne, that was Darlene! What did she say? What did she want?"

"I forgot that we're actually acquainted with someone in the county jail. Why would Darlene be calling our office? I don't know what she wanted. I didn't talk to her, just the operator wanting to know if we would accept the charges."

"What did you say?"

"I said no, of course."

"Oh my God—now she thinks I don't want to talk to her!" I snatch up my phone and begin searching for the jail's phone number.

"Well, sorr-eee. If you were expecting a call from her, you should've let me know. I've never received a collect call in my life. I didn't even know they still existed."

I wave her into silence because I've gotten through to the jail. "Hi, an inmate, Darlene Hayes, tried to call me and I wasn't here to accept the charges, but now I'm back. What do I need to do to get connected?"

"Inmates can't receive incoming calls. You'll have to wait until she calls you again."

"But she might not unless you tell her to try again. My assistant wouldn't accept the charges. Darlene might think I don't want to talk to her, but I do. It's important."

The guy on the other end sighs. "Yeah. It's always life or death. You gotta wait for her to call back, ma'am. We don't take messages for inmates."

"Okay, okay—I get it. I'll come to visit her. When are vising hours today?"

"No hours until Saturday."

"Saturday!" I can't come on Saturday—that's the day of the sale. "What happened to Thursday and Friday?"

"We don't have visitation seven days a week, ma'am. It's a staffing issue. Come on Saturday."

He hangs up.

Damn! After the way she treated me when I visited her, Darlene sure isn't calling me for social reasons. If she's reaching out to me, it's gotta be because she thinks I can help her. It's gotta be something to do with Tom Eskew's visit to her home.

While I'm trying to think how to handle the Darlene problem, Ty appears holding a scroll of art paper in front of him. I can see a faint pattern of colors from the wrong side. I wish I had a camera ready to capture the expression on his face: brow furrowed deeper than when he's doing Stat homework, lip curled higher than when he's disturbed a swarm of roaches.

"What's wrong? What is it?"

"You tell me." He turns the painting around. It's one of Rachel's distinctive watercolors, primitive yet compelling. I take a step closer to study the scene.

A girl in a pink dress lies on a bed, the same four-poster bed that's in the second bedroom on the right upstairs. Her arms and legs are each tied to a bedpost with colorful, fluttering scarves. Her mouth is open in a silent scream. A man dressed in doctor's scrubs stands beside the bed. With one hand, he's reaching into the girl's torso; with the other he holds a gory mass dripping giant blobs of blood. On the other side of the bed stand a man and woman, impeccably dressed. Their faces are dominated by huge red smiles, the same shade as the blood. They hold their hands out in front of them, palms parallel. To show that they're clapping, Rachel has painted tiny sparks of yellow and orange.

My eyes meet Ty's. "I was in jail with a dude whose son drew a picture of him gettin' shot up by a posse of Crips. Then the kid handed it in for Back to School night. That's what this reminds me of."

"What's the doctor doing to her, I wonder? Did something awful happen or was she just traumatized by having her appendix out or something? Rachel's so strange, it's hard to know."

"What are we going to do with it?" Ty asks.

I take it and roll it up. "Someone might buy her nature paintings, but no one will be buying this. I think I'll hang onto it though."

As I put the picture in my bag, my phone rings. "Audrey? It's Wes Tavisson."

I wasn't expecting to hear from him so soon. I hope he hasn't discovered the painting is damaged beyond repair. "How's the restoration going?"

"Huh? Oh, the Arthur Dove—no worries. That's not why I'm calling."

There's a long pause, so long that I pull the phone away from my ear to see if the call got dropped. No, he's still there.

Finally, Wes speaks. "I called Sloane Trevelyan."

"You did? I thought you barely knew her."

"I know. I can't believe I had the nerve, but ever since I talked to you I haven't been able to get Parker off my mind. I kept stewing over why he would have called me to tell me about the trouble with Sloane. It was almost like he was determined that I should know the truth, not the cover story. Finally, I couldn't bear it anymore, and I called a mutual acquaintance and got Sloane's private number. And now I'm calling you. Because what Sloane told me has me even more confused."

I hear him take a deep breath.

"There was no rape. She never accused him of anything. She loved him, so she did what he begged her to do."

"Which was?"

"Send that letter. She forged it on her father's letterhead."

"But why? Why would he want her to tell a terrible lie about him?"

"He wanted to transfer to Columbia. He knew his father would never allow him to leave Harvard. So he arranged the transfer, then got Sloane to forge the letter so his father would have no choice but to go along with the transfer."

"That's crazy! He could have been arrested if the letter became public. It could have ruined his whole future."

"I know," Wes agrees. "It blew my mind."

"And she told you all this freely?"

"Audrey, it was like a dam bursting. Once I got her started, I couldn't have stopped her if I tried. It's been weighing on her all these years. And she also has been thinking about Parker since his mother's murder has been in the news."

"So what made Sloane go along with such a wild scheme?"

"She explained it by saying they were kids. Even smart kids don't think about how their actions could come back to haunt them. And I guess the awareness of campus rape was totally different then. It was still the kind of thing that regularly got swept under the rug. They simply took advantage of that attitude."

I'm still stunned by the extreme nature of Parker and Sloane's hoax. "But why would he want to leave Harvard that badly? I thought he was brilliant. Was he so unhappy there?"

"He was a straight A student. He had plenty of friends. All he would tell Sloane was that he needed to be close to home. At Columbia, he was a forty-five minute train ride from Melton."

"He was *homesick*?"

"No, it can't be that. He'd been going away to camp all summer long for years."

"If he and Sloane were in love, why would they want to go to different schools? Was he trying to break free of her?" But even as I say this, I realize how nutty is it. If this were a scheme to dump her, why would Sloane go along with it?

"Sloane said they never fought, but after the transfer they drifted apart. She would write and call, and he would barely answer. He seemed preoccupied. Then he invited her down to Columbia for the weekend. They were supposed to spend a fun long weekend in Manhattan. Instead, after the first day, he announced he had to go home to Melton. Obviously, he couldn't take her with him. She was marooned in his dorm room until she finally gave up and returned to Cambridge. That was the end. Eventually, Sloane married someone else. They're divorced now. I think she never got over Parker."

"And she never found out what was happening at home? Where were his siblings?

"I know his younger brother and sister both went to boarding school," Wes says. "Only his sister Rachel would have been home with his parents."

Rachel again. What was the bond between Parker and Rachel? "What was Parker like around Rachel, Wes? Do you remember anything unusual about their relationship?"

"She was just his kid sister. She was always kinda 'off', you know, but Parker was very patient with her. More so than anyone else in the family."

"And Parker never talked to Sloane about Rachel? Discussed what was wrong with his sister?"

"Nope. Sloane said he just shut down. Wouldn't tell her anything about what was going on at home. By the end of our conversation, Sloane was in tears," Wes continues. "She was blaming herself, saying if she'd been more understanding, stuck with him through whatever the problem was, maybe…you know, none of it would have happened the way it did."

There would've been no Leonie. No pregnancy. No flight to Hilton Head.

Parker would be alive.

CHAPTER 33

Tonight, after a long day at work, I have to face the Coughlin siblings family meeting. Topic under discussion: how to deal with Sean and Audrey's wedding. Sean and I want to keep the guest list to under one hundred, which means a whole raft of Coughlin cousins and in-laws will be excluded. We need a strategy for informing Sean's mother, and that requires all the siblings to maintain a united front. No wavering in the defensive line.

When I pull up in front of Deirdre's house, there's no sign of Sean's car. Rats! I've beaten him here. I seriously consider keeping my foot on the gas and driving a few loops around the neighborhood to give Sean time to arrive. I still feel uneasy in the boisterous whirl of the Coughlin family, and I'm not sure how to manage it solo. But just as I'm deciding to move on, the kids tumble out of the house and spot my car.

"Audrey! Audrey! Audrey!" Three of them come charging toward me while a fourth leans back through the front door and bellows, "M-o-o-o-om, Audrey's here."

The kids surround my Honda, a gang of four-foot-tall carjackers. "She brought Ethel!"

A screech of excitement goes up, causing Ethel to cower in the back seat.

The kids fling open all four doors at once, but luckily Ethel is too nervous to run off despite the allure of a wide lawn and leaf piles. I clip on her leash and drag her out.

"Easy, guys. She needs to get used to you."

The girls wrap their arms around Ethel while the boys attempt to shove them away. Little fingers jab her ears and little sneakers tramp on her tail. Ethel bears it all stoically.

Eager to rescue her, I search the clutter of toys in the yard. "Hey, is that a Frisbee? Ethel loves to play Frisbee."

Ian, the oldest, scampers off to get the orange disk. He throws it with a smooth flick of his wrist, and Ethel charges in pursuit. She positions herself strategically, leaps, and catches it in midair.

The kids scream in delight. "Let me throw it! Let me throw it!"

Relieved, I sit on the porch steps to supervise. I'm in no rush to go in and make small talk with my future sisters-in-law.

The Frisbee game continues for a good twenty minutes. Still no Sean. Finally Ethel can't take it anymore and comes limping up to me with her tongue lolling. As I'm getting her a drink from the hose, Deirdre emerges from the house.

"There you are!" She hugs me. "Thanks for wearing the kids out. Maybe we can have a quiet dinner for a change."

I follow her into the kitchen. Dierdre's home is like a "before" picture from *Love it or List It* , while Adrienne's is the fabulous house that no one can afford. Where Adrienne has acres of gleaming granite and stainless steel, Deirdre's counters are so covered in piles of homework and mail and soccer schedules that I'm not sure what material they're made of.

Deirdre scoops a pile of papers off a chair and orders me to sit. Her gaze turns to the clock on the microwave. "Five-forty. Usually I wait 'til six to have a drink, but if we have something to celebrate we can start a little early." She pulls a big jug of pinot grigio from the fridge and unscrews the cap. "So, what are we celebrating?"

"Uhm…"

"No one had detention this week. How's that?" She fills two tumblers to the brim and pushes one toward me. We raise our glasses in a toast.

It's not that I don't like Deirdre; I do. But I'm still edgy that she might question me about how I managed to lose Chrissy at the carnival, but apparently that episode has been forgotten. In the front of the house, I hear Sean's other siblings and their families arriving, first Terry, then Colleen. Dierdre tells me a story about her oldest son's encounter with the principal, which I strain to hear over the increasing din of the arriving cousins.

I catch a whiff of charred meat. "Uh, Deirdre…could something be burning?"

"Shit!" She hustles over to the oven to check the damage.

Meanwhile, Chrissy barrels into the kitchen and skids to a stop beside me. "I'm going to make you a friendship bracelet. Let me see your wrist."

I hold it out.

"Green or pink?"

"Green."

"I like pink better."

"Pink."

She's wearing a Larchmont School Lynxes sweatshirt. "Chrissy, do you know a boy named Kenny Hayes?"

"No."

"Really? I think he goes to your school. He's handicapped."

"Oh, yeah—Stretch."

Deirdre drains a pot of potatoes. "What do you mean, Stretch?"

"That's what kids call him cause of the way he goes." Chrissy demonstrates the spastic movement of Kenny's neck.

"Chrissy!" Deirdre drops what she's doing and grabs her daughter by the shoulders. "That poor child has a health problem! He can't help it that he makes that motion. Don't you *ever* make fun of him."

Chrissy squirms out of her mother's grasp. "*I* don't call him that. I said other kids. Anyway, he doesn't go to my school anymore."

"He doesn't? Since when?" I ask.

"This week. The teacher said he's going to a new school where they can help him more. He's going to live there. We all had to write him a note so he won't be homesick."

Every hair on my body stands up. A residential treatment center? Where would Darlene possibly get the money for that?

"The teacher showed us a picture of the place. It was pretty. But I wouldn't want to go there. You wouldn't ever send me to boarding school, would you, Mom?"

Deirdre hugs her daughter. "Of course not, honey. I'd miss you too much. But I'm sure Kenny's parents are just trying to do what's best for him."

Chrissy's face lights up as she looks over her mother's shoulder. "Uncle Sean!" she squeals, and Kenny is forgotten. Sean comes into the kitchen and lifts his niece into his arms. She wraps her skinny legs around his waist and buries her head in his neck. Who can blame her? Sean's embrace is a great place to be.

"My three favorite women all in one room." Sean sets Chrissy down and moves to hug his sister. Then he crosses over to stand behind me and massage my shoulders.

"Four, Uncle Sean. Ethel's here too."

Sean peeks under the table where Ethel is curled in a tight ball, trying valiantly to make herself invisible to the growing horde of Coughlin children.

"Everyone who matters is here," Sean says. "Except, where are Brendan and Adrienne?"

On cue, Adrienne waltzes in, but she's alone. "I brought the kids. Brendan's coming straight from work." She gives Deirdre an air kiss and agrees to a glass of wine. I watch her wrinkle her nose at the first sip.

"How's the wedding planning?" Adrienne asks. "Have you found a dress yet? If you procrastinate any longer, you'll be walking down the aisle in yoga pants."

I have, in fact, ordered a very simple dress from J. Crew with the help of my best friend, Maura, but I don't want to announce it here. I can hear the squeal of excitement that will go up from all the Coughlin women. Then they'll insist that I find a picture on the Internet, and they'll fuss, and cluck, and crow. I don't want to be the center of all that attention. It makes me squirm.

"I'm closing in on it," I say, and Sean winks at me.

"I'm st-a-a-rving," one of the kids complains.

Sean checks his watch. "It's after six. What time do you think Brendan will get here?"

Adrienne shrugs. "I'm not my husband's keeper. I reminded him this morning and got accused of nagging. I'm done."

Sean's lips compress into a thin line. Not one of his more endearing expressions. Deirdre also notices and starts herding everyone into the dining room. "The pot roast is already overdone. Let's start eating and I'll fix a plate for Brendan when he gets here."

Deirdre's pot roast is the ultimate comfort food and the dinner conversation is all light-hearted banter about the Mets post-season, and the kids' soccer, and whether dressing as the Pope for Halloween would be sacrilegious. Ethel parks herself beside the

youngest Coughlin's booster seat and obligingly cleans up
everything he hurls to the floor. I attempt to hold up my end of the
conversation, but under cover of all the noise, I'm thinking about
Darlene's son going off to a therapeutic boarding school. How can
that be?

Eventually the kids head out to the backyard to eat their ice
cream sandwich dessert and play whiffle ball and still no Brendan.
Now Sean is actively angry. "No one else's time is valuable except
his? No one else is busy?"

Adrienne doesn't respond. She's not about to defend her
husband, but she seems to know better than to join in Sean's
attack. It's okay for the Coughlins to criticize one another, but woe
be to the outsider who has the nerve to utter a harsh word about
one of them.

The sisters try to smooth things over. "We can just settle it
ourselves and Adrienne can fill him in."

But Terry, who I've noticed likes to throw gas on every fire,
won't go along. "No. No point in doing anything without our big
brother here. You know Mom and Dad will only listen to him. If
Brendan says it's okay for Sean to get married by some Moonie
out in a cornfield then it'll be fine with Mom. Any of the rest of us
say it—no dice."

"Pastor Jorge is not a Moonie. And the rose garden of the
Palmer Arboretum is not 'some cornfield'."

I lay a calming hand on Sean's arm. Can't he see that his
brother is baiting him? Who cares if anyone in the family likes our
venue or our clergyman or our outfits? They can come or not come
as far as I'm concerned.

Up until last year, I always assumed that if I ever got married,
I'd simply elope. An only child with no mother and an estranged
father doesn't need a big wedding. I'd still elope, except now that
my father and I have mended our fences, I'd hate to deny him the
honor of walking me down the aisle. He started talking about it as
soon as Sean and I announced our engagement. Should he wear a
suit or a tux? Would we walk to the Stanley trumpet voluntary or
the traditional Mendelsohn? How can I disappoint him?

I suppose that's how Sean feels, only multiplied by two parents
and four siblings. The rational part of both of us wants to say,
"Screw you. We'll do as we please." The emotional part wants all

our parents there, beaming with joy. But pleasing my father is easy-peasy compared to pleasing every member of the Coughlin clan.

Deirdre has succeeded in distracting us all with a large apple pie. As she's passing the slices around, a car door slams and all our heads swivel toward the window. Brendan's Porsche sits gleaming in the driveway.

A moment later he appears in the doorway, red silk tie loosened and suit jacket slung over his shoulder. "Dessert already? Don't tell me I missed the main event!"

Adrienne pushes apples around and around her plate. Sean grinds his molars. Colleen twists her napkin. Deirdre leaps from her chair. "I kept your plate warm. Sit down and I'll bring it right out."

"All hail the prince!" Terry performs a mock salaam.

I decide to be the grown-up in the room. "Hi, Brendan. Was traffic bad? We were getting worried."

"Nah. Got pulled into a meeting just as I was heading out the door."

"You couldn't have called?" Sean asks.

"You'd still be pissed." Brendan grins as he digs into his pot roast. "This way, you're relieved to see I'm not dead."

I notice him try to make eye contact with Adrienne, but she keeps her gaze focused on her pie.

Brendan gives up on his wife and looks at Sean. "So, I hear we need a strategy for convincing Mom that your witch-doctor wedding in the park still counts."

"My God!" Sean pushes his chair back from the table. "People get married outdoors all the time. And every non-Catholic is not a member of a cult."

"I know that. It's Mom who doesn't believe it. Where did you find this Jorge character anyway?"

I don't feel like getting into a long explanation of how I first met Pastor Jorge when he helped an undocumented worker who used to do odd jobs for me. "He officiated when my dad married Natalie last August. He put together a beautiful ceremony, so we thought—"

Brendan holds up his hand. "That's a key data point: this guy is Audrey's father's pastor. Audrey's father is a college professor. Hence, his pastor is legit."

"That's not quite accurate. My dad's really not a church-goer at all."

Brendan waves off this objection. "Your father is one of the few men on the planet who impresses our mother. St. Patrick, the Pope, John F. Kennedy, Roger Nealon, in that order. Pastor Jorge's not going to be an issue." Brendan turns to size me up. "How old are you, Audrey?"

"Thirty-four."

"Old. Too old for you to wait around for the Vatican to give Sean an annulment so you can get married in St. Bart's."

"I don't want an annulment." Sean's face turns crimson. "Screw the—"

"Sean!" Deirdre claps her hand over his mouth.

"I know you don't. I'm just telling you, that has to be our strategy with Mom. Time is of the essence if she wants you to get down to business producing a grandchild. You're willing to have the baby baptized at St. Bart's, right?"

Baptized? We haven't discussed the timing of a pregnancy and we're already planning the baby's baptism?

Sean casts a nervous look my way. "We'll cross that bridge when we come to it."

Brendan spears a carrot and gestures at his assembled siblings. "Okay, I'm talking to Mom on Sunday. I guarantee she'll come around." He points the carrot at Terry. "But no going behind my back to get her riled up again, understand?"

"Who, me? I'm looking forward to something different. But I still don't see how you're going to get around the fact that second cousin Maeve and great uncle Paddy aren't invited."

Brendan grins. "That's easy. Mom won't want them present at a witch-doctor wedding in the jungle."

After that, a bottle of Glenfiddich appears on the table. The Coughlin brothers stay in the dining room having a drink while the women disappear into the kitchen to clean up. This is one thing that Adrienne and I agree on: no matter how enlightened our mates are in their own homes, it's maddening to see how they revert to their sexist roots when they're all together.

I've been watching Adrienne since Brendan's arrival. She has not uttered one word to him, nor has she made eye contact. I'm sure she hasn't had any heart-to-heart talk about their problems, and that leaves me in a bind regarding the Tom Eskew episode.

Adrienne is a meticulous, clean-as-you-go cook, and no matter how many Coughlins she's entertaining, her kitchen never looks like the ravaged battlefield that confronts us at Deirdre's house. Adrienne pulls a pair of long, yellow rubber gloves from her Louis Vuitton tote bag and snaps them on. Then she steps up to the load of dirty pots in the sink.

"Oh, Adrienne, just leave those. I'll take care of them," Deirdre protests.

"We can't get anything else done without a clean sink," Adrienne answers. She's right of course. Despite her other shortcomings, Adrienne is quite good at identifying the critical path in an overwhelming project.

"Unload the dishwasher, Deirdre. You know where everything belongs. Audrey, take out the trash and put a fresh bag in the can. Colleen, put away the left-overs."

We all fall into line, and within twenty minutes, the kitchen is cleaner than when I arrived.

Adrienne pulls off her gloves. The steam from the hot dishwater has frizzed her sleek hair a bit, but aside from that, she looks her glamorous self. "Thank you for dinner, Deirdre. I'd better get the kids home. I'm sure they have homework."

She nods to the three of us—no hugs—and steps into the backyard calling for the kids. I notice Deirdre and Colleen exchange a glance. Maybe it's because I'm not yet officially part of the family, or maybe it's because Adrienne is my employee, but they are reluctant to say anything in front of me. Then the guys come in.

"Where's my wife?" Brendan asks.

"She just left. Said the kids had homework."

A current of tension passes through the kitchen. Terry opens his mouth to make a wisecrack, but Colleen silences him by initiating the long round of Coughlin good-byes.

"It *is* getting late. We all have work tomorrow." She begins hugging and kissing her siblings. Sean falls in after her.

When we are finally at the door, I remember something and pull Deirdre aside. "You're active in the PTA at Larchmont, right? You know all the teachers and parents?"

"Hoo—too well!"

"Can you do me a favor? Find out what school Kenny got sent to."

CHAPTER 34

"Guess what the tuition is at The River School? Go ahead, guess." I wasn't expecting Deirdre to call until tomorrow, but we're barely back to Sean's place when she calls with the name of the school Kenny Hayes has transferred to. I immediately check out their website.

"I have no idea," Sean says. "Twenty thousand dollars?"

"Sixty-three thousand bucks a year! And it's one-hundred percent private. It says so right on the website: we do not accept vouchers or Medicaid. The day before Mrs. Eskew died, Darlene couldn't afford to buy her son a birthday cake. Now she's in jail, but she can afford to send him to a therapeutic school that costs three times her annual income. What do you make of that?"

Sean lifts his head from his paperwork. I can practically see the gears turning in his mind.

"See, now the fact that Tom Eskew was at Darlene's house does seem significant."

Before Sean can answer, I continue. "And Darlene told me her kids would be better off without her. This is what she meant. As long as she agrees to take the rap for killing Mrs. Eskew, Kenny gets the best therapy money can buy."

"That's a long leap, Audrey."

"But it makes sense. At first I thought Darlene confessed because she was trying to protect her oldest son. She was afraid he killed the old lady because he was in the house that day. Maybe Mrs. Eskew accused him of stealing her drugs and the silver. But what if I have it all wrong? What if the Eskews bribed her to take the fall? What if one of them did it? They figure if Darlene confessed, the cops would stop looking at anyone else. Isn't that the way it happens?"

"Not in a well-run investigation," Sean objects.

"But you said yourself that the guys running the investigation were jerks."

Sean grunts. "I was just blowing off steam because I didn't like the way they were treating me. That doesn't mean they aren't running a legit investigation."

"But Sean, you know that false confessions do happen! Look at that famous case in Manhattan—the Central Park jogger rape. The cops got those teenage boys to confess, and then they ignored the fact that the DNA found on the victim didn't match any of the guys who confessed. Fifteen years later, they found the guy who really did it, and he had nothing to do with any of the guys who confessed."

"And instructors in criminal justice classes use that case as an illustration of the dangers of false confessions. Good cops know to verify all the supporting evidence."

"But when you're sure you're right...when the other suspects don't seem to have a motive, and the person who confessed does...then you might be tempted to cut corners. You yourself said there was something fishy about that plea bargain."

Sean leans back and closes his eyes. "What are you asking me, Audrey?"

"How can we be sure that all the Eskews have an alibi for the time of the murder? How can we be certain that the detectives on this case actually verified the alibis? Poor people with lousy lawyers can be falsely convicted. You know it really does happen."

"I'm sure it's not happening here."

I sit down next to him and bring my face within inches of his. "You know something."

He extends his arm. "Go ahead. Sink your teeth into my arm. I swear, you're like Rex on the K-9 unit. Nothing will make him break his grip."

"Thank you for the compliment. Now talk."

"Here's what I've heard. Kara was seen all over Pittsburgh on the day of her mother's murder. Her husband was in his office all day—also plenty of witnesses."

"Okay. So they're off the list. What about Rachel and Tom?"

"Rachel Eskew lives in a small condo complex, in a second floor unit. Her downstairs neighbor claims he heard her walking around and heard her TV during the time Mrs. Eskew was killed."

"Rachel weighs about eighty pounds. Who could hear her walking around? She's crept up on me a few times at the house. That sounds like a pretty flimsy alibi."

"Possibly. Except, as you say, Rachel is tiny. Do you think she has the strength to pound her mother's head in? Anyway, Tom Eskew's alibi is the most interesting. He was at the Holiday Inn Express with his lover. His married lover. He refused to give the police her name—very gentlemanly—but the desk clerk identified him."

Thank God I've gotten up in search of a wine refill when Sean drops this bombshell. The cool air in the fridge hits my hot face and I grip the bottle so hard I'm surprised the cork doesn't blow off.

Sean keeps talking, oblivious to my shock. "The clerk says Tom comes there frequently in the middle of the day. He checked in about twenty minutes before the one-hour window of time when his mother was killed. The maid remembered seeing the Do Not Disturb sign on his door."

"When did he check out?" I finally feel calm enough to show my face, but my dinner, which tasted so good on the way down, is now staging a revolt in my gut. Adrienne is such a liar! She told me the encounter in the pantry was one minute of madness. Now it turns out she's been meeting Tom Eskew for sleazy hook-ups. Should I tell Sean right now? But what if Tom was meeting some other woman? It's quite possible he's got multiple lovers.

"There's no need to actually check out. He'd paid for the room upfront. Left his keycard on the dresser."

"Did anyone see him leave?"

"Nope. And there are several exits. You don't have to walk past the registration desk to leave the building."

I feel a sense of triumph that I may have discovered Mrs. Eskew's real killer and saved Darlene. Then the triumph deflates into angst—this information might torpedo Adrienne and Brendan's marriage. "That gives him enough time to get back to his mother's house. The cops haven't forced him to produce the woman's name?" To my ears, my voice sounds squeaky with worry, but Sean doesn't seem to notice. I don't see how I can save Darlene without throwing Adrienne under the bus. And what's going to happen when Sean realizes I've known all along that Adrienne is cheating on his brother?

"Tom Eskew's under no obligation to cooperate with the police. He might have given his girlfriend's name up if they had arrested him. But they certainly didn't have enough evidence to do that. He had a lawyer with him when he was questioned."

"Isn't that suspicious?"

Sean laughs. "No. It's what smart people do. Rich smart people." He comes up behind me at the kitchen sink and wraps his arms around me. "All this talk about hotel rooms is putting ideas in my head."

I allow myself to be led away, but I don't anticipate being able to focus on the matter at hand. I've got to talk to Adrienne. She might be hooking up with a murderer.

CHAPTER 35

When Adrienne reports for work at the Eskew house the next morning, I'm on her like white on rice. I've already settled on my strategy: tell her I know what she's up to, don't ask and give her a chance to squirm out of it. "Sit. We have to talk."

She glances at her chunky Michael Kors watch and keeps walking through the kitchen. "I'm sorry I'm late. Jimmy forgot his social studies poster. I had to drop it off at school."

"This isn't about being late." I dart around her, blocking her way into the hallway. "It's about screwing Tom Eskew in the Holiday Inn Express." My voice is louder and angrier than I intended. Adrienne drops her bag and slowly turns to face me.

"What?" she whispers.

"You were with Tom Eskew at the Holiday Inn Express on the day his mother was murdered and you never bothered to mention that?"

She opens her mouth. I can tell her first impulse is to deny, deny, deny. But the certainty of my statement stops her. "Who told you?"

"Sean told me that—"

"Sean knows?" Adrienne's voice sounds like a rabbit being killed by a fox.

"He knows that Tom was at the hotel with his lover. He doesn't know the lover is you. *I* know that."

Adrienne begins to cry. She slumps into a chair at the long oak table.

"Don't start. Do. Not. Start." I stand over her. "You begged me not to tell Sean. You asked me to give you a chance to work things out with Brendan. But when we were all together at Deirdre's, it was obvious you hadn't made any effort to resolve your problems."

"You think it's easy?" She thumps the table with the side of her fist. "He leaves every morning at six. Doesn't come home 'til seven-thirty. The kids are desperate to spend time with him. By the time they're in bed, he says he's too tired to talk. Then on the weekend he spends every waking minute at the kids' games or on the golf course or with his family. We're never alone. Brendan makes sure of that. He doesn't want to talk about our problems. Coughlin men do what they want and Coughlin women put up with it." She points a slender, manicured finger at me. "This is what you're marrying into, I'm warning you."

I'm in no mood for an analysis of Coughlin family dynamics, even though I've worried about those very same things myself. "Can you be honest with me about one thing? Is that possible? How long was Tom with you at the hotel?"

"An hour and fifteen minutes. I couldn't be away from work much longer or you would have yelled at me."

I let this pass. When have I ever yelled at Adrienne? When has anyone?

Adrienne stares at her clenched hands. "I sat in the parking lot waiting for him to arrive. Once he was up in the room, he texted me, and I went up the back stairs and met him."

"What time did you leave?"

"One-thirty."

"You're sure? You two were together from twelve-fifteen to one-thirty?"

"Yes. Absolutely."

But Adrienne has lied before. How can I trust her?

I pull up a chair next to her. "You'd better not be covering for him, Adrienne. You realize you could be sleeping with a murderer?"

"No, Audrey—Tom's not dangerous. He might have stolen that book, but I know he didn't kill his mother. He's very kind even though he's had such a hard life."

"Oh, horribly hard—growing up rich and spoiled."

"The Eskews were rich, but they were never happy. This house is creepy. You said so yourself. Remember those scratches we saw inside the cedar closet door?" She gestures to the upstairs. "When the kids were little, their father would lock them in there in the dark whenever they made him mad. Rachel was terrified of the closet, so he did it to her the most. She's the one who made those scratches. That's why Kara and Tom were so amazed when we found the key. They used to try to let their sister out, but their parents would hide the key in different places."

"That's horrible!" I think of how terrified I was locked in the pantry in Harold the Hoarder's house. I was an adult. How much worse would it be as a child, especially a damaged child like Rachel? And to know your own father had put you there. "Didn't Mrs. Eskew do anything to stop him?"

"She was as afraid of the old man as the kids were. Tom says his father was a terrible snob. All he wanted was to get the kids into the best schools, get himself and his wife into the best clubs…to make sure they had the most useful friends, whether they liked them or not."

Complaining that someone's a social climber! That's rich, coming from Adrienne. She must see the look of incredulity on my face because she starts explaining.

"It's not me, Audrey. It's Brendan, I'm telling you. It's Brendan who wants us to have all this stuff. That's why I like Tom. I can really relate to him. He went through what I'm going though."

I grab her by the shoulders and give her a shake. "Listen to yourself. You sound like a fourteen-year-old girl with a crush on the bad boy in class. Stop romanticizing Tom Eskew. I don't care what his childhood was like. Right now, he's a dissipated old playboy. You have nothing in common with him. Whatever problems you and Brendan have, screwing Tom Eskew's not going to solve them."

"What about this, Audge?" Ty asks, tracking me down in the kitchen. Adrienne has retreated to the powder room to pull herself together. "You gonna put it in the sale, or should I take it straight to the dump? You know no one ever buys old suitcases."

I stare at the purple, soft-sided suitcase. It's at least thirty years old, the kind of thing a teenager might have used in the eighties. It must have belonged to Kara or Rachel. "Where did you find that?"

"In the closet in Parker's bedroom."

"Really? I thought I had inventoried everything in there."

"I noticed a little trapdoor at the back of the closet. The kind that plumbers put in so they can get to the pipes from behind. Remember that house on Dormont Avenue had one, and we found that bag of silver dollars in there. You know how people like to hide good stuff in places like that. But all that was in this spot was this." He kicks the bag. "And all that's in the bag is a dirty old sheet."

Just then I hear car doors slamming. Ty and I lock eyes. Adrienne emerges, her mascara repaired.

"The early birds are here."

I nudge the suitcase into the maid's room, which is off-limits for the sale, and lock the door.

Ty and Adrienne and I head to the foyer.

It's show time.

Day One of the Eskew sale is the most profitable day in Another Man's Treasure's history. The line never lets up. Of course the regulars come, attracted by the promise of high quality art, antiques, and housewares. But the rest of the crowd are the curiosity seekers, drawn by morbid curiosity and the breath of scandal. The neighbors are here—I hear them discussing the house and the Eskews. I recognize some people I've seen at the café in Melton. Even the mailman that I've waved to as he does his rounds is here. But even if they came for the wrong reason, they're still buying—rugs, lamps, furniture, paintings; corkscrews, potholders, flowerpots, coasters—it all goes out the door in a steady stream. And still there's more to sell tomorrow.

At four-thirty, Ty does a sweep of the house, rounding up stragglers and telling them to make their purchases and leave. "If you can't make up your mind, come back tomorrow. We'll be here," I hear him say over and over.

As I finish the final transaction of the day, I see an elderly lady emerge from the back of the house. I've seen her roaming around throughout the afternoon. She looks like she could be almost as old as Mrs. Eskew, but she's nothing like her. Sturdy and sure-footed, she approaches me with a look of determination on her face, but nothing in her hands that she wants to buy.

"Can I ask you a favor?" she begins.

"We don't put anything on hold," I tell her, anticipating her request.

"Oh, no—I don't want to buy anything." She leans in and lowers her voice although there's no one else around. "I used to live here. I was the Eskews' housekeeper for many years. Rose Lubich."

My face lights up. What a great source of information has just walked right into my arms!

"You looked like you recognized me," Rose says. "Have we met?"

"I believe Kara mentioned you," I say to cover my excitement. "What can I do for you?" There's plenty I want to ask her, so I'm willing to be accommodating.

"I've been walking around the house, remembering old times." She smiles slightly, but her glasses are so thick, I can't tell if her eyes are happy or weepy. "I'd like to peek into my old bedroom, but you have it locked."

"I'm using that room to store things that aren't for sale. Come on, I'll open it for you."

Rose stands in the doorway of her old bedroom, which is now a holding area for items headed for the dump or Sister Alice. "Sorry it's such a mess," I say.

She lifts her hands. "Ach, the house—it's all the same, but all different. Funny how time plays with your memory. When the kids were teenagers I'd be asleep in here, and I'd hear them come in through the kitchen late at night, and I'd get up to make them a snack. I never minded. And when Parker first brought Leonie here, he brought her in through the back door and introduced her to me first."

Rose shakes her head. "Ah, Leonie—what an angel that girl was. So sweet, so appreciative. When she and Parker and that dear baby died, ach, no one was ever the same. Mr. Eskew had his stroke and Mrs. E—she simply stopped eating. Egg custard and applesauce—I swear that's all she swallowed for a year." Rose rambles on and I let her go. She's enjoying her morbid reminisces as we walk back into the kitchen.

Eventually, I hand her some of Rachel's sweet watercolors of birds and flowers. Rose studies them and a small smile twitches her thin lips. Then she bows her head. "Ah, poor Rachel! She

always liked to draw. How is she? Have you seen her here? I send
her a card every birthday and Christmas, but I never hear back.
Sad, sad."

"What exactly is wrong with Rachel? Did the Eskews ever
say?"

Rose shrugs. "Just not entirely right in the head now, is she? It
was hard for the parents to admit. They're the types who're used to
everything around them being perfect. But sometimes God has
other plans, doesn't he?"

I'm not so quick to put God on the hook for Rachel's problems.
"Were you working for the Eskews before the twins were born?"

"No, I came right after. They were both wee small when I
started. Soon we could tell that baby Rachel was way behind
Tom—crawling, walking, talking—and she never did catch up."

"What did the doctors say?"

Rose lifts her hands palms up. "Test, test, tests, and they never
could find a thing that I know of."

"No one ever mentioned Fetal Alcohol Syndrome?"

Rose's face constricts with worry. "Oh my, oh my! Is that
what—"

"You think it's possible? Mrs. Eskew was a drinker?"

Rose arches her eyebrows. "We-e-e-ll, you know what people
like the Eskews are like."

"Actually, I don't. That's why I'm asking."

"Martinis in the afternoon, wine with dinner, cognac before bed,
champagne brunch."

"So, the booze was always flowing. Was Mrs. Eskew an
alcoholic?"

"Now, now—I never said that."

Rose strikes me as the kind of woman who wouldn't say shit if
she stepped in it. She's not going to hang that label on her former
boss, even if she's dead. "Did anyone ever hint that Rachel's
problems were linked to her mother's drinking?"

"Oh, my—no! Everyone in the family was convinced if Rachel
just tried harder, she could be the same as everyone else. Everyone
but Parker."

"Parker treated her differently?"

"He was the only one with any patience. He encouraged her
when she had trouble keeping up. They say twins are supposed to

have a special bond, but Tom never took much interest in Rachel. I think he resented the extra attention she got."

"Seems to me Parker is the one who got all the attention."

"Yes, Parker was the star and Rachel was the failure."

"And Tom and Kara were just along for the ride?"

"Ah, families can be strange now, can't they? I was the middle child of seven. Always felt a little overlooked."

"Rose, do you remember the time when Parker left Harvard and transferred to Columbia?"

"Oh, his dad was worked up over that, yes indeed. But Parker turned out fine. Working on Wall Street and all. I knew he'd manage, no need to get so riled. But of course I couldn't tell Mr. E that. Not my place."

"Was there something going on with Rachel at that time, Rose? Is that why Parker wanted to be closer to home?"

Rose's brow furrows. "Well, Rachel was sick around that time. In the hospital for an operation. Then her recovery didn't go so well. The hospital scared her, you know, with her mind being so unsettled as it is. I remember Parker coming to sit with her."

"Operation?" My hand slides into my bag ready to pull out the other painting. "What kind of operation?"

"Female trouble."

"But she was only a teenager. Did she have an abortion?"

Rose puts her hands to her cheeks. "Oh, heavens no. Don't even say such a terrible thing. Mr. Eskew was a churchgoer. Never missed a Sunday."

"But they weren't Catholic?"

"Episcopalian, but that's almost the same."

She rocks back and forth in the kitchen chair.

"Rose, there's something I need to show you. It's a little…strange." I spread the gory painting across the table. "What was Rachel painting here, Rose? Why are her parents clapping?"

She gasps and her purse thunks onto the floor. "Oh, it wasn't like that! They, they did it for her own good, but—"

"Rose, what are you trying to say?"

Rose lowers her voice and leans forward. "Her parents had her tubes tied. They couldn't take a chance, you see. Rachel was so odd, so childlike. Boys, men could have taken advantage of her."

"What boys and men? Was she dating someone?"

"No-o-o-o..." Rose looks increasingly edgy as glances around her old domain. She puts her hand on the table to steady herself. I'm sure she wishes she'd never come.

My stomach churns. "There wasn't something going on...uh, sexually...within the family?"

Her hand twitches and an unsold glass topples onto the floor.

"Oh, how clumsy of me!" Rose slips around me to grab a broom standing in the corner. She comes back and starts sweeping like she's hell-bent on removing the pattern from the tile floor.

"Rose? Why were the Eskews so determined to prevent any possibility of pregnancy?"

Rose keeps her head down. Sweep, sweep, sweep. "It wasn't anything filthy, not what you think. Rachel would never have been able to care for a child. Her parents did it for protection."

The sweeping intensifies. Rose babbles on. "Because what if the problem were passed on? What if the baby turned out..."

Like her.

Rose can't get out of the house fast enough. Queasy and lightheaded, I plop onto a chair in the foyer to contemplate the awful scenarios. Rose is convinced that Marjorie and Gilbert had their teenage daughter sterilized against her will to keep her flaw from further polluting the Eskew gene pool. What a message her parents sent her: You're so despicable that the thought of you reproducing horrifies us. Ironically, Rachel's problem isn't genetic at all. Could her parents have known that?

But can Rose's explanation really account for Parker's decision to leave Harvard in such a bizarre way? Why was he so determined to be near home even after Rachel's surgery? Did Parker want to protect his sister, or use her in the most despicable way? Maybe that's why her parents had her sterilized—because a baby born from incest might also be terribly damaged.

I shiver. Either way, Mrs. Eskew had good reason to beg for forgiveness on her deathbed.

And then Leonie appeared. Beautiful, perfect Leonie creating a beautiful, perfect child with beautiful, perfect Parker. No wonder poor Rachel slashed up those baby clothes.

Ty comes down from the second floor. "Everyone's gone and I straightened up the bedrooms. Are we going out the back door?"

"Yes, let's lock up the maid's room again."

As I switch off the light, the bulging purple suitcase catches my eye. Maybe I better double check what's in there. Ty is so squeamish. It's a good thing he didn't discover King Tut's tomb—he would've pronounced it skeevy and sealed it back up.

Gingerly, I unzip the bag. After this many years, there's no strong smell other than a stale mustiness. The pink-flowered sheet is balled up, not folded. I tug on one corner, and some brown speckles become visible between the rosebuds.

"See what I mean?" Ty says. "Nasty. I'm not touchin' that."

I tug a little harder. The speckles turn into a solid brown stain, stiff and dry. I've seen enough. "I'm taking this home with me."

Ty's face twists in disgust. "Why?"

"Terrible things have happened in this house, Ty. And I don't mean just last week. That was the end. The beginning might be right here."

CHAPTER 36

The second Sean walks into my apartment that evening, I start babbling to him about the sale, Rose, and the suitcase.

As he hangs up his coat, I trail after him talking a mile a minute. "...and who should show up at the sale but this woman Rose who was the Eskews' maid for years and she told me—"

Sean nudges Ethel and me aside and heads for the server in my dining area. He opens the cabinet door and scowls. "All you have is gin?"

"Sean, what's wrong? Did something happen at work?"

I step toward him, but he turns away, refusing to meet my eye. His face looks crumpled, like he's moments away from crying.

All thoughts of the Eskews vanish. "Sean, what is it? Did someone get hurt? Did someone—" I can't bring myself to say "die."

He closes his eyes and rubs his temples. "My god, can I at least have a beer?"

I run to get it for him, and after he takes a long draw he speaks. "Something terrible has happened. Something that's made me question everything." He exhales. "Brendan is cheating on Adrienne."

"Wha—?" I'm stunned into speechlessness, but of course Sean doesn't fully understand why. "How do you know?" I choke out.

"I had to go to a bar in Summit today to follow up on a lead for the Task Force. I walk in, and who do I see making out in a corner booth than my big brother and some blonde chick who looks about twenty-two."

"Oh, Sean—how awful for you! What did he say?"

"That's what bothers me most. He wasn't even ashamed to be caught. He sent the girl home—get this, she's a nanny from Sweden who watches the kids of Brendan's lawyer—and then he told me not to get on my high horse. He says she's a harmless distraction. He says Adrienne has what she wants, so he should get what he wants." Sean pounds the kitchen counter and my unwashed breakfast dishes rattle. "I can't believe my brother would talk that way. Like giving your wife a big house and fancy clothes is your license to screw around. That's not how we were raised, not what our family stands for."

I want to throw my arms around him, but I'm afraid to touch him. And I know I'm about to make things worse, not better. But now I have to tell him what I know. "Sean—" My voice cracks. I swallow and start again. Spit it out, Audrey. "Sean, Adrienne knows their marriage is in trouble. She, she's been fooling around too."

Sean's eyes open wide. Before he can even ask a question I launch into a long and stammering account of Adrienne's dalliance, how I found out, and why I haven't told him until now.

Sean turns his head away from me. The anger in his voice is replaced by a barely perceptible tremor. "My first wife cheated on me. Your mother cheated on your father. Brendan cheats on Adrienne."

I put my hands on his cheeks and force him to look at me. His bright blue eyes are hazed with a film of tears.

"Maybe I'm naïve, Audrey," he whispers. "Maybe what I want—a long and faithful relationship—is unrealistic, unattainable. Maybe humans aren't meant to be monogamous."

I trace the fine smile lines that have started to appear in his fair skin. "I don't think monogamy is the issue. I think all of them weren't happy with themselves, so they couldn't be happy with someone else. I've been alone for thirty-four years. I think I know myself pretty well. I know what I want."

I kiss him.

"Can we do this?" Sean asks.

"Yes. We can."

A couple hours later, we emerge from my bedroom.

For the first time, Sean notices the purple suitcase in my living room. When I explain what it is, he frowns. "You're tampering with evidence. You should have called the Melton police."

"And tell them what? I found a twenty-year-old sheet with a blood stain in the back of a closet and I want them to investigate? They already think I'm crazy for insisting that Darlene didn't kill Mrs. Eskew."

"But if this does relate to an earlier crime, you're not preserving the chain of evidence," Sean complains. "You touched it and removed it from the scene. Anything you find is now compromised. It won't stand up in court."

"Court! All the parties are dead. I think this blood is Leonie's. I think she was already dead when she entered that plane. When Parker loaded her into it, I should say."

Sean scowls. "That would be awfully risky."

"Not really. Put the body in a duffle bag and load it onto the plane. There are absolutely no security checks for a pilot flying his own plane. I verified that."

I pace around the bag. "All we have to do is test the blood. Get a DNA sample from Clothilde and see if this blood is from a person related to her. A private lab can do that, right? And then Clothilde will know why Parker crashed the plane." I pause. "Not that it will bring her any peace. She still won't know why he killed her daughter. Why would he kill her a month before his son was due to enter the world?"

"Actually, pregnancy is a particularly dangerous time for women in abusive relationships," Sean says. "The abuser sees his power and influence slipping away as the woman gets more focused on the baby." He's turned his back on me while he speaks. Sean loves to tell hilarious stories about dumb perps who take selfies at crime scenes and post them on Facebook or crazy citizens reporting their neighbors as spies, but I've noticed that on the rare occasions he confides tragic details about his work, he'll refuse to meet my eye.

I slide my arms around his waist and rest my head on his back. "You've arrested men who beat up their pregnant wives and girlfriends?"

"Too many times to count. And the worst part is, the women stand there with their noses broken and their lips bleeding, cradling their stomachs and begging us not to make the arrest."

"But that's poor women who have no place to go. Leonie could have gone home to her parents. They would've helped her."

"It's not only poor women. When I was a patrolman, we got called to a big colonial on Magnolia Lane. Four-year-old dialed 911, but then was too scared to speak. Dispatcher could hear the whole fight going down over the phone line. We had to break the slider on the deck to get in. Guy had a knife and was threatening to cut the baby right out of her. He was a vice president at AT&T."

"And she didn't want him to be arrested?"

Sean twists around in my arms. "Said she loved him. Said she didn't want her kids' father in jail. When we cuffed him, she went ballistic. Bit me. I still have the scar." He holds out his powerful right arm. Beneath the downy golden hair and the freckles I can see two small white depressions.

I caress his arm. "What happened to him?"

"Guy had a great lawyer. Since he didn't actually cut her with the knife, and since she wouldn't testify against him, the judge ordered anger management classes."

"Does that ever work?"

Sean snorts. "Court-mandated treatment for abusers never works. Doesn't work for drug addicts like Amber Pileggi either."

"You're so cynical. You think people can never change."

"Not true. People can change if they themselves want to change. People don't change because someone else tries to make them change." Sean brushes my bangs away from my face. "Anyway, anger wasn't even this guy's issue. Power was his issue. He needed to be king of the hill twenty-four/seven."

"Could that have been Parker's issue? He was used to being the golden boy in the family and at school and at work. Maybe all the fuss about the birth of the baby made him violent. Maybe Parker slashed up those baby clothes. Then he lashed out at Leonie and killed her."

"And he covered up the crime and killed himself with the plane crash?" Sean ponders the situation. "A family annihilator. Could be."

"He couldn't face going to prison. He couldn't face being humiliated in the eyes of his family and friends and colleagues. I think it makes sense, but I don't know how I'd ever prove it. Clothilde says the bodies were burned beyond recognition. They had to use dental records to confirm the identities."

Sean pulls me into an embrace. My head rests against his chest and I listen to the most reassuring sound in my world: the steady thump, thump, thump of his heart. "Staging a fiery plane crash is the ultimate act of control. Destroy yourself and all the evidence in one fell swoop."

I pull away and study Sean's face. "Then why would he have left that bloody sheet behind?"

"Even smart criminals make careless mistakes."

"Careless would be forgetting about the sheet. Why make the effort to hide it in the house when it would have been much easier to take it away with the body?"

"So you think someone other than Parker hid the sheet?"

"Someone else knows what happened that night. I'm determined to find out who." I run my fingers through my hair.

"First, I have to finish the sale. Then I'm getting this blood tested. Then I'm going to the jail to talk to Darlene."

Sean breathes in sharply. "Oh, I forgot to tell you. Darlene got beaten up in the jail last night. She's in the hospital."

"Sean! What happened? Is she all right?"

"Unconscious."

CHAPTER 37

Day Two of the sale and the Eskew house has been picked as clean as a Coughlin family Thanksgiving turkey. Adrienne has worked hard all day, but for the past hour her kids have been calling every ten minutes to ask for help with homework, help with finding a lost doll, help refereeing a fight. Finally, I send her home.

The second floor is almost empty. Ty and I can finish ourselves.

As I descend the staircase, I hear raised voices.

"Can't you see I'm workin'? I can't take him now."

"Please, please, Ty. I wouldn't ask if it wasn't important. This is the third callback I've had for this job. He wants me to have coffee with him and the other person I'll be working with. I know he's going to offer it to me this time."

"Good. Maybe then you understand what it means to have responsibilities. I can't drop everything every time you need help."

"Ple-e-e-a-se."

"Get that lazy-ass friend of yours—"

Ty and Charmaine fall silent as I enter the kitchen. Baby Lo is sitting in his infant car seat waving his arms like he's conducting the argument.

"What's the matter?"

"Audrey, please can I leave him for just an—"

"I told her I can't—"

"—hour so I can go to—"

I ignore them both and head over to Lo. I stick out my index finger and he grabs it with his strong, tiny fingers. "Hey, big guy! What's happenin'?"

Lo tucks his chin into his Cookie Monster bib and looks at me through his long, dark lashes. What a flirt!

"Why can't we watch him, Ty?"

"I have three trips to make to the dump! I can't wait—"

"He can stay here with me while you're driving." The words are out of my mouth before I even realize it. What's come over me? Am I actually getting comfortable with baby care? Maybe I'm simply desperate for Charmaine to get a job so Ty won't have to worry about her so much.

"Thank you, Audrey! You're the best!" Charmaine crows.

I grab her arm as she heads for the door. "He's got food?"

"Two bottles. And I'll be back in an hour, two, tops."

After she leaves, I can tell Ty is mad at me. He moves back and forth between the back door and the van, hauling impossibly heavy boxes without ever meeting my eye. There's one stack of stuff going to the dump, and another smaller pile of kitchen tools, lamps, and small appliances that will go to Sister Alice in Newark on Monday.

"Why are you mad? Lo's no trouble. Look at him—he's happy just watching us."

Ty drops the box he's just picked up. "My sister needs to learn to make a plan. Why'd she wait until ten minutes before she needed to be there to look for a babysitter? You keep bailin' her out, all you teach her is that people are put on this earth to take care of her."

"But you want her to get a job. What's the harm in being generous and helping someone when you can?"

Ty's eyes narrow to slits. "World don't work that way."

He slams out the back door

I put my face in front of Lo. "Looks like it's you and me, buddy."

He gives me a gummy grin and waves.

An hour with a baby. I can handle this. I'm getting to be an old pro.

There are unsold items upstairs that I need to carry down. I decide to take Lo with me to the upstairs hall, then I can consolidate everything there and carry it down while still keeping him in sight. My plan works fine until I stay in one bedroom too long and Lo starts to howl.

I pop back out. "I'm right here. Relax."

But of course he doesn't. His body stiffens and he strains against the straps of the carrier seat. I take him out and bounce him on my hip. Immediately he quiets down, so I put him back. Immediately he starts to howl.

I sigh. Now I see what Ty meant. We'll never finish up here if one of us has to hold the baby. I pace around with him. Even try singing "Sweet Child of Mine," but Lo is not a Guns 'N Roses fan. Eventually, his head lolls on my shoulder. It would be a nice feeling if it weren't for the clock ticking in my brain. Two more trips to the dump before it closes. If we don't make it, then there will be no room in the van for all the items that need to go to various charities on Monday. Our contract states the house is to be empty and broom clean by 9AM on Monday. To make matters worse, I know Ty has a test that day, so I can't expect him to come in early to finish work that should have been done today. The tension in my gut must be radiating out into Lo because he begins to squirm and whimper. Maybe if I feed him and rock him he'll doze off and I can finish up before Ty returns.

I carry the baby downstairs and get his bottle. He sucks it down, belches and sighs. By the time I carry him back upstairs, he's asleep. I set him in his carrier and start to strap him in. Instantly, his eyes fly open. Taking a deep breath I try to summon some Zen calm. I rub his tummy and rock the chair and eventually his eyes grow heavy. I keep it up until his breathing grows slow and steady. His head is slumped over on top of the seat belt. No way I'm pulling the strap and waking him up. He can't fall out just sitting here on the floor.

Finally, I can work.

I spring into action, carrying loads into the hallway until every bedroom is empty. I glance at the door to the attic. Yesterday, Adrienne told me she brought everything down from there. But I'd better check. Lo is actually snoring. No way I'm moving him. I'll just pop my head up into the attic.

I scamper up the uncarpeted stairs and do a 360. Empty. Empty. Empty. Boxes. Three of them on the west wall. Damn that Adrienne!

I stride across and grab one. Heavy as sin. I look inside. Encyclopedia.

Shit. No wonder she left them here. But she could have told me. Maybe she told Ty and he forgot. I push the top one off the stack and shove it across the floor. Then do the same with the other two. Ty will have to take them from here.

I scamper down the attic stairs ready to start carrying boxes downstairs.

Twelve boxes wait for me in the hallway.

The infant carrier is empty.

CHAPTER 38

A knife of fear impales me.

I didn't strap him in. Could he have fallen out and rolled down the stairs?

But the carrier is nowhere near the top of the stairs. And Lo doesn't crawl yet. He only recently learned to roll over. Still, I run to the stairs and look down into the foyer.

Empty.

Surely Ty couldn't be back from the dump already, so maybe Charmaine is back. I grab the baby carrier and run downstairs calling as I go. "Charmaine?"

If Charmaine is back so soon, she must not have gotten the job. And on top of that disappointment, she's discovered her child unattended. This won't be pretty.

"Charmaine? Charmaine!"

I run from the foyer down the long hall into the kitchen. As I move, a worm of doubt gnaws at me. How could Charmaine have found us so quickly upstairs? She's never been beyond the kitchen in this huge house, and Lo wasn't crying or I would have heard him in the attic.

I skid into the kitchen and find it empty except for the boxes awaiting Ty's return. Neither Ty's car nor the AMT van is in the driveway.

My whole body vibrates with the pounding of my heart. "Charmaine? Ty?" But I know they're not here.

Who is?

I hold my breath and listen, every fiber of my body tuned to hear Lo's cry.

Silence.

I drop the baby carrier in the kitchen and slip back down the hallway, stepping silently on the plush carpet. Outside the door to Mrs. Eskew's former sickroom—her death chamber—I pause. Faintly, faintly, I hear a sound.

Did he whimper? Cough? Or is it just my need to hear him playing tricks on my ears?

Then I hear a keening moan, too loud and deep to have come from a baby.

I stand against the wall and reach across to open the door the way I have seen Sean do it.

"Go away, Mother! Don't you come in here."

The voice is louder, stronger than I've ever heard it. But unmistakably, it's Rachel.

"It's not your mother, Rachel. It's me, Audrey. Can I come in?"

"There's nothing in here for you. You've already taken everything. Everything."

I'm not afraid of an eighty-five pound woman even if she is bat-shit crazy. I step through the door.

There stands Rachel, holding Lo clutched to her chest. One pale white hand squeezes his plump brown arm while the other pushes his dark head against her bony shoulder.

"Hi Rachel," I try to keep my voice light and chatty. "I see you've met Lo. Isn't he cute? He's Ty's nephew. Ty, who works with me."

Her eyes open wide. "His name is Parker Eskew the second. Not junior. I named him after my brother."

Whoa. Okay, I can roll with this. All that matters is that Lo is safe. "That's quite an honor, to name him after your brother. Can I see him?"

I take a step closer.

Rachel rears back and squeezes the baby closer. He begins to struggle and whimper.

I stop moving. "I think he doesn't like to be held so tight."

Her eyes narrow. "I know how to take care of my baby. I know how to be a good mother. Not like you."

That's a barb that hurts more than Rachel could know. "You're right. I shouldn't have left him alone in his carrier."

"You cut me up. You ruined me. You said I couldn't have a baby, but I showed you. I showed you what I can do."

Don't argue. Don't try to reason. Just agree, agree, agree.

"He's a beautiful baby. You've done a good job. Can I see his face? Who does he look like?"

Rachel loosens her grip on Lo and gazes down at his face. At least now he can breathe.

"He looks like Parker."

I'm not seeing the resemblance myself, but I smile and nod. I know I could overpower her if all I needed to take from her was car keys, or a purse, but I can't risk lunging at her when she's holding Lo. She could drop him or fall on top of him. My best bet is to get her into the kitchen. When Ty comes back, he can subdue Rachel while I grab the baby.

Lo begins to fuss. "I bet he's hungry," I say, knowing that he's probably not. "Let's go get his bottle in the kitchen."

I see Rachel's eyes light up, and I lead the way pausing occasionally to make sure she's following. She carries Lo awkwardly but doesn't seem in danger of dropping him. Once we're in the kitchen, Rachel spies the diaper bag and begins pawing through it, fascinated by all the baby paraphernalia.

She finds the bottle and stuffs the nipple in Lo's mouth. He takes a few listless sips and pushes it away. I just fed him half an hour ago. All the poor kid wants is a little snooze.

Rachel's face tightens. She doesn't appreciate rejection even from one so young.

"How about putting him in his carrier so you can rock him?" I suggest.

But Rachel's having none of that. She sits in one of the sun porch chairs that didn't sell and sways back and forth clutching Lo. As she rocks, she talks to the baby in a breathy monotone. "I knew I could do it. No one ever believes me. Especially Mother. Only Kara can have a baby. Kara and Leonie, you said. Babies are for them, not for you, Rachel. That's what you said. But you were wrong, see? There was no baby for Leonie. And now there is a baby for me."

Rachel is calm and Lo actually has dozed off. So why do I feel a shiver of dread pass over me? I don't need to know this—not right now, not right here.

But I have to know.

"Why was there no baby for Leonie?" I ask softly, as if we're chatting about why there's no milk in the fridge. But I'm a ball of tension. I need to find out what happened to Leonie, not for me, but for Clothilde.

Rachel hums tunelessly. She strokes Lo's forehead.

She's not going to answer. Let it go, Audrey. Don't push her too far.

"I cut her open," Rachel says in her breathy monotone. "The way Mother told the doctor to cut me open. What's sauce for the goose is sauce for the gander. That's what Mother always says. Isn't it, Mother? Isn't it?"

"You had an operation?"

"I was fixed. Just like you fix a cat. Because too many kittens are bad. No one wants them. No will take care of them. Especially if they're not perfect. No one wants those. Right?"

So that's the operation Rachel depicted in her painting. Her mother really did force her to have her tubes tied. Sterilized her so she couldn't reproduce. Because she wasn't perfect.

I hear a door slam. Thank goodness. Ty is back.

A moment later, Charmaine breezes through the door. "I got the job! I start next week." She sees Lo in Rachel's arms. "Was he good? Smells like he needs a new diaper."

This isn't good. Why was I so sure Ty would arrive before Charmaine?

Charmaine reaches for her son. "Here, I'll change him." She tilts her head. "You a friend of Audrey's? I'm Ty's sister, Charmaine."

Rachel pulls the baby closer. "Get away from Parker."

Confusion, concern, anger flit across Charmaine's face in quick succession. I step toward her to try to explain. "We're having a little issue here, Charmaine. I think it's best to just stay calm until Ty gets back."

"What's wrong with her?"

"She's a little, uhm, confused. It's best not to get her worked up."

"You gave my son to a crazy person? And now you tellin' me to just *chill*?"

I put a calming hand on her arm. "I think it's best to wait for—"

She shakes me off and spins around in one movement. Charmaine is smaller than I am, but she's strong and in good shape. She seizes Rachel by both shoulders and pries her right hand off Lo. I have no choice but to pitch in. I grab the baby while Charmaine struggles with Rachel's left hand.

But Rachel isn't going down without a fight. She grabs Charmaine's braids and wrenches her head back. She's stronger than she looks.

"Bitch!"

I suspect Charmaine has participated in some catfights in her time. She knocks Rachel to the floor. I step back with the baby, who's awake and crying now.

Charmaine forms a fist and pulls her arm back ready to swing. This is not what we need. If Rachel gets hurt, Charmaine will be the one who gets in trouble. I see the job and the apartment evaporating all because of my carelessness. I set the howling Lo in his baby carrier and rush in to separate the two women.

After some tussling in which the three of us stagger around and knock over a tower of boxes, I manage to pull Rachel down and get her arms pinned to her side. She twists and squirms with the strength of an enraged cat. We're surrounded by a minefield of broken bowls and whisks and measuring cups.

"Get the baby and go!" I shout to Charmaine.

Charmaine grabs the baby carrier, but Lo isn't strapped in, so she pauses to secure him. Leaving him at her feet, she rises to open the back door. In that second, Rachel bites my hand. Her teeth sink into my flesh and instinctively I pull back. She breaks my grip.

Rachel rolls away from me, panting. My gaze goes to Charmaine and Lo. How close are they to being out the door?

A big dented skillet is blocking the door. Charmaine kicks it aside and opens the door, propping it with her foot as she reaches back for the baby carrier.

Rachel rises with a long shard of pottery in her hand.

I don't scream. I don't think.

I throw myself over Lo's body as the blade comes down.

White heat but no pain. A spurt of red, red blood.

Is it mine? Or his?

CHAPTER 39

The sitting room at Bretton Pines is stifling, but Clothilde awaits me in a cashmere sweater and pearls. Her eyes widen she sees the sixty-two stitches that stretch from my ear to my shoulder blade.

"*Mon dieu!* You look like Frankenstein's monster!"

Gee thanks, Clothilde. Tell me what you really think. "It looks worse than it is. She only nicked an artery." I sink into the wing chair across from her. "The plastic surgeon says I'll barely have a scar."

Clothilde keeps her hands clutched together in her lap. "Where is she?"

"The hospital. She's had a complete psychotic break. They're trying to stabilize her, but she may never be competent to stand trial."

"For attacking you?"

I shake my head. "What she did to me doesn't matter. There's a lot I have to tell you, Clothilde. I'm afraid it's very painful."

"The DNA test? The blood on the sheet belonged to Leonie?"

I nod. The police plan to speak to Clothilde once they have all their ducks in a row, but I wanted to talk to her first.

Her blue eyes meet mine, but I can see the tremor rising from her clenched hands. "Nothing can be worse than not knowing."

So I tell her what we think happened that night nearly thirty years ago. Parker and Leonie were staying at Eskews' house the night before their trip because it was closer to the Palmyrton airport where Parker kept his plane. Gilbert was traveling on business, but Rachel and Marjorie were home. Leonie had been sleeping in Parker's room, the room where we found the suitcase with the bloody sheet. Perhaps her pregnancy made it hard to rest comfortably and Parker moved to the guest room to get a good night's sleep before their flight. In the middle of the night Rachel entered the room and attacked Leonie and her unborn son with a knife. By the time Parker responded to her screams, it was too late. They were both dead.

Hours passed before Parker left for Palmyrton airport. We can't know, but he must've spent the time agonizing over what to do. The truth was so horrific that he must have decided that his own family and Leonie's family would be less distraught if they believed the three of them had perished in a plane crash. And Rachel would be spared a lifetime in prison.

Certainly, he had no desire to go on living himself.

Even eight months pregnant, Leonie was petite. Parker must have found a duffel bag big enough to hold her body. He probably intended to bring along the purple suitcase that held the bloody bedding, but in his grief he left it behind. Rachel was shrewd enough to hide the bag.

Then Parker flew to North Carolina and sent his plane into a nosedive on a deserted stretch of beach. The resulting fire destroyed any evidence of the attack on Leonie. Her bones, however, were found in the passenger seat.

He flew with her corpse beside him.

"She knew." Clothilde exhales the words when I'm done. "She was there that night."

"Marjorie Eskew? I don't think so. She was probably passed out drunk that night. She was an alcoholic, but no one acknowledged it. Her drinking during her pregnancy caused Rachel's problems: Fetal Alcohol Syndrome. But Marjorie considered her younger daughter to be incompetent and willfully immature. If she had known what Rachel did, Marjorie would have cast her off."

"Someone knew," Clothilde insists.

"Tom knew. After Parker died, he took over the role of Rachel's protector, but not willingly. Maybe the drinking and screwing around are his way of coping. When his mother was murdered, his worst fears were confirmed. He knew Rachel had done it. He knew what she was capable of.

"When the cops suspected Darlene, Tom saw it as a godsend. He struck a deal with her to plead guilty in return for paying her son's fees at the therapeutic school. Scandal averted and Rachel rescued once again."

"They protect this monster!"

Is Rachel a monster? I certainly don't relish defending her to Clothilde. Yet she should know that the attack on her daughter didn't come out of the blue. "There's one more detail you should know. It doesn't excuse what Rachel did, but…"

"What? What defense could there possibly be?"

So I tell her how Gilbert and Marjorie had had their daughter sterilized as a teenager. How they wanted to make sure that Rachel's shortcomings weren't passed along. How Rachel had had a breakdown requiring hospitalization when she realized she would never have children. How Parker had left Harvard to be closer to his sister.

Clothilde's eyes have grown a little misty, but she hasn't allowed the tears to spill over. Despite the horrors she's had to absorb, she's still totally in control. A Bretton Pines aide heads toward us bearing a tray of tea and cookies. Clothilde causes her to change course with one forbidding glare. "Why now? Why did Rachel kill her mother now?"

I take a breath. "There's more, Clothilde. Remember when you told me you felt there was a hole inside Parker, a darkness that surrounded the family?"

"So, it was not my imagination?"

"No. You wondered what happened to Myron Eskein, Gilbert's brother, after he went to prison. Myron was released from Attica in 1978, the year Parker was a senior in high school, about to apply to Harvard. He'd served over twenty years, and was well into his sixties. He was penniless and too old and tired to resume his life of crime. Of course, he'd never worked a legitimate job in his life."

"So he came to his brother for help?" Clothilde asks. "How do you know this?"

"Tom." I reach for her hand. I expect her to bat me away, but she doesn't. "He's here, Clothilde. Out in the lobby. He'd like to tell you this next part himself."

Now she does shake me off and draws herself up tall. "He expects my forgiveness? Never!"

"No, I don't think he expects that. He simply wants you to have some information that only he can provide."

She glares at me. "You know. You tell me."

"I know the facts," I concede. "But only he and his sisters know about the darkness."

Clothilde grips the arms of her pastel flowered chair, as if in preparation for the dentist's drill. "Fine. Bring him in."

Tom Eskew has aged ten years in the past week. His face is gray and haggard; his jaunty bearing has morphed into a dragging shuffle. I escort him across the sitting room, past two silver-haired ladies working a jigsaw puzzle and an elderly gent reading the *Wall Street Journal*. I know he hasn't seen his brother's mother-in-law since Parker and Leonie's funeral. He extends his hand to Clothilde, but she declines to take it. Disconcerted, he shoves both hands into his pockets and drops into a chair across from us.

"I've told Clothilde about your uncle, Tom." I say. "You can pick up from the night when you met him."

Tom nods. He focuses his eyes on a potted lily behind Clothilde's shoulder and starts talking. "It was an evening in late September. Still daylight savings time, so there was some light after dinner. I know it was a Monday because Rose, our housekeeper, had her day off and was visiting her sister. Mother had already gone to bed—passed out, as usual. We kids were doing our homework in the morning room when the doorbell rang.

"I was always happy for any reason to goof off, so I went to answer it. Rachel trailed after me. When I opened the door, there was a man who looked just like our father, except older and more worn out, and badly dressed. He asked if my dad was home, and his voice was just the same as our father's. That's when Rachel started crying—it freaked her out. Parker and Kara came running, and the four of us stood staring at the guy. He was obviously related to our father, but Dad had always told us he had no living relatives.

"So Parker took charge, as he always did. He sent the rest of us back to our homework, and he took the man to our father's study. A few minutes later, Parker came back, obviously rattled. But he wouldn't tell us anything. Kara sneaked down the back hall and came back to report they were shouting at each other, but she couldn't understand what they were saying. Parker forbade her to leave the room again."

Tom gazes around at the cheery chintz furniture and cozy gas fireplace in the Bretton Pines sitting room like he doesn't know what planet he dropped into. He takes a deep breath and continues. "About twenty minutes later, our father appeared in the morning room. At dinner, he'd been wearing a sweater over his shirt, but now he was just wearing the shirt. He was agitated and distracted. I'm sure he didn't realize there was a big, dark stain on his gray flannel pants, but I noticed. So did Kara.

"Dad told Parker to come with him, and told the rest of us to go up to our bedrooms and not come out until morning. Kara's bedroom and mine faced the backyard. I heard the back door opening. I looked out my window and in the last glimmer of twilight, I saw Dad and Parker carrying something between them. They stumbled and staggered and at one point, Parker dropped his end and Dad yelled.

"I knew where they were headed. That summer, Dad had decided to have a clay tennis court installed at the end of the garden. He wanted us to practice more and improve our games. That week the workmen had come with an excavator and dug out the spot. Then it had rained."

Tom pauses. When he resumes, his voice is weaker, breathier. "About an hour later, I heard the back door open and close again. I heard my father and Parker come upstairs. I heard their bedroom doors close. I wanted to go to Parker, but I was afraid. I remembered the look in my father's eye when he said we weren't to come out until morning."

We all sit in silence. The clock in the Bretton Pines lounge chimes the hour. Tom speaks again. "I was awakened on Tuesday by the sound of the workmen. They got an early start laying the clay surface. When we got home from school that day, we had a new tennis court." For the first time, Tom looks Clothilde in the eye.

"Dad made us practice every day."

CHAPTER 40

Clothilde rests her head against the chair and closes her eyes. "Gilbert destroyed his children while Marjorie stood by and did nothing. So their daughter destroyed my daughter. And my grandson. Yet both of them got to die not knowing the abomination they set in motion."

Marjorie Eskew had her head pounded in with a rock wielded by her own daughter; I wouldn't say she had an enviable death. Still, I see Clothilde's point. She thought the truth would bring her some peace, but believing that the Eskews died in blissful ignorance is galling.

I glance at Tom. "Do you think she knew?"

His eyelids are at half-mast. "Who knows? Mother was an expert in not knowing. She kept herself pickled so she didn't have to see, didn't have to hear, didn't have to act. Parker wrote me a letter dated a week before the crash. He mailed it to my college dorm. I didn't get it until well after the funeral. He told me to watch after Rachel when he wasn't there because Mother and Dad couldn't be trusted to do what was best for her. For years, I convinced myself that he really had written it well before he died, that all he meant was to ask for my help when he was busy. But as the years went by, I knew."

Tom closes his eyes completely. "Rachel attacked Kara with a hot curling iron two weeks before her wedding."

"That scar above her collar bone?"

Tom massages his temple. "A very unfortunate hair-styling accident, according to Mother."

Clothilde pounds the end table with her fist. "Willful ignorance! I want to rub her face in the truth. Why should she not suffer as I have?"

I feel helpless in the presence of her anguish. Could I relieve that pain, even if it involves stretching a hunch into certainty?

"In the days before she died, Mrs. Eskew was very agitated, Clothilde. She said something to me one day when I was in her room. At the time, it didn't make sense. Now it does."

"What? What did she say?"

"She was telling me that she was afraid, that she didn't have a choice about something. That she was to blame." Then she said, "Only Parker was brave."

I lean toward Clothilde and whisper, "She knew. She knew the sacrifice Parker had made. For Rachel. For her."

CHAPTER 41

When Ty and I roll up to their apartment in the AMT van, Darlene and Judah are waiting for us on their front steps.

Ty hops out and fist-bumps JJ. "C'mon, let's see what we gotta move."

They head upstairs, leaving Darlene and me standing awkwardly. Her face is still covered by an ugly bruise fading from purple to yellow.

"It's real nice of you to help us move our stuff. Doesn't amount to much, but it wouldn't have fit in the car."

"We're happy to do it. I'm so glad you got this new job. What a terrific opportunity."

Darlene gives a short bark of a laugh. " 'Bout time I caught a break. I thought Kenny would have to leave The River School at the end of the semester, but it turned out they were looking for a live-in aide to work nights and weekends. They have trouble keeping people. I told 'em they'll have trouble getting rid of me."

She gives her harsh laugh again, but I detect a little mistiness in her eyes. "I'll still be giving baths and handing out pills, but for kids, not old people. I think I'll like that. And I get to be near Kenny all day."

"What about Judah?"

"Counselor at the college got him hooked up with an old lady near campus who lets out a bedroom in her house in exchange for help with the yard and the garbage and stuff."

"And Rob?"

Darlene turns away. "Didn't your boyfriend tell you it was Rob's dealer crew that put out the hit on me to get beat up in jail?"

"He told me they were afraid you'd talk about how Rob

pressured you to take pills from Mrs. Eskew. But you didn't talk."

Darlene faces me with her lips pressed into a thin line. "I have to keep this job for Kenny. And for me and JJ. I can't let Rob ruin this." She clenches her fists into tight balls. "I hope your man arrests Rob. I hope he arrests him soon. Otherwise, Rob's going to get killed. He can't stay ahead of this trouble much longer."

I put my hand on her shoulder. "I'm sorry, Darlene. I wish…"

I wish what? That Darlene hadn't gotten mixed up with two different men who refused to father their children? That she could've had a shot at a job where she earned enough to pay the heat, electricity and phone bills all in one month? That she didn't have to choose between visiting her son at the cemetery or the jail?

She shrugs away from me as she hears Ty and JJ approaching. "I'll tell you this, my son might be screwed up, but he's not as screwed up as those Eskews."

The real estate closing is on one of those bizarrely warm November days that only happen in New Jersey. When Sean and I pull up at our new house after signing all the paperwork at the lawyer's office, the party is already in full swing. Never ones to be deterred by lack of a key, Sean's father jimmied the back door lock so the female members of the Coughlin family could arrange the potluck spread on the kitchen island. Grandma Betty is pushing aside some corned beef to make room for her fried chicken and potato salad. Everyone's brought their own lawn chairs, which are set up throughout the empty rooms. My dad and Natalie are here, perched on the folding canvas chairs awarded them for their NPR donations, looking a little shell-shocked as Coughlins swirl around them. The kids can't decide who's more fascinating, baby Lo or Ethel.

"Looks like the house is plenty big enough to hold us all," Sean says.

"Do you like it as well as the one we lost?' I ask him for the hundredth time.

He answers me the way he has the last ninety-nine times. "This is the house we were meant to have."

As I look at everyone laughing and talking surrounded by the shag carpeting that has to be pulled up and the flowered wallpaper that has to be pulled down, for the first time, I believe him.

"The king and queen of the castle have arrived!" Terry announces, pushing beers into our hands. "I sure hope you guys own this place now, or we gonna have some 'splaining to do."

"This is one hell of a way to impress our new neighbors," Sean mutters.

"Don't worry—we invited them," Deirdre calls out as she passes.

Sean cranes his neck to survey the crowd. I know he's looking for Brendan; he wants his big brother's approval for this landmark event in our lives. I know Sean won't find Brendan because Adrienne is here with the kids. Right now they're living apart—taking a breather, Adrienne says—and seeing a therapist once a week.

Ty lopes up. "Jill just texted me from the train station. I gotta pick her up. Be right back."

The gang's all here.

It's loud.

It's chaotic.

It's fun.

After an hour of nonstop eating, drinking, and talking, I need a break. I find Grandma Betty out on the porch swing. Baby Lo is sprawled across her lap, his mouth open, his tiny fingers loosely curled around the edge of a blue blanket.

"I do believe this child is the most beautiful of all my grandbabies. Don't you agree, Audrey?"

I know better than to point out that Lo is not technically a blood relation. If Grandma Betty has declared him a grandbaby, he's a grandbaby. "He sure is, Betty. He's going to be every bit as handsome as Ty."

Grandma Betty strokes Lo's forehead. "Yes, he is. And as smart as Ty too."

"So, you're helping out with Lo?"

"Wednesdays only. He goes to daycare the other days, but Wednesdays Charmaine has to work until seven at that ad agency. Helps to run a focus group, whatever that amounts to. I didn't want Ty watching the baby. He has homework to do."

I ease into the swing beside her. "You're a pushover, Betty."

"Hmmph. Takes one to know one."

"Charmaine seems to be doing very well at her new job."

"We'll see."

"You're not optimistic?"

"Optimism doesn't really enter into it, girl. Charmaine knows what she's gotta do: keep her head down and her lip buttoned. She's never been able to do that before, but now she's got this little man to think of, so maybe she'll wise up."

We sway back and forth, the only sound the squeak of the swing's chain, the party a dull roar behind us. After a while, I find the words to ask her what's on my mind.

"How do you know if you can be a good mother, Betty? How do you know if you're ready?"

"Ain't nobody ever *ready*. Doesn't matter how old you are, how smart you are—you're never ready to be a parent."

"Well, how can you know if you'll be good at it? Once you've got the baby, it's too late to turn back."

"You remember when John McCain ran for president against Barack Obama?"

One thing I've learned in my conversations with Grandma Betty—she's the queen of the non sequitur. I have to trust that this is going somewhere. "Uhm…yeah."

"I always admired McCain because of how he made it through being a prisoner of war in Vietnam. See, when he joined up in the Air Force, he didn't say to himself, 'I better not do this unless I'm sure I can survive being locked up in a cage in the jungle.' I'm sure there were many times when that young man wanted to just lay down and die. But he didn't. He made it out. And he went on to run for president."

"You voted for John McCain?"

"Don't talk crazy, girl. I voted for Obama." Betty puts her foot on the floor and stops the motion of the swing. She turns to face me. "What I'm sayin' is, you gotta just step up to the plate. You can do more than you ever thought possible."

THE END

Dear reader,

I hope you enjoyed *This Bitter Treasure*. Please consider leaving a brief review to help other readers discover this book. Thanks so much!

Would you like to be notified when my next novel is released? Please join my mailing list. Don't worry—you'll only receive ONE email when a book is released.

http://swhubbard.net/contact/

If you've read all the Palmyrton Estate Sale mysteries, it's time to try the Frank Bennett Adirondack Mountain mystery series:

Take the Bait

The Lure

Blood Knot

Dead Drift

ABOUT THE AUTHOR

S.W. Hubbard is the author of the Palmyrton Estate Sale Mysteries, *Another Man's Treasure*, *Treasure of Darkness,* and *This Bitter Treasure*. She is also is the author of three Police Chief Frank Bennett mystery novels set in the Adirondack Mountains: *Take the Bait, The Lure* (originally published as *Swallow the Hook),* and *Blood Knot,* as well as a short story collection featuring Frank Bennett, *Dead Drift*. Her short stories have appeared in *Alfred Hitchcock's Mystery Magazine* and the anthologies *Crimes by Moonlight, The Mystery Box,* and *Adirondack Mysteries*. She lives in Morristown, NJ, where she teaches creative writing to enthusiastic teens and adults, and expository writing to reluctant college freshmen. To contact her, join her mailing list, or read the first chapter of any of her books, visit: http://www.swhubbard.net.

Follow her on Twitter @swhubbardauthor or like her Facebook author page, https://www.facebook.com/swhubbardauthor/. Connect with S.W. Hubbard on Pinterest and Goodreads too.

Made in the USA
Coppell, TX
21 April 2022

76907028R00134